SPELL STARTER

ELSIE CHAPMAN

Scholastic Press   New York

All rights reserved. Published by Scholastic Press, an imprint of Scholastic Inc.,
Publishers since 1920. SCHOLASTIC, SCHOLASTIC PRESS, and associated logos are trademarks and/or registered trademarks of Scholastic Inc.

The publisher does not have any control over and does not assume any responsibility
for author or third-party websites or their content.

Library of Congress Cataloging-in-Publication Data available

ISBN 978-1-338-58951-1

10 9 8 7 6 5 4 3 2 1   20 21 22 23 24

Printed in the U.S.A.   23
First edition, October 2020

Book design by Maeve Norton

JESSE, MATTHEW, GILLIAN—
YOU ARE EVERYTHING

ONE

The inside of the bar is dim. Shapes of black-painted furniture form within the gloom, and there's the dull glow of unpolished fixtures. A thick gray haze fills the air, and through my mask comes the bitter hint of tobacco. I smell more, something sweeter—the scent of tea, floral and grasslike.

Chang's is inside the Tea Sector but located close enough to Tobacco that people come to the tea bar also looking to smoke. Customers hover around bar tables crowded with ceramic teacups and metal ashtrays. Classical music plays over the speakers, strains of violin strings mixing with the low rumbles of conversation.

A headache teases, and unease blooms, even though I haven't cast yet.

I know I'll have to. The inevitability hangs over me, as dense and suffocating as the smoke in the bar. It's how I'm paying for what I've done.

Old Chang knows of my parents, just like they know of him. Both his bar and Wu Teas are longtime establishments, though each place started out differently. My family's legacy traces back to the days of serving the finest teas to empresses and emperors, while the Chang business goes back to the pubs and taverns of old, to being barkeep to the staff of that same royalty.

When tea slowly fell out of favor, the entire sector fell into decline—it didn't matter who your clients once were. Wu Teas would still be just one more struggling business if I hadn't paid off all we owed.

On the surface, it's easy to see how finally being freed of debt gave us the chance to prosper again.

But Chang's fallen behind on his payments owed to my boss.

Saint Willow is why I'm here.

I let the front door of the tea bar fall shut. The sliver of pale sunlight disappears, returning the place to near darkness. The few faces that turn to look at Jihen and me glance away, already bored. In the back corner of the room is a shadowed pocket of an entrance—the owner's office.

Guilt comes at having to do this, anger at being cornered. Shame, too. It wasn't long ago that my parents were in the same position as old Chang is now.

Beside me, Jihen slicks back his waxed black hair and tries to look cool. "Shall we?"

I shake my head. "I can do Chang alone. Just wait for me over by the bar."

He gives me his greasy smile. "Now, Aza, you know the rules. Saint wants me to keep a close eye on you. Make sure you do what you need to do."

"I'm the caster, not you. And I know business owners. You don't."

My tone is rude and I don't care, just as Jihen's is smug and he doesn't care. We still hate each other, even though we both work for Saint Willow. We're stuck here together.

Jihen is the gang leader's cousin, and while family goes deep when it comes to gang membership in Lotusland, she hasn't been happy with him lately. I'm not here by choice, either, and he knows

2

it. Right now, his only enjoyment comes from my being a prisoner who is forced to cast magic on demand.

"Doesn't matter what you know," he says, "if you don't do as ordered."

"Getting the marks is the order."

"Getting the marks *using magic* is the order. Saint wants you back to casting the way you always have, and that's it." A snort of derision. "Ai-ya, squeezing without magic—anyone can do that. Even little beebees—screaming brats that they are—can find a way to do that. Even *I* can do that."

I nearly laugh at his clumsy attempt to insult me. Still, my pulse starts to race, dread growing along with it.

"I need more time." I'm still trying to get used to casting again. I'm beginning to doubt it'll ever happen.

"Yeah? Well, you're not getting more time. This is your third squeeze, and while I might be your babysitter, Saint says no more hand-holding. I've got my orders, same as you." With a leer, Jihen slides his eyes over my face. "So go in there and cast. And do it right."

Not wrong like my first squeeze job, when I refused to use magic at all. Facing Saint Willow's fury afterward left me cold for hours.

Or the second, when I *did* use magic, and half the roof fell in on us. At least the place was nearly empty, as most businesses in Tea tend to be nowadays.

Getting full magic back—magic that's not mine—hasn't been easy. In the month that I've been living with this strange and ugly new power in my blood, casting's become unpredictable. Every spell feels different. All the control I've ever learned is gone. Nothing but chaos remains, like I'm at war with myself.

Casting pain starts early. Sometimes while I'm still casting, making it harder to focus.

Recovery takes longer—bruises that stay until morning, headaches that follow me into dreams.

And then there's the planet. I'm destroying it more than ever.

The consequences are adding up, and I can't help but wonder about payment. The same way I can't ever forget how I got magic back, no matter how much I try to avoid the memory. I do my best to keep those thoughts away, but I still keep tripping over them. Falling in. Getting stuck in the past until I can crawl back out.

I'm silent for too long, and Jihen gives an impatient tsk. "Listen, beauty—"

"You really need to stop calling me that."

"Then cast." He clucks his tongue. The complaint takes shape on his lips: mah-fung. *High maintenance.*

I make myself nod. He's right—I *will* have to cast. What I did was terrible, but it's also in the past. Unchangeable and useless to me. Saint Willow is my now, wholly in my face and with the power to make everything even worse.

Still, it doesn't mean Jihen gets to watch again.

"I'll use magic," I say, "just like I'm supposed to. But I'm going in alone. It'll be easier for Chang to accept my coming here with less witnesses."

Jihen knows I'm talking about saving face. He might be a gang member, but he's also Chinese, same as me, same as Chang. Some concepts can't be shaken. They run deeper and longer than any gang rule.

He grunts, considering, and lets his gaze drift toward the bowls of free nuts on the bar. He takes out a shred of tree bark from the chest pocket of his suit jacket and casts. Just leftover magic, the only kind he—and most people of the world—can cast. The kind where there's no pain as a cost, no damage to the earth.

The shoulders of his black suit lift and neaten themselves, the lapels pressing smooth. His pinkie curls as he flicks away the depleted starter of the bark. It's the finger I broke last month, now completely better.

I had to cast with the new magic to heal it. There was a brief second when I hoped it would all go wrong—more pain for Jihen. It ended up hurting me more than him, but it was still worth it, since it finally got Jihen to stop whining about how I broke it in the first place.

"Make it fast," he says now as he heads toward the food. "We can't return to headquarters empty-handed."

I turn away, too, annoyed at his use of the word *we*. It's his way of telling himself he's still necessary and more than just my baby-sitter. I even go along with it when Jihen reports back the overblown version of his effectiveness. What do I care? Saint Willow is never going to let me go. Having me at her disposal is how she gets to control full magic.

It's why she forced this unknown magic inside me.

Why I'm no longer sure who I am.

TWO

I weave my way around tables until I get to the shadowed corridor in the back. A long drape of dark red silk is the door.

A guy—tall, run-of-the-mill face, arms too thick for the size of the rest of his body—steps out from the side to block my way. "Sorry, staff only."

"Saint Willow business," I say, meeting his suspicious gaze.

He hesitates.

Don't make me cast to get through, I think. My starter bag lies across my chest, messenger style, and I place a hand on it. *Please. It'll hurt me, but it will also hurt you, and this place. More than you can imagine.*

His eyes move to my starter bag. There's another beat of hesitation, and then he steps back.

I shove the silk drape to the side and walk inside.

It's a closet of an office. The walls are covered in faded blue paper where they aren't obscured by wooden shelving stuffed with yellowing file folders. The air is just as hazy in here, but the smoke comes from the burning of cheap incense and nothing else. Its scent is heavy enough that I know my smog mask will carry it all day. I'd have taken it off by now since I'm indoors, but this is a squeeze job—staying undercover helps keep this version of myself separate. She's a version of Aza I don't really want to know.

The song from out in the bar is also playing in here—straining violins.

Chang is seated at a tiny table at the other end of the room. His expression is grim, a blend of terror and resignation. He must be expecting this—he can't have lived in Lotusland this long to not know the price for holding out. The question, then, isn't why Chang is late—no reason has ever mattered—but what I'm going to have to do to make him pay.

He's older than I thought.

Cold sweat rises on my skin. Elderly people are frail, particularly vulnerable. They make my current level of control over magic—magic that won't listen to how I want to cast—especially dangerous.

"Who are you?" Chang's voice is a creak through the haze, snapping my mind free.

I take three steps until I'm standing in front of him. The incense burner is right on the desk, and the smell rising off it makes my head swim. "Your honor marks for the bar. I'm here to remind you that this month's payment is now overdue. Do you have them for me right here, today, to bring back to Saint Willow?"

He looks me up and down. Scorn dawns. It forms a shine in his eyes, sharp and cunning. "*You* work for Saint Willow? How old are you?"

"I don't want to hurt you, but I will if I have to. Do you understand? If you don't have the marks right now, we'll have no choice but to look into stronger . . . techniques of encouraging you to pay. Trust me, you don't want that—"

Chang laughs. "Trust you? *You?*" He makes a show of trying to peer around me. "Bring me someone who is important, and then I'll negotiate."

I sigh through my teeth, wishing I had some way of avoiding this and knowing I don't. I take out a slip of paper from my starter bag. I draw a six-pointed star on my palm and place the paper in its middle.

"What are you doing?" Chang is sputtering. "Stop wasting my time and leave before I call the police."

A flesh spell, I decide; a relatively small one to suit his aged heart, and hopefully it won't leave the gang with a body to bury.

"Saint Willow doesn't negotiate," I say quietly, "and neither do I."

I take a deep breath and imagine the red cloud of magic in my brain into a shape. A fist around a ripe peach.

I cast.

The floor trembles. Heat spears its way from my feet to my chest. From my arms to my hands. It builds in my one palm. Loose papers drift from the shelves as the incense burner clatters and jumps along the top of the desk.

A deep whooshing sound fills my ears. The taste of the incense smoke in my mouth intensifies, is acrid on the back of my tongue.

I imagine the pictured fist clenching just the slightest bit. The ripe fruit denting from the pressure.

And Chang's throat denting the same way.

The shop owner grabs at his neck, trying to breathe. His gaze is full of panic and disbelief. Shock at what I can do. *Full magic, here? Cast on me, and by you?*

My own shock is nearly as great. The correct spells aren't guaranteed anymore when I cast. Relief swirls in.

"I told you I didn't want to hurt you," I say even as casting pain finds me, thin whispers of it ebbing from behind my eyes, swallowing up any relief that had just been there. I let the depleted starter—the paper gone lacy and ash-like—fall to the floor. "Are you ready to talk about your late honor marks now?"

He nods so vigorously I'm worried about his old heart again.

I wait for the spell to run out. Six points—it should be any second now, and then he'll be fine.

Except the spell keeps going. My palm starts *burning*, the sensation so hot it's nearly icy. The pain behind my eyes bursts into a wide web of agony. Invisible fingers wrap around my skull and dig in.

Chang shoves his chair back—it leaves a gouge in the wall—and staggers to his feet. He begins clawing at his throat. The skin of his face goes mottled, the red parts as dark as the silk drape door to this office. His panic is frenzied. He knows he is dying.

No. No! Not again!

I lean across the desk, hands out. I want to shake him, like such a gesture is anything but useless.

The magic inside me, this terrible power I've accepted—I hate it the way I hate Saint Willow. I hate myself for ever thinking I deserved to have full magic again just because I once did. When I gave it away in the first place just to keep from ever having to use it to serve her.

Chang's eyes are wild and searching, full of his desperation to breathe. His fingers dig in harder.

Then he begins to cough, finally drawing in huge, hoarse gulps of air. I stumble back, the pain behind my eyes thickening even as the pounding of my pulse deep in my ears begins to let up. Over the sound system, the violins have morphed into flutes. I can't place the song, only that it's cheery and light and the very opposite of this moment.

"You"—he's gasping—"*you*—"

He stares at me like any second I might choose to cast once more. His terror is back, all signs of resignation and scorn gone.

"I do not have the honor marks," he wheezes. "Business has not been very good. But I'll get them soon, I promise."

"Promises of soon aren't enough." I struggle to speak above a whisper, pain coming in slaps. "Until you find a way to pay, the bar's going to start failing health inspections, your suppliers will cancel contracts, loyal customers will stop coming. Do you understand?"

Chang nods, still pale in his cheeks. At least he's not dying anymore.

"This place has a safe." I hold out my hand. The stink of incense turns my stomach and makes the room tilt again. "Empty it of marks. And if there's nothing inside, then empty your wallet."

"My wallet? But—" Everything about him seems to shrink. "There's nothing else."

"And still it's Saint Willow's," I say. Then I make myself shrug, as though I don't care at all about his situation. But really, I understand everything about his despair. Saint Willow has me trapped by my family's legacy, too.

Wu Teas, always within her reach if I don't obey.

THREE

I shove marks into my jacket pocket as I leave the office. It's nowhere near what he owes, even though I left his safe and wallet bare.

Jihen's at the bar, his ugly white sneakers so bright they practically glow against the beaten wood floor. He swigs back the last of his drink as I approach through the haze of tobacco smoke.

"Tea's not bad at this place," he says. "No Wu blend, of course"— he winks, and my stomach rolls again—"but good enough. Ho-goh mo yeh."

Better than nothing.

"Let's go," I say. Everything is louder out here because of my headache. Laughter is the pounding of drums. Flutes turn into chain saws. I long to sleep off the effect of casting, but that's going to have to wait until after we're done reporting back to headquarters.

Jihen burps. "Got the marks?"

"Everything he could give me."

"You going to throw up in my car?" His smirk spreads across his face, oily and wide. "Ha-mai beng? Feeling sick? Maybe you should walk."

I wonder just how bad I appear and how much of my pain shows. Jihen looks for my weaknesses the way treasure hunters collect clues.

"I'm fine." I push down the pain, hiding it out of sight. Away from him. "Never been better."

"Well, beauty, one thing's for sure—you cast magic after all, just the way you were supposed to. So I won't have to rat you out, at least." He gestures across the bar, where workers are sweeping up glass and ceramic. A huge crack has split the back wall, tearing a shelf loose and sending cups and dishes crashing to the floor. It was only luck that no one was sitting close enough to get hit.

I leave the bar first.

It's a ten-minute drive from just past the midway mark of the sector down to headquarters on its south side.

I sleep for all of it, burying my headache beneath oblivion. I wake up only when Jihen's already out of the car and slamming the driver's door shut.

I slowly sit up, blinking. The pain is better, I tell myself.

Sunlight is thin and bright, the smog that's layered into it a longtime staple of the world. Beneath it, Lotusland is as wet and gray as ever, the city's dampness one more thing no one living here ever escapes for long. It's summer, but it'll probably be raining by tonight.

We're parked outside a dim sum restaurant. It looks as vacant as it did the first time I saw it—covered windows, dusty and dingy brick, a faded sign above the front door.

No one would ever guess that the sector's powerful gang leader schemed and worked from within. Which I guess is probably the whole point.

Across the street are the pink woods. The scarlet trees lie along the bottom of Lotusland like the frill on a skirt. It's the part of Tea that forms the city's southern border.

The pink woods have been this way for over two hundred years. A permanent reminder of magic that was too powerful to harness, the scar of demanding too much.

A group of casters—full of magic but inexperienced, thinking of dares and of showing off—wished to make a mark of some kind. To bring beauty to a world that was falling apart all around them. They cast in unison, believing danger spread thin was nearly no danger at all. That they would be safe and live to tell a tale. Instead, none of them were, and the acres of trees have grown pink ever since. Their tale, told by trees.

That was also the year that a typhoon hit Ena Island and hundreds of people drowned.

One more way full magic made its mark.

I get out of the car and walk toward the restaurant. I don't bother knocking before I pull open the door. For better or worse, I'm part of Saint Willow's gang now, and who knocks before entering their workplace?

Only a month, and already everything inside is too familiar. The amber lighting, the gold-papered walls, the red-and-yellow lotus-print carpeting. The round black tables and matching chairs. Scents of tea and perfume and cooked rice. And live music—Nima, bent over the piano at the back of the restaurant.

The two of us don't speak. Not since the powerful gatherer of dark spells helped Saint Willow put magic back into me. Not since that night, a night I'll never be able to shake myself free from. Or deserve to.

Nima lifts her head as I step inside. Her orange eyes are a bright flash in the dim. They're the only visible proof she's an Ivor, her full magic turned useless because casting again would break her apart. This fact matters little to Saint Willow. Nima is still her gatherer, a tool for her to use as she likes. What does she care if Nima can't cast as long as she still has the ability to collect the world's most dangerous spells?

Nima drops her gaze and goes back to playing the piano.

The gang leader is seated at the center table.

Saint Willow is elegant and striking the way cats are elegant and striking right before they attack, all liquid lines and sleek muscles. Her clothing is the same, always silks and satins, each piece perfectly draped over her body. She's flipping through a glossy magazine, appearing bored.

Sitting on either side of her are her two most trusted men, Luna and Seb. I tell them apart by how Luna hates jackets and wears his white sleeves rolled up, while Seb is never without a full suit and tie. They're playing cards, their favored hobby between jobs.

I'm sure they know Jihen would kill to take over for them, just as I'm sure they aren't worried about it. Jihen isn't clever enough to figure out how to do it without Saint Willow knowing who's behind it. And Jihen would hardly be her first choice to replace them, anyway.

She flips a page in the magazine and asks coolly, "Any problems with Chang?"

Meaning, did I squeeze using magic? It's her only concern, making sure I'm at my most powerful so she will be.

I stay by the front door and wait for Jihen to begin the report. He loves every chance to prove his importance to his powerful cousin.

He pulls out a chair and sits himself down across the table from her. "No problems at all. Ho hoong-yee. Simple as anything. And Aza squeezed just as you asked."

Saint Willow nods. "I'd like to speak to Aza, please."

She still hasn't looked up from her magazine. But the order is more than clear, so I head over, slowly tugging my mask down over my chin. Fresh trepidation tingles along my spine—what might she want to hear from me that Jihen can't tell her?

My headache from Chang's bar comes roaring back. The slow song Nima's playing isn't helping, every single note heavy and thunderous, pounding away just as my head does.

Jihen settles into his chair, seeming unconcerned. "Sure, and she can tell you how before she cast, it was me who—"

"I want to speak to her alone."

Still yet to say a word, Luna and Seb simply lay down their cards, get to their feet, and leave for the kitchen.

Jihen stares as they go, his mouth flapping in surprise. "But we still have to give you our full report. About Chang."

"Aza can give it to me." Saint Willow's long black hair is wound into a bun, and it sits on the top of her head like a crown. "And on your way out, go ask Xu in the kitchen to bring out some tea."

Another flap of Jihen's mouth, and he pushes back his chair. He gives me an ominous glare as he gets up, as though I have any say over the sector's gang leader.

As soon as he's gone, Saint Willow shuts the magazine, lays it down on the table, and watches me.

Piano notes continue to sound, breaking up the silence. Saint Willow never asks Nima to leave, the way pet owners will keep their pets alongside them regardless of who else is around.

"Sit down."

I slip into the seat Jihen just left and place Chang's marks on the table in front of her. Unease stirs—from the headache that's a fist inside my skull, from the taste of the words I have to say next. My report on Chang will be nothing but an echo of Jihen's own report on *my* family. Back when he was squeezing *us* for marks we didn't have, staking out the teahouse, and threatening all of us. That person is me now.

Saint Willow's eyes pin me into place. "Did you *cast* on Chang?"

I give her a harsh smile. "Did I have a choice?"

Her expression stays elegant, her eyes unmoving. "Good."

"I still don't see why I have to do it every time. When it's not necessary."

"It's always necessary."

The memory of old Chang clawing for breath. I push it away.

"The shop owner was old," I say. "I could have found another way to get the marks." One without pain. "You're wasting my casting."

A single crease appears between Saint Willow's brows before being entirely smoothed away an instant later. She leans back in her seat, as casually observant as before.

I was meant to miss it. This extra careful shuffling of her thoughts, like caution slipping through.

But it's also like she's holding something back, and I shudder.

Whatever she wants to talk to me about, it's not some routine squeeze job. And she knows I won't like it.

"Tell me, Aza—why do you think I wanted you to have full magic back?"

To control me, I wish I could spit out. *To pretend my magic is actually yours.*

But then Xu comes out of the kitchen pushing a dim sum cart, approaching us with food.

I stare down at the black wood of the table, thinking fast.

What does the gang leader actually want to hear? The head of the Tea Sector only asks questions that have answers she can accept.

Xu sets out a pot and cups, little bamboo baskets still steaming through their lids. Saint Willow asks about har gow and sticky rice pouches.

On the other side of the dining room, Nima's piano-playing changes. This new song is an up-tempo one, every single note nearly a sparkle, as though she's trying to assure me that whatever is coming isn't all that terrible.

I can't believe her.

The last time I heard her play music like this—music that made things seem like they would be fine—was just over a month ago, when I went to go see her at the Tea Chest Hotel. That was when I first asked her about a gathered spell to steal magic, the cost of which turned out to be my ability to cast. My own magic, torn from me.

I can no longer remember if our hope was real or if we somehow knew, deep down, that we were just pretending.

Neither of us knew that Saint Willow was set on me getting magic back or how she would make it happen.

I shudder again.

Nima playing this happy song right now?

It brings me right back to the real cost of our plan. Of everything we've done.

FOUR

I could have won the tournament on my own. But simply winning had stopped being enough. Between Rudy's death, finding out the truth about Shire, and then what happened to Kylin, it wasn't just the championship I wanted to take from Finch. I wanted to take his magic from him. To strip of him of the one thing he cherished most. And to do that, I had to make a deal with Saint Willow.

I thought I'd outsmarted her, too. Agreeing to be her caster, then giving up my own magic in order to take away Finch's. The price I was willing to pay—it should have solved everything. What use would I be to Saint Willow without the power to cast?

Heading home after the tournament was over, I should have known. Should have remembered that some things still weren't finished. That Saint Willow isn't Saint Willow because she lets people walk away from deals they've made with her.

Pure fear ran through me at the sight of her and Nima waiting for me outside the teahouse that night.

Saint Willow held out the blue bead starter on her palm as though it were some kind of offering. And it *was*. A rare gift, even. But that bead—the gathered spell that would put magic back into me—was also a trap.

Knowing that changed nothing.

"Okay," I said to her. It was the only answer I could give, because it was the only one she would accept. I had promised to cast for her, and she was going to collect.

Saint Willow pocketed the blue bead. Her teeth glinted in the dark. "I'm glad you can see reason."

"Whose magic is it?" I asked.

"Impossible to tell." Nima's eyes were shrouded—by the contacts she wore to hide her orange Ivor eyes, by the darkness of the night. "It's collected from the air, as I gather all spells. It is no one caster's as much as it is everyone's."

There was a loneliness to her words, the way someone could still feel lonely despite not being alone, and it pierced me deeply. I thought of my magic adrift out there, a part of me gone forever even as I appeared unchanged.

"How does it work?" My voice was flat from behind my smog mask, trying not to shake. The rain was cold; my skin was as numb as I felt inside. "None of us can cast."

"The spell is self-casting," Nima says. "Since you once had full magic, you only need to have the gathered spell in hand to release it."

"It can't be that simple." Regaining magic should be as hard as losing magic. It should be even harder. All magic has a cost.

"Except that it *is*." Saint Willow's words were sharp, full of barbs. "Aren't you fortunate that most of the work lies in the gathering? Just as you are fortunate that my gatherer was happy to do it."

Nima stayed quiet behind her smog mask. Her fear of the gang leader was something not even the dark could hide. I didn't want to imagine how furious Saint Willow must have been to discover

Nima had helped me give up my magic. I remembered Nima's confession that she didn't want another caster at her boss's mercy. Yet there we were, the both of us more trapped than ever.

I hugged my starter bag closer, shivering as the rain came down. The bag was new, made of soft red silk, given to me just that day. A message from my parents that they were starting to trust me with magic again, the way they had trusted Shire before she died.

Saint Willow slipped on a smog mask. She blew against her palm, and leftover magic slipped the hood of her jacket over the black waterfall that was her hair—Lotusland's most powerful gang leader, careful always to be hiding in some way.

"Be ready for when it's time," she said to me. Her voice was icy.

"How will I know?" I was already aware that Saint Willow was not the kind of person you simply contacted. She was the kind who chose to contact you.

"You'll know." The gang leader let her gaze slide over to Nima, waiting until the gatherer dropped her head before coming back to stare hard at me once more. "And, Aza, no more tricks. Or your parents *will* pay."

With that, she turned and left, disappearing into the night. Without facing me again, Nima followed, and soon I was alone once more.

FIVE

"It seems my question is more difficult than I mean it to be."

Across the table in the dim sum restaurant, Saint Willow is concentrating on uncovering bamboo baskets. But still I sense her tracking my reaction, the way snakes can smell with their tongues. I have no clue how long ago Xu disappeared back into the kitchen with her dim sum cart. I struggle to return from that night; the horror of the memory dug into my mind like claws.

Saint Willow's question . . .

I take food—a mini char sui bao, a square of turnip cake—and place it on the plate in front me, just to keep my hands busy. I'm not hungry in the least. My headache thrums, wound tight into aching knots behind my eyes.

"I think you wanted me to have full magic back because you wanted a caster of your own," I finally say. My answer can't be wrong if it's just stating the obvious. Still, I'll have to tread carefully until I can be sure about what she's really asking me. I gesture to the pile of marks—Chang's—still on the table in front of her. "You wanted me to get it back so I can be your squeezer with magic."

Her laugh is soft and low and absolutely full of contempt. Her dark gaze narrows, and for a second it's disappointment I see there before it turns back into her usual disdain. Like she's been secretly mentoring me and I've failed to pick up on something she assumed I was ready for.

"The problem with you, Aza, is that you're naive like a child." Her lips curl humorlessly. "You search the sky for the sun even as you know you'll never see it, because you've been told it exists. When all that does is keep you from looking to see what else the smog around us is hiding."

I drink tea—noticeably *not* a Wu blend—and wait for more. My hand is clenched so tightly around the cup that I'm half expecting the ceramic to shatter.

"You sit here, detesting me for making you work as my caster, when really you have no one to blame but yourself. For seeing only what's right in front of you."

This is the part of the game I've already learned to play, following when Saint Willow decides to lead. Not because I don't know any better, like she says, but because I have no other real choice. She's taken away any and all others. And she knows it. It's how *she's* learned to play this game.

In the background, Nima's piano playing goes on, notes still jarringly exuberant.

"It *is* true that no other gang leader in the city has a full-magic caster of their own. It doesn't hurt for my reputation to grow among the other gangs as stories of your power—and therefore mine—spread throughout the sectors." Saint Willow's teeth gleam as she smiles, predator-like. "But, Aza, everyone knows I'm always able to collect what I'm owed, whether it's by magic or other means. You being able to squeeze for me is a given, the obvious. It's the fact of the sun—with no one thinking to look around the shadows."

I go stiff. The smugness in her tone adds danger to the air. Saint Willow is loving this.

"Tell me what you see in the shadows, then," I say.

Saint Willow takes a sip of tea. "I know you fight using magic."

Fear trickles down my spine.

Saint Willow isn't supposed to know about fighting and casting. The Guild of Now has always kept those hidden.

The gang leader, slithering her way into dark corners everywhere.

I pretend not to understand. I focus on breaking open the pork bun on my plate and tell myself she knows less than she does.

"I don't need to fight as your squeezer, either," I say, my voice somehow steady. "I could have convinced Chang by just talking to him."

"That's not what I'm talking about, Aza, and you know it." She pours me more tea, elegant as ever.

I shut my eyes hard for a second. If Saint Willow knows about the tournament—

"Nothing about Lotusland stays secret from me forever," she continues gently.

The pain in my skull pounds and pounds. I drop my hands into my lap. She pulls one of the still-steaming baskets closer and begins to unfold its pouch of sticky rice.

"It was Jihen who gave it up. I'll admit, he was able to keep it a secret for far longer than I would have given him credit for. But after you nearly slipped away, my temper got the best of me, and so my men felt the wrath." She peels away steamed lotus leaves to reveal the soft heart of rice nestled inside. "Appointing Jihen your baby-sitter seemed an appropriately humiliating kind of punishment for his underhandedness, don't you think? The perfect amount of pettiness for my empty-headed cousin."

I knew she wasn't happy with him. It makes sense now, Jihen always being there with me for my squeeze jobs. It's because Saint Willow found out he was going behind her back.

Still, he's probably lucky to be alive, family or not.

I watch as she stabs her heart of rice with chopsticks. My chest tightening, I pick up my own chopsticks with cold fingers. I break off a bit of turnip cake and wait for the rest.

"I've been quite busy this past month," Saint Willow continues, "ever since finding out about the underground tournament. It got me thinking about trying something new, a different kind of challenge. Power, if not properly and regularly fed, dulls. The threat of weakness nears."

Power. The word creeps along my skin. Saint Willow thrives on power most of all.

She smiles, her beauty cutting against the restaurant's low amber lighting. She sets down her chopsticks and picks up her tea. "I will never let my power diminish. I've spent too long building it to let it just wither away. It's time for it to grow."

"There's nothing left for you to take." There isn't. She has stakes in every business in the sector, has planted seeds throughout the rest. Ownership, loyalty, fear—Saint Willow's power is always present.

"But there is."

"You can't." I blurt this out, too surprised to stop myself. "Whatever Jihen told you about the tournament, he didn't tell you enough. You need too much."

"Jihen told me enough to make me want to find out more—and so I did. For the last month, I've had my men squeezing for a very specific kind of information—details about fighting stages, backers and bets, all the rules of how it works."

It's too easy to see. The Tea Sector's gang members in the streets of Lotusland like stealth rats in the night, sniffing for scraps. I shouldn't have missed it, except I've been too caught up in worrying about this new magic, unwanted and intrusive.

I make myself sip tea and act like none of this means much. "There's no way you'll be able to do this." Guild members like Embry are as good as ghosts, their most significant secrets as underground as they are.

A short and dismissive laugh, and Saint Willow inspects the dark paint on her nails. "Many people have gone to these tournaments. And past viewers, past fighters—they all talk if given enough incentive."

More smugness, and my stomach turns again. Nima's song, back to stormy and thunderous, plunking out stirrings of doom in my blood. "So many people wanting another real tournament worthy of their bet money. So many past fighters wishing to prove themselves again. So many casters desperate to use their magic."

My hand trembles around my cup.

"And you, Aza, will be my fighter."

SIX

Ceramic clatters as my cup falls. "I won't."

"You will."

Gold-papered walls push inward, wanting to crush me. The room's amber light dims, and black creeps over my eyes. I struggle to breathe as panic swells and swarms.

Snippets of past fighting rings flash across my mind—the stink of blood, the cracking of bone. The pain and pleasure of casting, the line in between as fine and treacherous as the edge of a blade. Kylin, burning. Finch's cold green eyes digging into me as he aimed to kill.

All of it is both faded and too vibrant, like the worst and most jagged seconds of old nightmares.

To have to fight again? I'd be bringing those nightmares back to life. I'd be making new ones.

"I'm giving you back your days," Saint Willow continues. "No more squeeze jobs for now. But at night, you will fight for me. Jihen's reports tell me your control isn't perfect, but still good enough for what matters."

What does Jihen know of control? What does the gang leader? Neither of them will ever know how wrong it feels, this strange magic that is no part of me. That makes me want to climb out of my skin.

"I almost died," I finally say. "I hated fighting and casting magic."

Another low peal of soft laughter. "Except you didn't die. You became tournament champion. As for hating it, that's a lie, and we both know it. You can no more turn away from casting than you can decide to stop breathing."

"I gave up magic!"

"And yet here you are."

Hearing her say it, I know it's true. I was cornered and out of choices, but I still never felt more powerful than when I was in the ring.

The ache in my head swells and recedes, waves of an angry ocean. My face goes hot at how, again, I have to do what she wants.

"Who is Rudy?"

I go still. There's no real reason not to tell her. Rudy left no family behind for her to find. Plus, she's not asking about Rudy Shen, the now-deceased owner of Shen Apothecary. She's asking about "Rudy" in the ring. About me fighting as him.

"I needed a ring name," I say.

Her eyes lock on mine.

"You will fight as Aza from now on. I, of course, will be your backer." Her expression is as self-satisfied as when she forced unwanted magic on me. "Play this my way, and the payoff will be huge. Much more efficient—and fun—than chasing after dozens of debts."

The truth explodes from me.

"It's too dangerous for me to fight with this magic."

"All magic is dangerous."

We finally agree on something. And yet it still means nothing. Not in the face of her power.

"What if I cause a quake or something?" I sense my hope

draining, even as I keep arguing with her. Nothing I say will change anything. "What if I hurt someone?"

Her gaze hardens, goes pointed. "That never stopped you from fighting before, did it?"

I shake my head, wishing I could deny it. Deny the destruction I've already caused to the world. Scars on the earth, fallen buildings, annihilation. Most recently, that night, the worst of it all—

Saint Willow drinks tea and then smiles. "Wouldn't it be unfortunate if your parents' teahouse's recent success suddenly came to an end?"

I push away from the table. Fury is the wild beat of my pulse, battering at my neck. There's a kind of shrieking in my skull—the pain of my headache, my uselessness against this woman—and I want to scream out loud. To run, when there's no escape.

I stare down at Saint Willow. I'm stuck, but maybe I can improve things for my family again. At least that part worked last time.

"I want a cut of the bet marks you make off me." I'm nearly breathless, rage a quiver in my voice. "For every single match I fight for you."

Her smile thins. "Ten percent. To be paid after the match."

"Fifty. I'm the one fighting."

"Twenty. I own you."

"Forty. You can't do this without me."

"Thirty. I own your *parents*." She lifts the lid of a still-covered bamboo basket. Instead of food, inside is a small white envelope. She hands it over. "The address for tonight's fight. Don't be late."

I shove the envelope into my starter bag and get up to go. I'm shaking all over; the soft haziness of the restaurant only makes me feel more shattered inside.

"Also, Aza?"

I stop, pull up my smog mask, and force myself to wait.

"I've put a lot of work and thought into this endeavor. And not just for me, but also for you. I hope you appreciate it."

I hate her.

For a few long seconds, our eyes lock. Clash. A battle of wills. The room falls completely silent. The piano notes come to an abrupt halt—even Nima knows to stop playing for this.

Finally, unable to hold on, I drop my gaze. I swallow my rage, tell myself: *Later.*

Nima begins to play again.

"Good." Saint Willow grins. "To prove your loyalty, I want you to wear a ribbon around your arm whenever you're in the ring. Just as you did before, but for me this time. Choose a pattern that will make me happy."

SEVEN

I find the train with the longest route.

It's one that nearly circles the entire city, heading north, then dead east, then back west along the southern border. The entire loop takes more than an hour.

I climb on, find an empty seat in the back, and fall asleep. By the time I wake up, my headache has quieted to a small, muffled throb, and my stomach says it's nearly time for dinner. I would call my parents to tell them I'm going to be late, but casting full magic kills cells. I haven't had a working phone since before Shire died.

I peer outside the train window.

It's the Paper Sector. The streets are lined with bookstores and stationery shops and newspaper kiosks.

My train's made better time than I thought it would, given the never-ending track repairs and reroutes through an ever-crumbling city.

Soon the shops begin to change, from books and paper to clothing and fabric, from bland milky hues to bursts of saturated violets, crimsons, ultramarines.

The Textile Sector.

I get off at the next stop.

The day's waning, but it's summer. Sunset is still just a hint—the faintest orange tinge in the smog. That tinge *is* sunset now, since the sun hasn't shined clearly for decades.

The Mothery is about to close for the night. I slip inside to find the shop empty except for Piper, cutting fabric on the table.

She looks up, red hair carefully done in fat waves. Her makeup is as immaculate as always. She's clad in a blue sequined jumpsuit, so sparkly it nearly washes out the rows and racks of glossy fabrics lining the shop.

I haven't seen her since the tournament. I was set on never seeing her again. I didn't realize until this second that I actually miss her. I tug down my mask and smile.

"Aza! What a surprise!" She comes forward and gives me a hug.

How can I ever fight for Saint Willow the way I fought for Piper? Both can cut you down with a single look, but Piper is like a soft fuzzy spider, while Saint Willow is pure viper.

"Hi," I say into her shoulder, sequins crinkling beneath my cheek. Tears come, surprising me, and I blink them away fast as I step back. "Big plans tonight?"

"Honey, I dress like this just for me. What brings you by?"

"I can't just come by and say hello?"

Piper's eyes flutter. "Yes, except that you haven't. What's kept you away?"

For a second, I'm sure she knows what I've been up to since the tournament ended. That she even knows about that night and the price I was willing to pay to have full magic back. But her expression stays too pleasant, and I let out a deep breath.

"Sorry, I've been working," I say. "My parents have a teahouse—Wu Teas—and it's been busy."

The talk of profits makes her grin. "How nice for all of you."

I nod. "I wanted to ask if you've heard anything about a new tournament."

"I *have* heard, and through good sources." A wink with one perfectly made-up eye. "Whoever is in charge knows to at least give the impression they know what they're doing." Then Piper waves a hand. "But most knockoffs never last long—they mistake how smoothly the Guild's tournament runs for simplicity instead of skill and strength."

"This isn't the first one?" I wonder if Saint Willow knows just how deep the underground runs.

"Far from it. But they come and go, never leaving much of an impact. It's why I've never had an interest in going."

But, Piper, none of those had Saint Willow. Or me.

Now her gaze narrows, and I know I'm not hiding my tears as well as I thought.

"Aza, why are you upset? It can't be over a tournament that means nothing."

"I have to fight in it." It's all I can do to not look away, to hope she buys my half truths. "I . . . made a deal with someone. Something for my family."

"For Wu Teas?"

I nod. Isn't it always? The family legacy, hundreds of years old, rich with the blood and dedication of my ancestors—and its survival hangs in the balance.

What if the weight of a legacy only ends up pulling you under? What if the only way out is to swim away? To abandon the past in order to see a future?

My parents would never see it that way. Shedding the teahouse wouldn't be freedom; they'd feel defeat. A loss of dignity, a great humiliation. My parents live and breathe that fear every day, just as our ancestors did when they built our teahouse.

I love my parents too much to wish for their downfall. The recent boom in Wu Teas sales and the promise of more only make it worse. Failure after great success is its own special kind of defeat.

Piper's tapping her painted lips with a just-as-brightly painted fingernail. Confusion has filled her face at my obvious reluctance. "I've seen what you can do, Aza. Your magic made you a champion. You'll be great even under these circumstances."

"This magic isn't—" I stop, remembering that Piper doesn't know I even lost mine in the first place. "I would just rather be fighting because I want to, I suppose."

"Well, that's understandable." Still, she stays watchful.

"I have a new backer, too."

A knowing smile. "Aah, now I see why you're upset. Business is business, Aza. I'm not unhappy with you for that."

I don't know if this makes me feel better or worse.

"I might be curious enough to go tonight after all," she says. "Would you mind?"

"I'll look for you."

"You won't be able to miss this." She casts, and leftover magic fluffs her thick curls. I let myself laugh as she spins in a circle so that the sequins of her jumpsuit flash beneath the shop lights. The shine of her fabric reminds me of why I'm here in the first place.

"Piper, I need a ribbon for tonight."

"Of course." She leads me toward a cabinet that's bursting with rolls of brightly colored fabric.

We find a pale green satin with a willow tree pattern in white. Saint Willow can't say I didn't try to make her happy—the print is perfect. I roll up the ribbon Piper cuts from the fabric and stuff the silky material into my starter bag.

Dread turns my fingers clumsy—to have to be Saint Willow's in the ring, too. How much is too much?

My fingers brush against a different ribbon.

I take it out—pink-and-red peonies on cream. It's the silk ribbon I wore all during the tournament to show that I was backed by the Mothery. I've left it in my bag ever since. Unwashed from the fight I thought would be my last, the fabric is worn and still stained in parts. I run my thumb over streaks of blue mud from the ring, over the dried blood from my veins. Both Guild magic and true magic, back when mine was still my own.

What kind of magic will Saint Willow show us at her tournament tonight?

I hold the ribbon out to Piper. "I should probably give this back to you, since I have a new backer now."

Piper laughs, but the laugh isn't an unkind one. She takes the strip of silk, rolls it up so it's neatly coiled once more, and places it in my hand. "No other fighter I've backed has ever wanted to return their ribbon to me. You should know by now that this is yours far more than it's mine."

I fold my fingers over it. I can't deny I'm glad to have it back.

"I'll see you tonight, Aza Wu." A flash of coldness—competitive, cutting—in her eyes. I know it's not for me, but it chills me anyway.

It's a reminder that Piper doesn't go to tournaments for fun. *Business is business.* "Whoever your backer is, I hope they never forget they're backing a champion."

That's the problem, I want to tell her.

Saint Willow knows it all too well.

EIGHT

Leaving the Mothery, I head northeast to get back to Tea. The sector is close, the next one over if I cut across diagonally, and so I walk instead of catching a train. My headache is mostly gone, and I want the alone time. Ever since becoming Saint Willow's squeezer, too much of my days are stuck with Jihen, going back and forth. Or I'm at headquarters, forced to report and listen and accept. I'm hardly ever alone.

The sidewalks are still crowded, even though the light's nearly gone and the air's cool. I cut across the top corner of Tobacco, and its scents drift past the edges of my mask—nutty, oaky. Then the smells change over, turn into the scents of clean grass and mild honey, and I'm back home in the Tea Sector.

As I head toward the teahouse, I take out the envelope from Saint Willow and tear it open. Inside, there's a slip of paper with an address on it:

Midnight
August 19
Waterfront Station

There's a small pang in my chest as I stare at the words.

Waterfront Station is where you go to take the seabus out to Rockland. The outcrop is the only thing in the water that's between Lotusland and the High Shore Mountains up north. The city decided the span of flat-topped rock was large enough to turn it into a city attraction. So they built the station and the seabus—a leisurely ten-minute ride across the waters of the Upper Inlet, and you could pretend you were in some quaint seaside town.

The last time I was out at Waterfront Station, Shire was still alive. We were both still kids, and we begged our parents for a day trip out to Rockland.

It was windy; I remember the seabus swayed until I felt sick. Shire secretly cast full magic, a stillness spell to make me feel better. She covered up the faint bruise of her casting pain with her jacket sleeve, hiding it from our parents.

We picked barnacles off the low posts of the quay, their strange mottled blue color a sign of how they were slowly getting sicker. There was a growth of shrubs, somehow still vibrant and green, which we agreed was our favorite part. We ate popcorn shrimp (mock only; the real stuff was too expensive) for lunch at Moby's, and then a dinner of fake-fish-but-real-chips at the Fishmonger, with sesame ice cream in between. We didn't leave Rockland until dark.

The air out there still smelled okay back then. Still more like the sea than like chemicals. Not the way it does now.

This past winter, Rockland began to slide into the sour waters of the inlet. The city eventually determined the whole thing would be swallowed up before long and it would not be a good look if anyone was on it when it happened. So now the place is condemned.

The small hotel that once boasted water views from every room is all boarded up, the eyes of its windows forever shut. The ice

cream stands and imitation seafood restaurants have been disman-
tled. The only thing yet untouched is the fake lighthouse, a beacon
to nowhere.

With nothing left out there to see, seabus service came to an end.
And with no seabus, Waterfront Station was also closed. The city
talks about plans to scrap both, but because it's Lotusland, nothing's
happened yet.

I peer inside the envelope, wondering about a key starter, about
marks to buy starters for the ring. Frustration comes—how can
Saint Willow not know about those?

I flip over the paper.

There are more words scrawled on the back.

Surprised, I read:

black box

What can *this* mean?

Black box, black box—I say the words to myself again and again.
But I still don't understand.

I flip the paper back over to read the address once more, deciding
to focus on the one thing I *do* know.

Waterfront Station is in the Spice Sector.

The Spice Sector is also where the Salt Lick is.

Where I'd find Oliver, if I wanted to.

He's been trying to reach me all month, ever since I stripped his
brother of his magic at the cost of my own.

How to explain to him what I am now? A squeezer, a tormentor,
holder of stolen magic—a killer. How can I say that and look him in

the eye—Oliver, who willingly gave up magic for his brother, someone who's been able to live knowing he'll never have magic again?

I can't.

I fold the paper, tuck it back inside my starter bag, and climb the front steps of Wu Teas.

The sign on the door is flipped to CLOSED, and inside, my parents are cleaning up after the day. My mother is clearing the dining area that's one part of the shop, while on the retail side, my father is going over the till and the day's receipts.

The stack of receipts is tall, taller than I ever remember it.

We're getting a taste of what it was once like for Wu Teas, back when our name was spoken with reverence.

The dining room is still tiny, but everything else is new, from the tables to the serving dishes to the cutlery. The walls of the shop have been freshly papered in a honey shade and the floors laid down with polished wood. Outside, the name WU TEAS is painted in glossy green letters across the storefront window. Proud again.

Our in-store sales have tripled this month. We can barely keep up with the new accounts. My parents are talking about hiring help, something they've never, ever had to consider.

I should be happy for them. For the shop and everything it stands for. I mostly am. But it's hard to not see Saint Willow wherever I turn, her fingerprints on everything.

Mom walks over with a tray of dirty dishes in hand. She's wearing a new outfit, one of the few she let herself buy after years of going without. She even looks younger, the lines at the corners of her eyes and around her mouth eased away along with the worst of her worries over the teahouse.

"Honestly, Aza. Couldn't you have asked someone to call for you to let us know you'd be this late? You don't work alone, after all."

I sigh inwardly at the idea of asking Saint Willow or Jihen to call home for me so I don't get in trouble. "Sorry, I left late for my last delivery, and then the train broke down on the way home."

Mom tsks as a reply. I can tell she's torn between being proud of my job with Saint Willow—the leader of the city's most powerful gang, after all—and wishing I could just work at the teahouse now that it's so busy. But there's nothing we can do about it—my parents would never consider turning down Saint Willow's request that I stay on as her courier.

"We saved you some dinner—you can eat out here." Mom turns and heads for the kitchen in the back.

I move to the front counter, where Dad's working. He's brought out the teahouse's ancient calculator. It's one of the few things he won't consider upgrading.

Your great-great-great-grandfather used this—change everything else in this room if you like, but this stays.

"Other than running late, how was work?" he asks.

"The same. How about here? Nothing but busy, I hope." I shake the tip jar. It's full.

He grins and keeps working through bills of sale. "Very much so. We really should hire someone if this keeps up—and let's hope it does."

"I can help you find someone, if you want."

"With what time? You're as busy as we are and barely here."

"Actually." I set down the tip jar, remembering Saint Willow saying I won't have to squeeze anymore. "I'm going to be around more during the day from now on. Saint Willow is training some-one else to help out as courier."

"Oh?" Fresh concern crosses his face—the possibility the gang leader doesn't need me anymore. Or even worse, that I've done something wrong. Either way, it would mean shame on the family.

I smile and hope it reaches my eyes. "I've been doing such a good job, I can have some time off for now."

"Well, isn't that nice of him." Dad looks more than impressed.

I stretch out my smile. It's probably way too close to being a gri-mace. "Sure is."

My parents—like most of the city—are still in the dark about who Saint Willow really is. Not only do they still think the gang leader is a man (I did, too, until she allowed me to meet her), they still think she's well meaning. They believe Jihen's visits were never shakedowns but simply the price we must pay to remain under her protective watch. For the greater good.

This is what they've learned to see in order to go on. And now that things are so much better for them, I can't see any reason for telling them otherwise. I don't even know if they'd believe me.

"If he's training someone to share courier duties," Dad continues, "then perhaps it won't be long before you're back here full-time."

Not likely. But I nod, reaching over to a shelf and straightening a row of Wu Teas branded mugs. They're the latest addition to the shop, untested merchandise now considered creative rather than a risk. "Hope so. It'd be nice, that's for sure."

Dad's still punching buttons on the calculator. "You know, you're quite lucky, having Saint Willow for a boss. If there's ever trouble, there's no one more powerful you can have on your side. Never forget that."

I can barely keep from laughing. I finally manage a reply. "I know I'm lucky, Dad. I remember every day when I go to work."

"And your mother and I know we're also very fortunate." He gestures outward at the teahouse, a soft sheen of appreciation in his gaze. "Being under the protection of Saint Willow has only paid off."

Another silent scream is building in my head, wanting to unleash itself to block out Dad's words. The depth of his gratitude toward Saint Willow, his cluelessness about just how much power she holds over our all our lives—my stomach churns. I've freed us from her grip, yet I still have to let my parents keep believing as they do in order to keep them safe.

Mom walks in with the tray, now with a bowl of hot rice on it, and vegetables and beef fried with garlic. "Eat before it gets cold. You can tell us about your day while we finish closing up for the night."

My parents are trying hard for us to feel like a family again. For a long time, I know they stopped seeing me, unable to look past their pain. But time has helped heal the wound of Shire being gone while I'm still here, still alive.

Now their happiness only makes lying to them even more difficult. Their trust is just another burden I have to carry.

"Thanks," I say, moving over and taking the tray. "I really am sorry about being late."

Mom tsks again, but I can tell she likes the apology. "Next time, just call."

"Aza just told me Saint Willow is giving her some time off," Dad tells her from behind the counter. "He says she's earned it."

Mom's smile says she's as grateful as he is. "That's so kind of him."

I sit down and shove food into my mouth, unable to taste one bit of it. "It is, yeah."

NINE

Three hours later, I'm in my bedroom, attempting to tie the willow-printed ribbon around my upper arm. My fingers are stiff and uncooperative despite the warmth of the air.

I try not to think about what lies ahead. But doing that only makes my thoughts race, chasing me down so I can't miss them. My arms and legs are shaky, and I imagine the magic in my veins already at a froth, already promising it won't obey.

With this new and unwelcome magic, everything Shire told me about casting, everything Rudy taught me about control—it's all useless now.

An image of Kylin burning away in the ancient baths pops into my head, and my new tournament ribbon slips from my hand. The memory batters at me, fresh and vivid.

My eyes blur.

I already showed that I was capable of horrible things with my own magic. Now I'm even more out of control. More unpredictable. Dangerous to everyone and everything.

A single pact with a kid—and I refused her. Why didn't I just do it? Then maybe she'd be alive. Maybe I would never have fallen for Finch's trick. Maybe—

I shake the image away and take a deep breath. Okay.

For Kylin, I have to fight tonight as hard as I ever have. Even if it means doing the impossible, which is trying to control this strange magic stuck inside of me. Because I'm the one still here.

I swipe at my eyes with my sleeve and bend over to pick up the ribbon. I start winding it around my arm once more, but then I stop. I take out my old ribbon from my starter bag. I run my fingers over its pattern of peonies on cream—over raised dried splatters of blue mud and blood—and start wrapping the silk around my arm. When I'm done, I take the new ribbon and wind it over, covering the first one completely. The result is a bit bulky, but I leave it, unable to explain why I feel better. Only that I do.

I open my bedroom door a crack. The hallway outside is darkened, and I listen for a minute, making sure my parents are asleep. I shut the door and pick up my starter bag from my bed, slinging it on across my chest. I tug on a fresh smog mask and click off my lamp.

I walk up to my bedroom window and peer through the glass.

Nothing but night. The shimmering outline of my face reflects back at me, a pale and frightened-looking oval.

I shove the window open and silently climb outside. After jumping down to the ground, I turn around and slide the window shut. Three steps and I'm at the row of tall snowball bushes that separates our backyard from the rest of the city. I push through the hedge's branches, green leaves and white petals drifting down to my sneakers, and step out into the alley.

It's merely habit now, sneaking out. I no longer have to hide what I'm doing from Jihen. But it's a habit that's hard to shake, that still feels smarter to keep than break.

There are muffled sounds of traffic. Nearby houses and shops press close.

I stay back against the hedge for a minute, going still and just waiting, listening. But the shadows stay shadows, so I head toward the street, toward the fight.

TEN

Lamplight haloes down. I keep outside its edges, trying to disappear into the dark. Tiny alleys beckon, and I duck into them before emerging somewhere on the other side. Detours and double backs and turning from people I pass on the sidewalk—I do all of this without thinking. Noise spills outs from open tea cafés, and cars zip by. There's the occasional train rumbling in the distance.

I keep heading west, weaving my way through Tea, then Flower. I'm still trailing heavy scents of rose and lilac when I reach the border of Spice. Then it's dry peppery heat that's in my hair, a swirling saltiness against my skin like someone's carried in handfuls of the Pacifik and rubbed them onto me.

Instead of turning into the sector proper, I veer north, toward Waterfront Station. It's the farthest north you can go in Spice and still be on land. After that, it's nothing but the murky brown waters of the Upper Inlet.

"Fighting on water again," I mutter out loud as dread slips in. The last time a fight had anything to do with water, it was the baths, and Kylin, and—

My mind fumbles, steers around the memory.

This is not the same thing. The baths were part of the finished ring, not the outside world it was cast from. And it was cast by the Guild. I have no idea what to expect tonight.

I think about the Salt Lick, which is just blocks away. How

Finch once tried to feel whole with fighting and magic, and how he might want that feeling back.

What if he comes tonight? Would Oliver let him come alone?

Then I'm at the end of the sector. The High Shore Mountains on the other side of the Upper Inlet are completely invisible, obscured by night. What's left of Rockland is just as hidden, the outcrop still sliding away by the day. The smog's helping to obscure it, too, hiding being the thing it's so good at. Like most people, I've never seen a star outside of a picture and I'm not going to see any tonight.

Wind whips and lashes at me freely, no buildings around to break up its path. I smell brine as air pushes at me, and beneath the scent, a sharp sourness that seeps through my mask and into my nose. It's the water out here, home to warped fish and strange creatures that could once be classified but are now beyond naming. It's the ruins of our magic, the cost of our greed.

Just ahead of me is Waterfront Station. The building is completely dark, and I can barely make it out against the midnight black of the water. Dome-shaped, the mostly brick-and-concrete structure sits on top of wooden barges that float next to the sandy shore. Parked right up alongside it is the seabus, the boat with a passenger capacity of three hundred.

I remember having to board it from inside the station, remember Mom admonishing Shire for turning the turnstile around and around instead of just going straight through. Dad held my hand as we stepped onto the rickety connecting bridge, the cracks between the boards seemingly big enough to slip through. The water below shimmering and soft-looking, its depths nothing but mystery.

I head toward the station, moving carefully in the dark, trying to convince myself that nothing about tonight's fight will really be new. I'll be used to it all.

It might not be *my* magic, but I still know magic. This might be Saint Willow's tournament and not the Guild's, but I survived last time. More than that, I *won*.

And yet.

My heart pounds too hard, and my pulse is erratic, the magic rushing alongside it already feeling defiant. My mouth is as dry as the sand I'm kicking up with every step. I'm not touching the water, but the sense of drowning surrounds me.

I reach the entrance to the station and yank at the handle of the glass door. Locked. No surprise there.

I press my face close and peek inside.

The space is empty, lobby-like. Wide windows climb up toward the ceiling. Linoleum flooring peters out into darkness. Everything looks locked in time.

A quick glance around reveals I'm alone on the shore. Wherever the crowd is for this tournament—wherever the other fighters are—they aren't here with me.

I open up my starter bag and feel for the paper with the address. My fingers tremble as I hold it and read the words on the back again:

black box

I shove the paper back in the bag and examine the door to the station.

Nothing but smooth glass and metal.

I get closer, swearing under my breath and wishing I had thought to leave the house earlier—everyone else must already be inside. Trying not to feel frantic, I scan every inch of the door, looking for even the tiniest bit of black, for something that hints at being part of a box.

Nothing.

I swear some more and step back, now looking at the brick walls of the building around the door. Maybe I was looking *too* closely, thinking too small. What if this black box is huge? Maybe this black box is actually around the *entire door*—

Just like that, I see it.

Not a real box at all, but the image of one.

A black box the same size as a starter is graffitied on the wall, off to one side of the door frame. It's simple spray paint, applied unsteadily, the three-dimensional cube a bit distorted. But it's still obviously a box. And my way into the ring.

But now that I've found the key starter, I can only stare at it, scared anew.

Saint Willow, how are you planning on holding everything together?

Not that this new magic inside my blood can be trusted, anyway. I don't know what casting to get inside this ring tonight will cost. The ground might shake itself apart. Each and every one of my bones might turn into dust.

Or, or, or.

I draw a six-pointed star on my palm and place it over the painted black box on the wall.

I cast.

The wall in front of me starts to fall apart. Bricks slowly begin to jostle loose. As though connected by invisible hinges, they all swing open as one, forming the shape of a doorway. A black box.

I'm still busy watching this, trying to guess how much magic such a spell would have needed, when casting pain hits.

I jerk back with a cry as heat races along my skin. Explosions like fat pinpricks of fire go off against my arms. I wince at the feeling of bruises forming.

The worst of the heat passes. I yank up a sleeve to look, wanting to be wrong but knowing I'm not.

Marks like small plums are painted onto my skin. The bruises appear nearly black in the night. Not just on my arms, but on my legs, too—I feel their burn.

I knew to expect this, but still. A kind of baseless, useless anger fills me. I want to blame this on Saint Willow and how she has no idea what she's doing. Who knows what kind of information her men squeezed from people to put this tournament together? What if they have no idea at all about protective magic?

And just as badly, I want to blame this *other* magic. Because I can't trust it to play by the rules. For not letting me control it the way I once did my own.

Saint Willow. The magic now in my veins. There's no escaping either.

I shove my sleeve back down, step through the doorway and inside the station. The full heat of fire fades from my skin and is replaced by a thin buzzing, as though my limbs are still half asleep and struggling to wake up.

It smells like brine inside the building, too. It's that same ugly sourness that says we've messed up the earth. There's also a heaviness in the air, a weighted sense of abandonment that creeps into long-empty places. Wide beams of wood cross overhead to leave behind the faintest hint of mildewed cedar. Outside the windows, smog hangs, a gray shawl wrapped around the shoulders of the blackened inlet.

My shoes squeak just the slightest bit against the linoleum as I walk through. I tug my mask down, and my breathing seems too loud in all the quiet. I reach a set of heavy inner doors. As I grab one of the handles, it vibrates against my hand. An even stronger vibration emanates from the door itself, a thrumming that is both noise and motion.

It tells me I'm no longer alone.

I pull open the door.

ELEVEN

This room is the heart of the station. The last of the land before you were shuttled north onto the water. Walls make up three of its sides, while the fourth is a series of gates, each marked by a turnstile. Beneath the station's high domed ceiling, dozens of bulbs hover midair, their insides cast alight. Not by the Guild this time, but by some other magic.

Here is the crowd, as well. People swarm in all directions so that everything feels charged.

As I keep walking, letting my eyes adjust.

Just as with the annual Tournament of Casters, there are tables set up along each of the three walls. Counters for bets, registration, and starters. Noise fills the air as spectators catch up on who's already registered and who's just shown up, on who they hope might still come at the last minute. Loudest of all are the calls for bets.

"Ten minutes to get your bets in! Who's it going to be tonight for you? Bets start at five marks, just five marks!"

"How are you betting tonight? Status- or technique-style bets? *Who* are you betting on tonight? Choices are yours, so get your bets in!"

"Forty on Tau, two skin spells!"

"Twenty on Luan to bow out!"

"Get me ten marks on Indy to cast a blood!"

I head toward the registration counter, feeling both sick and relieved. This tournament feels just like the real thing, the one I know and beat. But the thin buzzing beneath my skin from casting my way in still lingers, nagging and constant.

Until I bent the rules and lost the Guild's protection, casting as a fighter in their tournament meant I didn't feel as much pain as I would have otherwise. The Guild aimed to keep all their fighters whole, their tournament a celebration of magic. What reason do I have to believe Saint Willow will do the same? What desire could she have to keep fighters safe? To prevent the earth's destruction?

As long as she stays safe, the answer is none.

The sense that I have to prepare myself as I never have before hits me keenly, like I've badly jarred my funny bone and the ache of it is zapping me throughout.

Casting in her rings—it's going to hurt. Everything will be treacherous.

I move along, trepidation a growing fist in my chest. I listen to more bets being made. The ring name Luan sticks in my brain, somehow familiar. Then his face comes back to me. The first fight of the Guild's tournament. Piper's fighter until I knocked him out to advance to the next round.

If he's here to fight in Saint Willow's tournament, how many other fighters from the Guild's will also come? Who will I recognize? And who might recognize me? I never thought I'd see any of those fighters again.

Then I hear this:

"Eighty on the reigning champ, *eighty* on Rudy the Champion to win!"

The sound of my ring name—of *Rudy*'s name—nearly makes me jump.

That's me. They want me here, expect me. They think I can keep winning.

My face flushing, I yank my mask back up.

Rudy the Champion.

My stomach flutters, gone empty of everything but pure nerves and a jumbled mix of pride and resentment. I wish I could tell everyone to keep their marks and to bet on anyone else. Forget winning—I don't even want to cast. Not with this trespasser of magic. I'll be lucky to get out of this alive.

I scan the crowd for Saint Willow's men, trying to decide who the gang leader might send. She won't show—her face is her best-kept secret. I'm reminded of all the years I spent picturing her as a man because no one could ever talk of knowing her.

No Saint Willow means no Luna or Seb tonight, either, since they never leave her side.

Perhaps Jihen, I think. He's gone to tournaments before. He might even have been ordered to report back about the fight—to keep his usual eye on me.

I hope it won't be Nima. She and I—nothing lies between us but destruction.

The crowd presses closer as I keep walking, and mild panic filters into my brain. There must be more than two hundred people here, maybe even close to three. Whether Saint Willow got her men to recruit people with threats or promises, it makes no difference, because it worked. A packed crowd for the opening fight of a new tournament—she will be pleased.

I pick out fighters in the crowd, ring names written in white ink blazing bright from their cheeks. Spectators slow down to stare as they pass, giving the fighters as wide a berth as possible. I still remember them doing that to me. Awe and fear—it's how a lot of people feel about us. It'll probably always be this way.

When I spot a caster with something scrawled on *both* cheeks— ring name on one, a zero on the other—I stop to get a better look. I never saw anything like that in the Guild's tournament. But then I pass a second caster with that same zero, and a third, and I know it's something new. Just as Saint Willow came up with her own kind of key starters, this is one more thing she's thought up.

I pass other fighters, scanning their names along the way.

Vetta. A lady in her thirties, hair dyed pink, skin tanned like she lives at the beach.

Indy. The new fighter I just heard the bettors talking about. A teenaged girl, just like me. Only taller and thinner, with brown skin and black hair worn cropped instead of down her back.

Bardem. A guy maybe a couple of years older than me. Dark blond hair and sleepy-looking gray eyes set deep in his pale face.

Tau. Early twenties, pink-flushed skin, hair mostly hidden beneath a leather ball cap.

There's no sign of Piper.

And I actually don't recognize anyone here, no fighters from the last tournament. Maybe the Luan I heard about earlier is someone different? It could be any Luan. Even the two people shouting at spectators to place their bets are unfamiliar.

But it's obvious that the most important things are the same at this tournament. I'll still have to walk into a ring. Will have to fight. To win. When I'm supposed to be done with all of this already.

A rush of recklessness freezes me into place. Defiance that tastes as good as the air tastes bad.

What if I don't fight? If I just turn around and walk out of the station? No one here can stop me. No one here can keep me.

But then I shake my head.

If I don't fight, I lose everything. Saint Willow will make sure of that.

I'm still swearing silently at the gang leader, my hate for her brimming full, when I notice the room is emptying.

People are streaming out through the turnstiles. The corridor on the other side is also lit up with bulbs, guiding people in the right direction.

We're taking the seabus to get to the fighting ring.

The realization leaves me uneasy. Such an unnecessary elaboration will take serious magic—not just to cast but to *keep* casting. It lines up with Saint Willow's need for power. Still, I can't decide if such a show is more foolish or impressive.

"Leaving for the fight in five minutes!" a man calls out in the distance. "Five minutes! Last call for bets! All winnings to be picked up at the bets counter after the fight!"

I walk over to the registration counter and get in line. More of the crowd streams through the turnstiles as I wait. Impatience and anxiety flow around me.

"Next!"

I take off my mask and move up to the lady standing behind the counter.

"My ring name is Ru— My ring name is Aza. But it used to be Rudy."

Saint Willow ordered me to use my own name, but I would have switched anyway. Rudy wanted me to move on. Fighting with uncontrollable magic—it feels wrong to use his name after he trained me to use my own. "Can you mark that down so anyone who bets on Rudy will know I'm Aza from now on?"

The lady looks at the paper on her clipboard, then stops when she reaches my name. It's clear on the sheet, easy to spot. But still I have to blink as though I'm not quite sure I'm really seeing it here. If Saint Willow instructed the bets counter to call out the name Aza instead of Rudy, I don't blame them for already forgetting. *Aza* doesn't mean anything to a tournament. Not yet.

From behind the counter, the lady holds a pen to my name, moving it slowly across each letter as she speaks. "Sorry, dear, can you confirm this spelling? *A-Z-A?*"

I grit my teeth. "Yes."

She sets down the clipboard, picks up a white marker, and writes on my cheek. The letters feel especially gigantic, like she's worried everyone's going to miss it. But I know it's just my imagination. The name feels bigger because it's my own, the first time I'm using it in a fight.

When she lifts the marker, I start to pull back. But she stops me.

"Not yet, almost done." She draws on my other cheek.

I already forgot. The zero. "What's it for?"

"The tally of how many fighters you eliminate. It's cumulative, so everyone will come to know how powerful a fighter is by looking at their tally. Or not powerful, of course. Helps spectators decide on betting, too."

A mark of power. Another way for Saint Willow to pressure me.

My hand wants to reach upward and touch my cheek. I'm used to the feel of ink on the other. Not this one. Not both. "What if it smears away by accident?"

"It shouldn't." She glances around almost conspiratorially, like she's about to spill a secret. Her voice lowers. "It's part of the magic."

I nearly roll my eyes. She's probably right that the ink will stay, though, if Saint Willow's managed to make it close to the Guild's.

The lady straightens. "Don't forget your starters."

Another fighter approaches the counter to register, so I move away. I find the starter counter and head toward it, unsure how it works here. I'm not about to spend marks of my own to fight in Saint Willow's tournament.

The guy behind the counter starts to ask me my name, then catches sight of it on my cheek.

"Aza, Aza," he mutters, looking at his clipboard. "Here you are. Your line of credit is four hundred marks. That will buy you forty single-use starters."

A line of credit? I'm almost amused, in a sickened kind of way. This is just one more way Saint Willow is getting others indebted to her. These ambitious casters can enter on credit, dreams of a big payoff in their heads. Doing so costs nothing up front. And after spending the last month squeezing for her, I know exactly how everyone's going to made to pay when their time is up.

But her greed might backfire with this. Collecting from full magic casters won't be easy.

And I bristle when I consider more carefully the line of credit she's given me. Four hundred marks for forty starters. That's way more than what's needed for a single match. Or even for a few. I didn't come close to using that many in the last tournament.

Saint Willow sees no end to my fighting for her. Her greed with me is the same as her greed for power.

I buy ten of each kind—red for blood spells, white for bone, gold for skin, and silver for breath. There's an additional texture to these ring starters. A fine, luxurious grain. Piper called Saint Willow's tournament a knockoff, but if she felt these starters, she might describe it differently. An upgrade. The deluxe version.

Still, making them fancy doesn't mean that they'll work. I'd rather they be made of the plainest plastic in the world and do what they're supposed to.

I slip all the coins into my starter bag.

Two minutes to get to the seabus.

I head toward one of the turnstiles. The faintest image of Shire as a little girl racing around appears in my mind's eye.

Wherever I'm headed out there on the water, it won't be as fun as Rockland back then.

The image of my sister—of the past—fades. Leaving only the now.

I take a deep breath and push through.

TWELVE

I follow the streaming crowd along the short corridor. It ends when the building does, and then we're filing onto a skinny wooden bridge that shakes with each step.

Here is where Dad held my hand, promising me I wouldn't slip through and into the sea. The fear seems silly now, but as I cross the bridge and look down, a shiver still manages to wash over me. The water is as black as ink, its depths greater than I want to think about. If something happened, could magic save me?

I tug my mask tighter, trying to keep out as much of the salt in the air as I can. It continues to build into a noxious little bouquet right beneath my nose. I'm relieved when I step onto the seabus, despite longing to be anywhere else.

Rows of seats, nearly all full. Outside, the smog hangs in the air, writhing and twisting against the glass of the windows. Bulbs bob beneath this ceiling, too, and rays of cast light flow from each. The lights are no brighter than the dimmest of candle flames, flickering like there's a wind coming through.

It's all nearly romantic-looking, if you forget this thing is practically a ghost ship. No one's set foot in here for over a year. A heavy air of abandonment clings to the dusty and darkened corners, forms an invisible sheen over the worn seats.

The childhood trip to Rockland suddenly feels beyond the past.

As though it's from a different timeline altogether, one of some other lifetime.

"Aza."

It's Nima, murmuring my name as she steps closer, leaving the thick of the crowd behind.

Immediately, I tense up, willing her to back away. To disappear from view again.

The last time we were together in a crowd, we left chaos in our wake. Stirred up a darkness. It's been a month, and more nights than not, my mind finds its way back to a crowded Lotusland street, its pavement and buildings drizzled damp with a cold summer rain, the sound of screams filling my ears. Nobody to blame but myself.

I want Nima gone. Away from near me. Away from here, where there are too many people.

The orange of her eyes is invisible, carefully concealed by the contacts she always wears outside headquarters. Tonight, her gaze is light blue.

Her hand skims mine in the half dark of the seabus. A fold of paper presses against my palm, and then she slips back into the crowd, where the shadows are thickest.

Nima wouldn't seek me out unless it was important—the weight of that night must rest heavily on her, too.

I'm tempted to read the note right away.

But clearly, whatever's on it is meant to be a secret. I can't be sure who's watching me here. Or watching her.

I fold the note and slip it into my jacket pocket.

Waiting for the seabus to get going, I head off to one side and lean against a panel of wall between windows. Cool night air drifts in, leaving my skin chilled.

Still no sign of Piper.

I think about Oliver and whether he's heard about the tournament. If he's come here to check if I have. I wonder if Finch is nearby, my former rival, desperate to get close to real magic again.

The seabus rocks and sways in place, still tied to the shore as more passengers climb on. The wooden barges creak and groan below. There are mutters about getting seasick, and again the old memory of Shire casting me better drifts across my mind. People call out concerns about maximum passenger capacity, since the seabus feels way too crowded. And though no one else is asking, I can't help but question if this magic of Saint Willow's is really as capable as that of the Guild.

The stink of the water down below flows upward in broad rushes. I breathe through my mouth, trying not to think about how only a thin sheet of metal separates us from the depths of the sickly inlet. Metal that's been unused for a long time.

Overhead, the bulbs wink out and then back on. The flickering is slight and uneven, the kind right before a power outage. When you're no longer debating *if* the dark's coming but *when*.

A brief dazzling surge.

The sudden brightness reveals Jihen in the crowd. He sees me first, and he gives me his usual leering grin. I watch him mouth the words *hello, beauty*. I ignore him, turning my shoulder so I'm facing the windows. Nearly everyone's on board.

Keeping my hands low and out of clear sight, I unzip my starter bag and find the metal holder for my starters. There are still a few attached to it, leftover ones from the last fight of the Tournament of Casters. Useless to me now.

The holder was once Shire's, her own invention, and using it is way more effective than having to yank out starters from your pocket each time you cast. One second can be the difference between knocking out another fighter and getting knocked out yourself. Between advancement and elimination. Between living and dying.

Working by feel with my fingers still hidden inside the bag, I tear off the old starters and attach the new ones. I sort them by color onto their correct loops—red, white, silver, and gold. I fit as many as I can, then attach the entire holder to one of the belt loops of my jeans. The weight is comforting despite my wishing I didn't have to be doing this. I pull the hem of my shirt over it.

A few seconds later, a metal screen along the side of the seabus slowly drops, closing off the entrance—no more passengers. Without warning, we begin to glide across the water. The smog parts like a cape being swept open, only to close back around us as we drift. Beneath my feet, the floorboards are dead still, the motor guiding this thing absolutely silent.

We're moving by magic.

The crowd applauds. All complaints are forgotten.

I stare outward, as though the gray outside can tell me what to feel. I'm still torn, as deeply impressed as I am alarmed. Already, Saint Willow's debut has proven it has great magic running it, and that's exactly the dilemma. Embry would declare all of this a waste, casting so much unnecessary magic outside the ring. Full magic has limits, no matter how strong its caster. Things on the surface can appear perfect, until you dare to scratch and see the mess beneath.

I wouldn't mind discovering Embry here right about now, sneaking on board to see what all the rumors are about. He's one of the most intimidating people I've ever met, but he's also reassuring, a promise that he knows what he's doing. It feels wrong that he's not here.

Overhead, the bulbs flicker again, the floorboards give a long, rattling groan, and Jihen gets to his feet.

He's dressed in one of his many black suits, along with his usual white sneakers. A silver handkerchief is tucked into his chest pocket, as though to mark the night as a formal occasion. He makes his way toward the center of the seabus, smiling all around so the passengers can't miss him. He holds a stack of notecards.

I choke back a snort of disbelief.

Jihen is the face of Saint Willow's tournament.

Equal parts horror and laughter begin to bubble up in my throat, and I cough to cover any sounds of snickering that might be escaping.

Satisfied everyone is getting a clear view, Jihen claps his hands, and the passengers fall completely silent, waiting.

His grin is wide and smarmy as he begins reading off his top notecard.

"Hello, hello, and welcome to the first annual Founders Tournament. My name is Jihen. I'm the group's Head Speaker. You all hear that? *Head Speaker.* That means if any of you here have any questions, you come to me, got it? Because I am *Head Speaker*, and no one here better forget that."

He looks up and down all the rows, making sure to make as much eye contact as possible. To be as intimidating as Saint Willow, as smooth as Embry.

Passengers react by glancing in confusion at one another, like they're waiting for the rest of the joke. Slowly, they start to clap.

My hands stay clenched into fists at my sides as new questions form in my mind. A single word keeps circling my brain:

Founders.

Who are they? What kind of group is Jihen representing? What are they supposed to do?

Oblivious to the crowd's reaction, Jihen grandly flips to the next card. I catch a glimpse of bullet points and scrawled arrows. Despite everything, I have to stifle laughter again.

"Let me explain to everyone how this tournament is going to be run, all right? First off, this isn't just going to be a once-a-year event." Jihen sneers. "Nothing so small as that, you got me? No, the Founders Tournament is going to run *all year round*. That's right, a fight every night for as long as we like. Each fight will take place in a different spot around the city. Every single ring will be cast by the Founders using the most powerful full magic that still exists anywhere on earth."

More clapping. Louder this time. A loud and appreciative whistle. Jihen, winning everyone over with the announcement of fights every night.

I barely hear any of it. My alarm from earlier gets louder.

Who are these Founders that they believe they can cast full magic on a wide scale every night without effect? Don't they know magic always has a cost? That it must always be paid for in some way?

The lights overhead flicker more and more.

I'm scared to try to guess how powerful this magic harnessed by Saint Willow really is. How reliable.

Jihen flips to the next card. He's licking his lips and grinning, fully enjoying finally getting to be in the spotlight.

"Only our starters will work during fights, along with whatever other stuff comes from the ring. To keep Scouts from finding us out, Founders will cast diversion spells to hide everything from the outside world. We'll also be casting protective magic over the fights themselves, so fighters won't get hurt casting and we won't break the world. Of course, we can't promise no accidents will happen, but if something does, it won't be our fault. Got it? So don't blame us."

More applause, hesitant at first before becoming more boisterous. Someone hollers, and Jihen positively swells.

He turns his awful grin toward me.

Look who's in charge now, Aza.

He starts in on rules. A fighter is eliminated when they bow out or are knocked out. There's no time limit on a fight. Every fight will follow a free-for-all, last-fighter-standing format. All bets must be made and collected on the premises. There will also be fun surprises along the way. *Nothing but the best for the best, am I right?*

I've nearly tuned him out. Am unable to follow along. Because all I can think about is how dangerous all of this is.

Saint Willow hasn't just created her own tournament based off the Guild's—she's spilling all their secrets. She's revealing details and insider information the Guild has built up over centuries.

Who's to say who is here right now, absorbing every single word Jihen spills? Not everyone is loyal. Any Scout would love to learn all of this.

If Embry knew, I doubt he'd dismiss this tournament. He'd be furious. So would the rest of the Guild. Leaving Saint Willow's tournament to collapse on its own might be too much of a risk. But starting some kind of magic war against Saint Willow and her Founders wouldn't be any safer.

Who are these Founders to equate themselves with the Guild? To agree to work for someone like Saint Willow?

The seabus speeds up, rocking, and my stomach rocks with it. Outside the window, the smog is swirling fast, like moths' wings beating hard at the glass. Water streams across it in rivulets, assuring me we're really moving.

I steady myself as other passengers reach out and grab hold of the backs of seats. Some whisper, glance around, and I read the questions on their faces:

Who is doing the casting?

Can they really be strong enough to cast all this magic?

What can't *they do?*

Jihen flips his cards and continues.

"Also, any caster can fight on any given night, whether they won or lost the night before."

The loudest cheers yet.

"One last rule. The most important rule of all." Jihen winks to charm. A sour taste climbs up my throat. "We're at a full house already. So, no talking about the tournament and the fights in the outside world. It would truly sadden me if any of you were to . . . disappear if that happens. Is that clear? No mistakes. And no second chances."

More glances throughout the crowd. Flashes of uncertainty mixed with fear.

Suddenly, half the hovering light bulbs blink out, and they don't come back on. The seabus shakes and shudders and gradually comes to a clumsy, halting stop.

Passengers murmur, fearful and uncertain again.

One thing's clear. The Founders might have more than enough magic—and tons of flash on top of that—but they're still not nearly as polished as the Guild.

The gate on the side of the seabus scrapes itself open.

The dark outside lifts with it. Night is now day. Clean sunlight filters in instead of smog, wafts of sweet grass and green fields instead of sour brine.

"Whoa," a passenger drawls. It's Bardem, the sleepy-looking caster I walked past in the station. "What *is* this place?"

Jihen flips to his next notecard and reads off it.

"Welcome to the Founders Tournament fighting ring number one. Otherwise known as the historic—and long-gone—Bamboo Maze of Daiyu."

The last of the light bulbs go dark.

THIRTEEN

Jihen starts to lead everyone out when a small stampede happens. Eager to see the past come back to life, passengers push and shove in their hurry to get off the seabus. The site is an illusion, but that doesn't make it seem less vivid, less real.

My head suddenly spinning, I take a step back. Then another, falling back farther. The crowd surges past me as they head the other way. I glimpse Nima slipping out, disappearing into an illusion where soon I'll be forced to cast for real.

I can think of a million other places I'd rather be right now. Accepting this latest order from Saint Willow—I thought I was ready. I *need* to be ready.

Yet here I am, my fear of casting back in full force. At war with myself. Magic is supposed to be a fighter's best ally, but it's my biggest enemy.

I'm last on the seabus. I step off.

The earth is green again.

It's all bamboo, forests and fields of it. Wood-like stalks as thick as tree trunks soar higher than any tree I've ever seen in Lotusland. Their tops are lush and feathery with leaves, curling over so they sway back and forth. Some have woven themselves together to form mini canopies against the sky.

As the stalks sway, a slow and deep creaking sound fills the air, as rhythmic as a heartbeat. The wind carries scents of mown grass and fresh oats. I imagine sitting out here all day, doing nothing but getting warmed by the sun.

I've only ever seen bamboo in tiny bits. Miniature versions of these stalks grown in pots, with just a single stem or two. There's a store in the Tea Sector that sells them, priced as the rarity that they are. Only the wealthiest can afford to buy. It doesn't seem real that such great amounts of it—the vastness of this forest—used to exist.

I reach out and grab a stalk. It's cool to the touch and as smooth as polished wood. Its hold in the ground seems absolute—a shake, and the thing doesn't budge at all. I smell my fingers—grass, the faintest hint of earth, baked-in daylight.

I've never seen reality cast so perfectly before.

My skin prickles like pins and needles are traveling around within it. More remnants of the pain that came from casting my way into the ring. I rub my arm, my thoughts whirling.

The memory of the light bulbs going on and off on the seabus. That hard bump of a stop when we arrived. Cracks in the illusion that are glaring if you know where to look.

Protective magic means nothing if it doesn't work.

I brush away inklings of dread and instead kick hard at the ground. Testing it.

The heel of my sneaker brings up nothing at all, the earth here packed as solid as the bamboo growing from it.

I glance over and notice that the seabus is gone. Where it was only seconds ago is now just more bamboo. The *inlet* is gone. Its brown-black murky waters full of strange warped creatures—also bamboo.

I turn back toward the crowd.

Everyone's already loosely organized themselves. Fifty fighters stand together. Twice as many spectators are in their own sprawling group. And stalks of bamboo, growing in the thousands, wherever you look.

Jihen places himself in front of the spectators, so he's between them and us. He's still holding his stack of notecards. He reaches out with his free hand and raps his knuckles against a bamboo stalk. The sound is deeply cavernous as it echoes over the crowd. Everyone falls quiet.

Jihen clears his throat again. He throws out a look that is supposed to say he's powerful, but instead it's really just him squinting and pursing his lips, like he's eaten something bad. He begins to read off a card.

"Fifteen hundred years ago, there was this great battle in the Maze of Daiyu. When the end came, it was really bloody, sure. But it wouldn't have ended at all if not for magic. So here's how it started, all right? The city of Shulan got bored and invited themselves over to this city called Daiyu. The Shulanese decided they liked Daiyu enough to stick around and take it for themselves. And so they invaded. And the Daiyunese guys, you know, they hadn't fought a war for decades. Their king was as old as dust, their military soft and lazy. They had no chance in hell of fighting off the Shulanese, who were known to be pretty good fighters. People everywhere called them the Two-Legged Locusts, because that's how the Shulanese lived—they took over lands, milked everything dry, then left to find some other party. Also, the Shulanese were really good with swords. So you can see why the Daiyunese were freaking out like beebees."

Jihen's voice is as smothering as oil. I tilt my head to stare at the bamboo tops, at the sight of their cool green leaves waving in the breeze. When a wisp of a cloud shifts the light, the hair on the back of my neck shifts, too.

There are faces in those leaves. Set into them the way wood has a grain. I only caught sight of them because of the glare—the same way glare can bounce off dust motes and make them sparkle.

I stare harder at one face that seems familiar.

It is.

It's Wilson.

A familiar face that is now part of the ring up there instead of down here with us as a fighter, the way he was in the last tournament.

My mind races as I think of the members of the Guild. How they were always at the ring but invisible, casting their magic from out of sight.

Wilson is one of Saint Willow's Founders. Wilson, whose enthusiasm for fighting eclipsed his finesse in the ring. Who maybe saw his best chance to become something bigger and couldn't say no. Not as a Guild member but as a Founder.

If Wilson's the kind of caster Saint Willow has recruited for her Founders—casters responsible for building her tournament's fighting rings—then maybe all those bulbs flickering is just the beginning.

Anger flows, and a disappointment that nears betrayal.

Wilson, you fool.

I dig my heel into the forest floor again, my skin now abuzz with apprehension as well as old casting pain. The ground seems so solid, but what if it's just thin crust over something closer to liquid? The bamboo didn't budge an inch when I tried shaking it, but bamboo is hollow inside. Nothing but air.

Jihen continues, flipping cards.

"But even before the Shulanese crashed the party in Daiyu, the Daiyunese knew they'd become a bunch of loafers from taking it so easy. They arranged for a dozen of the land's best casters to live nearby in the king's palace, just to do their bidding, like fetching them things and stuff like that. As it turned out, these same casters saved their butts when the Shulanese invaded. The king got his casters to use magic to grow bamboo overnight, forming a giant hidden maze that changed *as* it grew. When the Shulanese soldiers attacked, Daiyunese soldiers led them into the maze. There, they trapped them and killed them."

A ripple of admiration goes through the crowd.

I scan the bamboo tops again. Sunlight dances, and faces shimmer in the breeze. How many others might I recognize?

I scan the crowd.

Pav.

Another familiar face, his nervous grin that I remember so well from the Tournament of Casters.

A kind of relief comes as I smile back.

Pav sneaks over toward me, tapping me with his elbow when he gets close enough.

I don't want to fight Pav; he cast the way he grins—without confidence. But it's better than him being a Founder. Better for him to get eliminated every night than choose to work for Saint Willow.

Past him are some of the new casters I saw back at the station—Vetta, Indy, Bardem, Tau.

And there among the spectators, I spot sequins glittering in the bright sunlight, the reflections of dozens of tiny mirrors.

Piper.

Jihen keeps reading, his voice close to shrill against the soft creaking of the swaying bamboo.

"The death trap of the maze convinced the remaining Shulanese to surrender. The Daiyunese—seeing as they had already won and really just wanted to get back to their nice cushy lives—decided to play nice and let the rest go. Still, thousands of warriors had already been killed in the maze, and the bamboo there soaked up all the blood from the ground, so their stalks grew red for a while. The Daiyunese casters ended their spell, and the maze went still, its paths never to change again."

I stare harder at the walls of bamboo surrounding me, curious about old secret paths that once wound their way around before being stilled. Wondering if they've left their shadows burned into the depths of green, the same way light dances on the insides of your eyelids after you stare at it for too long.

I look *through* all the stalks, letting my eyes go unfocused. The bamboo blurs together, and what's left behind sharpens. Grows clearer.

Then I see them, because it's impossible *not* to. Shadows shooting through the stalks like thread needled through fabric. Paths that no longer exist.

"Really bad drought hit this place seven hundred years later and destroyed it," Jihen reads. "Very, very sad, of course. But those palace casters got a pretty good deal out of it, since they became legends and lots of songs and stories were made up about them. Even all those dead Shulanese warriors got pretty famous with stories of their own. One legend is that kids playing in the maze before all the bamboo dried up forever were said to see warrior ghosts stumbling around, dying all over again."

He reaches over and tears a low-growing leaf from a stalk.

Bamboo sap flows from the wound, but it's as red as blood.

"Nice trick," a fighter calls out. It's Vetta, pink-haired and smirking.

Jihen lets the leaf drop and winks, clearly impressed with himself. "The Founders Tournament promises never to be boring."

I have to snicker.

Then Jihen comes over, and I glare at him, trying to guess what he's up to now.

"Aza Who Used to Fight as Rudy." He gives me his grin. "Considering you might have a bit of standing coming into this tournament—"

"Um, she's reigning champion of the Guild's official annual Tournament of Casters," Pav says, gone huffy on my behalf. "I think that's more than just a *bit*—"

Jihen throws him a dirty look, and Pav stops talking. A deep flush climbs his cheeks, then creeps down into the pretty bird tattoos that lace his arms.

"I know who she is," Jihen hisses sulkily. He shoves his stack of notecards into Pav's hand. "Here, hold these—least you can do for being a distraction."

Next he tugs out the silver silk handkerchief from his chest pocket and holds it out to me.

Up close, I see it's not a handkerchief at all but something like a Chinese fan, the handheld type that opens and closes. And instead of being whole and pleated, the panel is made up of dozens of stiffened silk strips.

"Pick one," he orders, pointing to the strips.

"What am I picking?" I ask, wary as always because it's Jihen wanting something of me.

"One last thing that proves we're so much more interesting than *other* tournaments out there." He smiles and scans the crowd dramatically. "The *twist* to tonight's fight."

Oohs and aahhs.

There will be surprises along the way.

I frown, hesitating. I can't be the only one who doesn't like surprises.

Jihen scowls at my hesitation—I'm not cooperating as I should. Spoiling his moment. "We're keeping things interesting, remember?" He mutters something else under his breath. *Mah-fung.* Calling me high maintenance again.

I'm still unsure as I stare at the silk strips. So many possibilities to choose from. What lies down this particular path? How deep does it go? How winding is it?

Finally, I touch one of the strips. "This one."

He brings the fan closer to his face and reads whatever is written on the other side of the strip I touched. "Couldn't have chosen better myself, beauty."

The glee in his voice tells me I chose badly.

"What is it?"

Ignoring me, he returns the fan to his pocket, takes back his notecards from Pav, and faces the crowd once more.

"The twist for tonight's fight is that *no shield spells will be allowed.*"

I freeze, shocked.

Shield spells are basic. Dull and far from flashy. But they're also defense. To not have them in the ring is like deciding you can stay dry in a storm using just your hands.

Beside me, Pav shrinks. Once he was a big user of shield spells. I guess he still is.

A shout from a spectator. "C'mon, what if some of us just bet marks on fighters to cast a bunch of shield spells?"

Jihen shrugs. "Win some and lose some. That's what betting is all about, right? Like I said, we keep things interesting."

He takes one more step back toward the spectators, so that there's now a clear division between where they're standing and where the fighters are standing.

The ground beneath Jihen and the spectators begins to rise, climbing higher and higher, forming a brand-new hill in the earth. Bamboo pulls up with it, like a carpet of grass being grabbed and tugged upward. Its giant green blades are bamboo stalks, all growing sideways now.

The air is no longer creaking but *snapping.* It is the sound of rocks and millions of bamboo roots slipping and shifting inside the dirt.

Some of the spectators grab on to nearby stalks, their expressions shocked as they're lifted high into the air. A few panicked screams mix with stunned giggles of awe.

Finally, everything goes still.

Jihen and the spectators are standing on the top of the hill, now at a safe distance from the magic we'll be casting as we fight on the ground. The tops of the bamboo around them seem ready to disappear into the sky.

I lift my hand to the metal holder of my starters.

With a dramatic flourish, Jihen releases his notecards so they spin downward to our feet like unwanted confetti.

"The fight starts now," he calls down. "And watch the bamboo."

FOURTEEN

My fingers are about to grab a starter when all around us the bamboo begins to fall.

A terrible cracking sound fills the air as giant green stalks collapse one by one. They smash into one another, wood and fiber shredding apart. The thuds they make as they hit the ground travel up into my legs—I feel the force of their landing in my back teeth. Stumps left jutting out of the earth are raw and jagged, the hollowness inside gaping mouths.

I swear out loud and start dodging, trying to think of a plan. It's the first fight of a first tournament with a power-hungry gang leader in charge—of course Saint Willow's going to be putting on a show. Everything is going to make an impact. She won't appear, but her presence will still be felt, with no escaping it.

More crashing of bamboo. The wind cracks and shrieks. From above, spectators are cheering and clapping. Nothing but commotion all around.

Someone shouts to run. As the ground shakes, there's the scattered flurry of feet. Fighters are taking off in all directions, climbing over fallen stalks and heading deeper into the maze.

Fear traces my spine at the idea of going in there. The thick walls of bamboo that can topple at a whim. The winding paths that only lead you farther in. Until you're trapped.

The yell comes from somewhere behind me.

I spin around and see the bamboo falling from overhead first. A split second later, I see the fighter who yelled, his cheek turned away so I don't know his ring name.

He casts on the stalk headed directly toward him. And me.

His finger running along his palm. The glimpse of a gold starter winking in the sun.

The falling bamboo splits apart in midair, as though invisible lightning has struck it.

Hunks of broken bamboo as heavy as concrete fly in all directions.

I duck my head as the pieces hit the ground, leaving small dents. The earth opens up around the marks, and fresh stalks of bamboo begin to grow from the gaps. Bamboo stretches toward the sky with a thin screeching sound that hurts. Then these stalks begin to sway, too, held upright by the Founders until it's time for them to collapse.

A cold pit opens up inside my stomach.

How am I supposed to fight other casters while also defending myself from this ring built to attack? Pav mentioned me being a champion, so now everyone knows—no doubt there's a huge target on me. And to fight without using shield spells at all? With this magic that doesn't belong to me? A grim hopelessness looms.

I scramble away like a hunted animal and drop to a crouch behind a mass of broken bamboo. My breathing is jagged. I peek out and see fighters running everywhere, trying to stay ahead of a forest cast to keep coming down on top of them. There's yelling and screaming, the sounds of pain and fighting a constant roar in the air.

On cheeks, I see flashes of numbers—no longer zeroes but ones, twos, fours, magic keeping a tally and continuously rewriting them as casters are eliminated.

My zero is unchanged.

I turn and catch sight of a fighter staring at me. Her eyes are huge even from here, her expression stunned. Like she can't believe who she has to fight. Her ring name is Misha, white letters still easy to read.

A blur of silver slips from her hand—she's just cast. But before I can react, Misha's the one flying backward.

She's just tried a shield spell.

The Founders aren't just canceling our shield spells—they're punishing us for them.

Misha lands hard on top of half-broken bamboo and screams in pain.

I drag my gaze away. I'm still crouched over, looking for a way out. Only my reputation saved me. Misha could have planned an attack instead, but she froze when she saw who I was and could think only of protection. Could think only of a shield, the Founders' warning forgotten.

My eyes scan the maze as I try to decide.

The forest in there is darker, so much denser. There are places to hide inside, maybe, nonmagic ways to work around having no shield spells. A two-second sprint, and I can buy myself some time before having to start casting with this magic.

But all those paths. Going in circles until you're lost deep in the maze. Where those thousands of disoriented warriors all died.

Bamboo whistles and thuds onto the forest floor just behind me.

I gasp, then slide down another inch. I look over the line of broken bamboo in front of me with eyes that feel wild. My pulse rockets. My mind screams for me to run.

Hide in the maze, Aza. Wait this out. No one gets hurt if you do nothing.

Except I know I can't do that. I know I have to cast. Saint Willow's made clear that if she's not happy, I won't be, either. And while casting with this new magic might go completely wrong, I'm also out of choices.

It's my best chance—my only chance.

I move ahead, eyes still wild, looking out for fighters, for the danger of collapsing bamboo—

The blow lands on my back and pushes downward, like a giant's footstep. It presses harder and harder, the ground grinding away so I'm sinking. More, deeper. I can't breathe, can't move. The world is nothing but dirt and lack of air.

A skin spell, cast on my entire body. To make me stay down.

This is it. I'm out. Everything's going gray. Any second, the Founders are going to change me into marble, keeping my body safe until the end of the fight. I struggle to focus on the distant sounds of cheers and applause from the spectators, the blurred motion of other fighters around me casting on one another.

Your own fault. You waited, and someone got to you first. Now you're going to have to answer to Saint Willow.

A thunderous crack comes, and the foot lifts. Air comes in gusts, filling up my lungs.

I turn over, breathing hard.

The fighter is still stuck beneath the bamboo that knocked him over. Not one of the bigger stalks—he's still conscious, still in the game—but big enough to end his skin spell on me. He can't hide how he's favoring one side as he squirms free. A broken rib.

I see his ring name on one cheek—Riv—and the number one on the other.

Cast. Do it. Or he will.

Stumbling to my feet, I draw a six-pointed star on my palm with jagged motions. I tear a white coin from the metal holder at my side, gripping it tight.

I cast.

The forest floor trembles again, this time from the strange magic inside me. I will it to pull more from the earth, magic that is shapeless and without form but that I see as a red cloud in my mind. It seeks me, and I let it.

Beneath my shoes, the forest floor is hot, and the heat burns upward, filling my veins from the inside. Fire in my arms, in my hands, my palm with its waiting spell.

For Riv, a bone one.

Another rib can go.

But instead of curling over with pain, he slowly stands straighter. His hand goes to his side, pressing on his broken rib, and a strange expression fills his face. Shock, but no pain. He meets my eyes, and when I see the laughter building in his, I'm the one who is shocked.

My bone spell *fixed* his rib instead of breaking a new one.

I *helped* another fighter.

The magic in my veins, the one I can't control—my biggest enemy in this whole forest.

My hands shake, and the used-up starter drops to the ground. I'm taking a step back even as Riv takes one forward. He's reaching for a fresh starter when casting pain comes at me.

It should be almost nothing, an ebb of an ache that comes and goes and is barely remembered. Because I only drew six points. Because the Founders have promised protective magic.

But this magic is turning on me yet again. While everyone else might be okay.

The pain bowls me over.

The world reduces to a core of agony. It lives in me, then stretches outward. Bits and pieces of the ring swim through—shades of green, hot dry sun, the sweet scent of blood.

I fall, vision going gray, everything twisted.

FIFTEEN

From within the haze of my pain, another fighter appears from over the fallen bamboo.

A girl, face bloodied, limping.

I stare, my breaths nothing but pained gasps, as her head swivels back and forth. From me to Riv and then back again. Her face says it all. She wants to be the one to eliminate a champion, especially with me already down.

Except that Riv is also here, standing in her way. Calculation crosses her features as she thinks about trying to beat him.

Her hand goes to her pocket just as Riv grabs hold of his own fresh starter.

They cast at each other at the same time.

Grunts and shouts as magic flies. They both duck low, then scrabble back upright, reaching for more starters.

As the girl and Riv keep casting on each other, I crawl away to hide behind more fallen stalks. Still gasping, I twist around to look. The zero on my cheek burns.

The maze. With its promise of dark shelter, of being something close to a shield spell.

Fine.

I teeter over.

Just inside the mouth, I collapse into the thick bamboo, hiding but not hidden. There are other casters in here, running and searching, with more coming near. I have seconds to recover. To be ready again.

The pain is so slow to leave. And it does, but not the way it should. Like waves receding from the shore while the sand stays soaked.

I pull myself up and stagger farther into the maze. One step, two. The maze widens, different paths veering off in all directions.

Then the paths *change*. They morph and blur away, only to reappear and head elsewhere. Bamboo stalks shuffling along the ground as a deck of playing cards will splay out between two curved hands.

I want to rub my eyes, be sure this isn't happening. That it's a play of light. My pain, already beginning to break down my mind.

But it's the Founders. It's their magic and this ring. A re-creation of a battle famous for its dark paths, capable of moving as snakes can move.

Just how many more tricks can the Founders have the power to pull off?

I keep going, turning as the maze turns, my breath searing my throat as I pant. Through the blur of shuffling stalks, I catch snippets of faces, hear snatches of yells, and turn from them, too.

Then, right in front of me: the fighter named Tau. She's standing over the crumpled heap of another fighter as she breaks him down, pushing him that much closer to submission.

I jerk back, fumbling as I pull away.

Dozens of spent starters litter the forest floor. They shine beneath the bamboo-filtered sun, as pretty as ancient beach glass must have been. There are bodies of eliminated casters everywhere, transformed into marble statues stuck between stalks of toppled bamboo like food caught in teeth.

Not marble. No.

I look more carefully.

This material isn't marble. That was the Guild's magic. This is jade stone, and it makes me think of precious gems more than rock. It's probably the exact effect the Founders are going for. Fancy frills to mark a bigger and better tournament.

Meanwhile, I'm still hurting. That buzzing sensation beneath my skin lingers and clings.

From the hill in the sky, spectators scream and cheer. I hear names, telling me who's still in the fight—Bardem, Vetta, Pav.

Mine, stretched out so it's *Aaaaazaaaa.*

Something twists uncomfortably in my chest at the sound of my name in this tournament. Saint Willow's tournament.

Bamboo keeps slapping down to the earth as the Founders keep us hopping, making sure we put on a show. My heart drums heavily, loaded down with fear and adrenaline. I slip between stalks, weaving back and forth as the paths do, looking out for fighters so I can catch them before they can catch me.

My mind replays that bone spell I cast on Riv, and my throat goes dry. I was worried about this strange magic being too harsh. I never guessed it could be good. Kind. But used against me, both are equally dangerous.

I let out a shuddering sigh as I keep moving. Defeat pushes back. Telling me to quit.

Kylin's voice floats to the surface of my brain. *You're strong, Aza. Stronger.*

Screams of fighters break through, leaving the green all around me trembling. Bamboo whistles as it falls and crashes. From outside the maze, cheering swells to drown out all else.

So much enjoyment. Bitterness sits on my tongue as I move faster, circling, leaves slapping my face as I shove through. I wipe sweat from my eyes and force my breathing to slow. It's too loud in here, likely to give me away.

A deep war cry rings in my ears.

Instantly, I drag a star on my palm.

But it's too late.

My legs are completely numb, and they fold like an accordion.

I reach out to brace myself. Just in time. My face is an inch away from meeting the ground.

Some part of my mind is trying to decide if it's a flesh spell or a bone one. The rest is shouting, *Who cares, Aza. WHO CARES! You need to get out of this!*

A pair of worn, dusty high-tops appears on the ground. Still winded and half gasping, I turn my head and peer up.

A guy. His severe buzz cut doesn't go with the baby fat hugging his cheeks. I can just read his ring name from this angle: Mack. His smile is huge, like he's never had such fun before. And maybe he really hasn't, if this is the first time he's ever gotten to cast full magic freely. That feeling of it filling you up, nothing around to stop you from using your own power.

In the ring, he's my enemy, but he's also like family.

The five on his cheek tells me he's having a good night. But it's no reason to be standing here grinning instead of casting.

I reach over and place my palm on a nearby fallen bamboo

stalk. Plants are of the earth, just as flesh of casters is of the earth—a natural pairing of starter and spell. I brace myself, preparing for anything to happen. From nothing to everything, from good to bad.

I picture branches being snapped in half.

I cast.

Mack's arms go limp. They fall to his sides, useless.

"Hey, c'mon," he whines. "It's like cheating, keeping someone else from casting."

I want to tell him that makes every spell a cheat, but I don't bother. His spell on my legs finishes, and I stand up, teeth gritted. I wait for the pain of casting to build behind my eyes. For the headache to come, a nosebleed, anything, because everything is possible now.

Nothing.

Another beat of a second.

Still nothing.

It sure would be nice to know ahead of time if this was going to happen.

I draw again before my flesh spell on Mack wears out. Seven points this time. In my mind, Kylin's nodding.

A red starter.

I picture the twisting of a tap, the gush of the flow.

I cast.

Blood is a fountain from his mouth, gurgling as he falls to his knees. He misses the bamboo that's fallen there and bounces sideways. His eyes flash with panic as he tumbles nearly straight onto his face.

"Better bow out with your elbow or foot something," I tell him. "I don't know if you want to risk—"

Agony slices across my skull. A giant invisible hand is inside there. Squeezing it. Wanting it to shatter.

I bend over, retching. When I can stand up again, Mack is disappearing into the bamboo. He's still bleeding, too pumped up to consider the possibility of bleeding out before my spell's done. He'll chance waiting it out if he can come back to fight some more.

Beyond the waves of pain lapping at me, the ring's quieted. Bamboo is still falling, but not so quickly anymore. Paths have stopped shuffling. The casters who are still fighting have spread themselves throughout the rest of the forest, so most of the shouting is distant, muffled. Even the spectators have calmed now. There are lumps of jade stone everywhere, pale green against the near-emerald of bamboo.

I crawl over, lean against a still-standing stalk, and wonder if I might actually be dying. If this new stolen magic is finally done with me and stealing itself back. To float away and find the caster it first came from, the same way organs always fit best in the bodies that grew them in the first place.

The temptation to simply bow out reaches for me.

But instantly I turn it away. Impossible. However bad the pain, I can't give up.

A dark shadow darts through the bamboo on my right.

A caster.

My head pounds, a thousand sticks coming down on drums, as I try to figure out this caster's next move. What's the point of circling around me when they have the chance to cast?

Just show yourself already! Obviously I'm not going anywhere!

I yank a silver starter from my holder. Bile rises at the idea of casting again. Untrustworthy magic, more pain—I fight back another retch. The world swells and recedes.

The shadow creeps closer. This time, I get a glimpse of them as they run along the maze's path.

A warrior, dressed in ancient armor, sword in hand.

Fear dances along my skin, and my breath is stuck somewhere in my throat. Then the fear changes, goes darker. Fury at the Founders stabs me as sharply as the pain does.

Casting up tricks like bloody sap and self-generating bamboo? Moving paths and ghosts? Frills like textured starters and jade stone?

I picture the state of the city, and nothing but disaster fills my mind—floods, fires, quakes. If any of that happens, how much of it will be the fault of the Founders because they didn't have enough magic left to protect it? How much would be mine?

Someone steps out of the bamboo and stands next to me. A real caster this time. It's the fighter named Indy. A number seven glows on her cheek.

Her eyes go to the zero emblazoned on mine.

A huge wave of noise from the spectators.

I'm not supposed to lose.

Indy draws on her palm, grabs a starter from where she's tucked them into a wide band of cloth at her waist, and casts.

My hand is still fumbling at my hip when the seven on her cheek changes into an eight.

I turn into jade stone. Only then does the pain stop.

SIXTEEN

Coming back from stasis-by-magic after a fight is simpler than I would have thought. I've never been knocked out before, so I didn't have a clue what to expect.

When I open my eyes, I'm still sitting on the floor of the bamboo forest.

As I drag myself to my feet, there are still echoes of casting throughout my body. A faint headache and aching limbs. The very last of that strange buzz beneath my skin runs on, the way a low-grade fever can.

I didn't know that some of the pain comes back with you. Maybe it was like this with the Guild's protective magic, too. Maybe not. Either way, the pain has been dialed down to bearable. I can think clearly again.

I touch my cheek. It feels like the zero is radiating off my skin, as bright as the sun must still be. Not only did I lose, but I also failed to eliminate anyone.

Saint Willow will be calling for me.

I leave through the mouth of the maze. No sign of Indy yet. I wonder how much longer she lasted after she knocked me out. No more warrior ghosts, either. I hope the Founders are focusing their magic on keeping things together long enough for us to get out of here. Other casters are stumbling out alongside me, glancing at one another's cheeks, feeling their own as though touch will tell them.

I keep my head down and walk.

The stalks thin out and the light thickens, and here is the hill. Its base is already crowded with fighters. The last few are straggling over from throughout the forest.

I pick out familiar faces from those already waiting—Pav and Bardem. Vetta and Tau. None of them have zeros on their cheeks.

I unhook the metal holder from my hip and shove it into my starter bag. I untie both ribbons from around my arm and fold those in there, too. The whole time, the tips of my ears are hot.

Jihen grins down at us from the top of the hill, a showman and his audience. The growth of bamboo behind where he's standing with the cheering spectators is unmarred and perfect. It's in stark contrast to the rest of the ring, with most of the forest floor heavily strewn with shattered bamboo.

Every bit of it is a reminder of just how much magic the Founders cast to create this ring.

Does Wilson believe that magic has limits? How sure is he that Saint Willow won't push her Founders beyond breaking?

Then the earth rumbles and the hill begins to flatten out. The ground slides beneath my sneakers, the carpet of giant-bladed grass slowly being yanked flat.

Jihen lifts the arm of a fighter.

Indy. The number ten is scrawled on her cheek.

"Everyone," Jihen calls out, "the first official winner of the Founders Tournament!"

Beneath the blood on her face, Indy's expression is nothing but shock. She didn't expect this at all.

It'd be easier to resent her if she were even a bit smug.

When the crowd chants her name, she goes red. Uncertain of what to do, she waves, and everyone claps.

I clap along, willing no one to notice how I've lost. If the bamboo would grow back, I'd find a way to hide within it. Even better, I'd sneak off if I could, but I'm absolutely stuck here on this side of the inlet. The only way to get back across the water is to get on the sea-bus along with everyone else, then wait for the Founders to cast magic to get us home.

The crowd roars. Congratulations and whistles. I hear someone call out *Indy the Champion!*

Then:

"Did you see her take out Aza?"

Whooping and laughter. Cheers and boos.

My face is on fire even as the rest of me goes icy. I knew it was coming, but hearing it out loud is hard.

It'll be just like this tomorrow night if I lose again. And I *will* lose again, since I still can't control this magic. That makes me the weakest fighter here.

I have to find a way to cast the way I used to. To accept that I'm probably dealing with more casting pain than any other fighter here. There's no way to be sure without asking, but asking would only reveal my weakness. Not exactly the smartest move I can make.

Jihen, not hiding how he's enjoying my humiliation, gives me his slimy grin and motions for quiet. He's holding a notecard and now reads from it:

"Tomorrow's fight will be in the Tower Sector, 717 Endeavor Way, fifteenth floor. Look for the blue sphere to get inside. Time is set for midnight—show up late and you're out of luck!"

I blink, and the seabus is back. It's parked off to the side, waiting, and soon enough we've all climbed back on board.

The air inside is just as it was on our way over, salty and sour and somehow unwell. The scent of the forest has faded completely, its grassy sweetness already difficult to recall. Cast light bulbs still hover beneath the ceiling. Outside the windows, the smog is back, swirling gray billows. Behind its curtain, it's night once more.

The metal gate of the seabus slides shut with a bang, and we begin to move.

Back to the outside world.

The return trip is surprisingly choppy, and some of the passengers don't bother hiding their displeasure. I hear someone guessing that the Founders just used too much magic too fast.

My headache comes back. Putting on my smog mask, I slip away from the windows and head for the seabus's least crowded, darkest corner. I want to stop thinking about the Founders and their magic. I want to disappear. The idea of someone coming over to ask how I feel about losing makes me feel sick.

The idea of dealing with Jihen is just as bad. He won't bother to hide his smugness.

I duck even lower so Piper can't find me. What if she can't help but reveal just how glad she is to no longer be my backer?

When the seabus finally slows, my relief is palpable. I'm not going to bother checking at the bets counter—I can't imagine much of a cut after tonight's fight. I move toward the gate, wanting to be one of the first off.

Nima's already there.

I hesitate. I want to leave as quickly as possible, but I also don't want to go anywhere near her. Memories of that terrible night press close, pushing away even my thoughts of tonight's fight. Suddenly, I'm seeing a crowded street instead of an emerald forest. Hearing the screeching of traffic instead of the crashing of bamboo.

I back away, pulse fast. Passengers move past me and stand in front of the gate.

Then I remember Nima's note from earlier. Still unread.

I dig inside my pocket for it, only half hoping it didn't fall out during the fight.

My fingers hit the folded edge of paper.

A tiny bit disappointed I have to deal with it, I wonder once more what Nima might want. The best thing for the both of us is to never speak again.

The gate screeches open, and Nima steps out. I go to the rear of the shuffling crowd and follow it off the seabus.

I wait until I've walked through the station and am standing on the mostly secluded shore before taking out the note. Making sure no one's close enough to see, I open up the now-wrinkled paper. It's dark enough that I have to squint to read:

> Meet me tomorrow
> at the Tea Chest Hotel, 9:00 a.m.
> Tell no one.

I'm so confused, I read it twice.

But the note doesn't change. And my confusion stays.

What could Nima need to tell me that must be kept a secret from everyone else? Doesn't she realize she shouldn't want to see me, either?

It's too late to catch up to her now. If I want to know any more, I'll have to go to this meeting.

I rip up the note, walk to the very edge of the sector, and let the bits of paper slip into the sour black waters of the inlet.

SEVENTEEN

I turn away from the water and head back toward the main part of Spice. I'm not being careful enough in the dark, and my feet slip and slide on the slick rocks. But I don't care. What's a trip and a fall after fighting in the underground?

Any one of us could have died tonight. I think of Shire, of Kylin. Every time we fight, we risk everything.

I think of Nima being there.

All of us could have died tonight.

I walk until there's no more sand crunching beneath my sneakers. Then I turn southeast, deciding to cut my way through Flower to get back to Tea. It's past two in the morning, and exhaustion pulls at my eyes. Just as heavily, soreness from the night's fighting weighs me down. My mind skirts away from the possibility of still feeling this way in the morning. I try to forget that I'll be fighting again in a matter of hours, whether I'm in agony or not.

When the rain starts, I don't give it much thought—in the city, rain's as commonplace as the smog. And I'm only twenty minutes from home, since I'm already in the middle of Flower. I pull the hood of my jacket over my head and keep going, scents of rose and lavender and lily heavy in the air.

But then the *wind* starts, strong enough that I find myself bracing against it.

A moment later, hail as big as marbles bounces along the pavement.

Thunder and lightning.

The air goes thick with the scents of smoke and fire instead of flowers. And my stomach wraps itself into a knot of dread, because I *know*.

This storm is our fault.

The uncontrollable magic inside me. The Founders casting beyond their means. A gang leader obsessed with power.

The earth is paying for all of it.

I duck into a twenty-four-hour gas station. Inside, the store clerk is watching the news on the television behind the counter.

A massive electrical storm is centered over the Spice Sector. The original weather forecast called for dry skies all night. It came as a complete surprise, so no one was prepared. There are at least two dozen fires from lightning strikes in Spice alone. Smaller ones are scattered throughout the neighboring sectors of Flower, Meat, and Tower. Shops have been destroyed. Some homes, too.

I push open the door and rush from the gas station, going back the way I came.

I'm out of breath by the time I get to the Salt Lick. Standing on the corner outside the shop, I wipe rain from my face.

I need to see for myself that it's okay.

There are hundreds of other buildings in Spice. The chances of the storm damaging the Salt Lick are tiny. It *is* fine. Completely untouched while other parts of the sector continue to burn. In the near distance, orange light glows as fire slashes through the night. Ash mixes with rain, and the smell of smoke is everywhere.

But it *could* have happened. Oliver could have been inside. The image of Kylin burning is forever seared into my mind. Burning because of me.

"Aza?"

I startle and turn around.

Oliver's headed toward me. He's in a rain jacket, hood tugged low over his eyes. But I don't miss his expression of complete confusion at finding me outside his shop in the middle of the night.

"What are you doing here?" He stops when he's still an arm's length away. He looks as uncertain as I feel.

"I—I heard about the storm," I manage. "About the fires here. I thought about the Salt Lick." *And you.*

He frowns, still confused. "You came here in the middle of the night to check if my shop is on fire?"

I tug my own hood lower, glad for the dark and how it's hiding the flush on my skin. I struggle for some kind of explanation. "I was . . . nearby."

His expression stays the same.

My face gets hotter. Grasping, I try to switch tacks. "Why are *you* out here in the middle of the night?"

"Also checking. It's a short walk over, and the storm was loud—I couldn't fall back asleep." Oliver eyes the Salt Lick. "This rain might keep going for a while. Do you want to talk inside?"

"No, it's okay. It's late, like you said." I take a step back, my worry and relief already gone, only to be replaced by embarrassment.

And fear. He's been trying to reach me for weeks, and I've been ignoring him. I couldn't let him see me. I was sure he'd take one look at me and know how I've changed.

"I'm glad the shop is fine," I add.

A brief smile. "Me, too. All the fires are bad, but hopefully the storm will be over soon. It can't stick around as long as the Summer Souper, anyway."

I shut my eyes hard at his mention of last month's great fog. Breakthrough magic also led to that bout of freak weather. And Oliver's too smart not to eventually connect the dots between the oddness of that event and tonight's sudden storm. Especially if he's heard about the new tournament.

How long before he connects *me* to all of that?

When I dare to look at him again, I can tell he's already making the connections.

"Aza, this storm coming out of nowhere"—his eyes are more thoughtful than anything else as he watches me—"doesn't it remind you of what happens after a tournament fight? Breakthrough magic showing up in some way?"

I don't react. I should probably lie just to keep him away from all of this.

I also want to tell him everything.

"I've also heard rumors about a new start-up tournament," he continues. "Have you heard anything?"

"I— Yes." Something deflates inside me with the admission, even as relief prickles. "I've heard."

I should have realized I couldn't keep my secrets from him for long. People talk in the underground as much as they do in the outside world. A single person mentioning how Rudy the Champion is fighting again, now as Aza, and he would know. If he went to a single fight, he would know.

"Wasn't it supposed to be happening tonight?" he asks.

I nod.

"Well, that's why you're out here so late, isn't it? You went to watch."

"I was there." I let out a breath. "But not just to watch."

He goes dead still. Emotions cross his face, each as clear as day. Shock. Anger. More confusion.

"Impossible." His voice is tight. Rain slips down his face. "You gave up your magic."

"I got other magic back."

"How?"

A shudder racks me. He knows how to return to magic; he gave his to Finch a long time ago. He knows the cost. That's what his question is really about—cost. The idea of telling him *that*—

I don't know how much I can make myself say. The moments of that night haunt me, sit there in the back of my mind the way ghosts lurked deep in that bamboo forest.

For Oliver to see those same moments would hurt. Would burn us the way fire is burning his sector.

"Aza. *How?*"

I swipe rain from my face with a hand gone numb. I decide to pick and choose from the truth. For both our sakes.

"A gathered spell," I half whisper, all too aware that he already knows this part. Loose magic gathered back together from bits of other magic, magic not my own.

The idea suddenly dawns on me that Oliver's magic could be mixed up with the magic inside me. That he's now in my blood. Part of me.

I can't decide if that possibility makes me feel more like a thief or a victim.

"A gathered spell, obviously." Oliver exhales. His hazel eyes are dark with questions. "But *why*?"

"I was forced to take new magic. I gave up my own to pay for taking your brother's away. But I was still in debt to Saint Willow. Now I have to cast in this new tournament for them."

Please understand. I had no choice. I had to do it for my family. Same as how you've sacrificed for your family. We both know what it's like to give up magic and live with the consequences.

He shakes his head. "You shouldn't be fighting in that. It took the Guild of Then years to perfect their magic for the original tournament, and that was when the earth was stable. It took the Guild of Now even longer. Whoever is running this new one is likely learning as they go. It's too dangerous."

"I have to fight. If I don't, I won't be the only one paying. You know who Wu Teas serves."

I can tell he's struggling, angry with everything about this.

"So you're okay with fighting in a tournament that might end up blowing this city apart?" he asks.

"Of course not." At least he's not asking me how the new magic is. How I'm doing with it. "But—"

"You have no choice. I heard you."

"Oliver, please—"

"I do get it, okay?" He takes that one step between us so we're close again. Rain catches on his mouth as he gives me a small, defeated smile. "But I don't have to like the risk."

"Is that why you didn't go watch tonight?"

"I was never interested in the fights. I went for Finch. And he hates anything to do with magic now. I think that's probably the best thing for him."

I'm glad Oliver will never watch. I don't want him to see me cast the way I have been. And Finch—I'll be happy never seeing him again at all.

"I'm sorry I didn't come see you," I say, wanting to give him another bit of truth. "I know you came by. I was just waiting for a better time, I guess."

"I'm glad it's finally here, then." A full-fledged grin that makes me smile in return. "Even if you're only here to check on the shop."

Something in my chest burns. "It wasn't all because of the shop, okay?"

A flash of heat in his gaze. I turn to go, wanting to leave it at that. I'm afraid he'll talk me out of fighting. That he'll ask me how I did tonight. If I won.

Half walking, half running, it's not long before I've crossed the border into Tea. All the rain has drowned out the sector's regular scents. But it's still not enough to dampen the raw smell of fire. By the time I get back to the teahouse, climbing in through my bedroom window soaked and shivering, the sound of sirens has filled the air.

This electrical storm might have happened even if I didn't fight. Breakthrough damage is always a risk when you use magic.

But as I crawl into bed and try to sleep, pain settling into me like rust on steel, this is the fact that chases me into dreams:

It's all my fault.

EIGHTEEN

Nima's note made it clear that our meeting is a secret. But getting out of the house in the morning—and away from my already-awake parents—won't be so easy. Why didn't I wait a day to tell them I would be able to help out around the shop?

"You're up early." Mom smiles as I walk into the kitchen. She casts over a full cup of tea so it slides across the work island toward me. "Ready to get to work? It'll be a long day—we even have rushes now, if you can believe that."

I don't need to drink the tea to know which Wu blend it is—Perk, meant for mornings. The whole room smells like someone's been peeling fresh mandarins.

"I have to go, actually," I say. "I have to meet someone. I'm sorry, I forgot. I'll rush back and work then."

Dad looks up from his toast. "Who are you meeting? And so early?"

My mind is still bleary from lack of sleep, still hammered dull from the soreness of casting. The next fight is hours away, but a smattering of dread is grinding into my bones. I will have to fight hurt, because this isn't going to get any better.

"I . . . There's someone that I—" I'm fumbling, and my voice fades as I try to think of someone.

"It's okay if you're going out to meet a boy, you know," Dad says ever so casually.

"Or a girl," Mom adds, refilling both their teacups. "Or anyone, really."

This is my parents trying to be cool about dating. I guess they're trying to show they're more relaxed now, more trusting.

"It's nei—" Then I stop. Why not? "Okay, fine, it's a boy. But we're really just friends, so can you not be weird about it?"

Dad looks genuinely hurt. Which makes me feel bad, since nothing I'm saying is real. "How are we being weird?"

Mom smiles. "Is it that boy Oliver who called for you a few days ago? Did you call him back?"

Hearing her say Oliver's name is so odd that it takes a second to register. I've always been so careful to keep these two halves of my life separate. Aza the caster and Aza the daughter.

"I— Yes, it's him. Oliver." Simpler just to go with what they already assume, especially when the truth is way more difficult. "I have to go."

My mother puffs a breath against her palm, casts, and the lightest of winds smooths my hair. "Take your time. And when you get back, you can help out in the dining room."

"I will. I promise I'll be quick."

I pull a smog mask from my bag as I leave the kitchen and head toward the front entrance of the teahouse. I nudge open the door and glance around carefully before stepping fully outside.

But it's clear. No sign of anyone at all. Squinting against flat gray sunlight, I go down the shop's front stairs and cross the street.

The neighborhood's late-night teatini bars and tea cafés are closed now, patio chairs stacked upside down on their tables. They won't open again until evening. And most other shops—including the teahouse—won't open for another half hour, so street traffic is also light. Still, I can't help but make my usual detours. I get to the Tea Chest just before nine.

The hotel isn't Lotusland's most luxurious, or even its most luxurious boutique one. But it's the city's *oldest* boutique hotel, and the place has gained a bit of fame for being so strangely resilient against the quakes that have wrecked many newer and better-constructed hotels. Most people say it's just a mix of design and luck, but there's also a story that the original head builder didn't die of old age—it was from years of constantly feeding the site full magic.

It's only been a month since I was last here, but it feels longer.

Walking from the lobby to the lounge, I follow the sound of the piano, because that's where I'll find Nima. A part of me feels like how an animal might feel when they see a trap and sense the danger. When they can't help but get closer anyway because they're hungry.

It doesn't mean I can begin to guess why the gatherer wants to meet.

Except for Nima, the lounge is completely empty. Even the adjacent bar is closed, the sign saying it doesn't open until lunch.

Relief that no else is going to be around—that there's nothing that will even hint at a crowd—makes me nearly cheerful.

She doesn't look up as I walk in. She doesn't stop playing, either. I wonder if someone can be driven mad by their own piano playing. Or maybe I've got it backward. Maybe she plays because it keeps her sane.

"Hello, Aza," she calls out over the music. I don't know the name of the song, but I recognize the tune. People play it during happy occasions.

Nothing in her voice indicates how we've been careful to side-step each other. Trying to avoid the ugliness we've left in our wake.

I guess I can pretend, too. For as long as this meeting lasts, anyway.

I move over to one of the sunken couches and sit down, tugging down my smog mask. Watching her play here instead of at the dim sum restaurant, I realize it's the first time I've seen her be anything but Saint Willow's gatherer. Is this where she goes when she's not at headquarters? Does she live upstairs in the hotel?

"Do you work here part-time or something?" I ask.

"Not officially. They just let me play their piano. Sometimes I'll fill in a shift for them here at the lounge. When I'm not needed at the restaurant, this is where I usually am."

I get a glimpse of her necklace of blue beads and feel my face go pale. Each round bit of plastic represents her work, a banished and destroyed piece of dark magic that she's gathered back together.

Such treacherous spells should never have existed in the first place. I believe that now more than ever.

Nima catches what I'm looking at and keeps playing. She has brown contacts in today to cover up her orange Ivor eyes.

"I want to make a deal with you," she says.

I go still.

I've already made too many deals. How can Nima of all people ask me to make another?

"I had to wake up extra early to meet you here on time," I say, the words stiff. The gatherer must have, too, but she didn't have to fight last night. She's not sitting here with an ache beneath her skin like a saw working on wood. "Please tell me it's for a good reason."

"Do you enjoy being Saint Willow's caster?"

I frown. "Seriously?"

"That was a rhetorical question."

Piano notes fill the air as I wait to hear more. I'm hesitant to say too much to Nima. I know how dangerous she is. How powerful despite not being able to cast. I've seen it firsthand. Gathering is a level of magic that even full magic casters have tried to banish.

"Aza, I'm getting out. But I can only do it with your help. That's why I asked you here." She's still playing the piano like this conversation is anything close to normal.

I want to tell her to leave me alone, but I can't. I think of all that Saint Willow has stolen from me. How she continues to strip the recognizable parts from my life. The idea of finally taking something from her has already dug its way into me. A hunger. And now I can't shake it free.

"Stop playing," I say to Nima. "Because I'm listening."

NINETEEN

Nima's hands go still on the keys.

"Once," she starts, "I thought I was lucky to have found Saint Willow. My family was terrified of full magic—terrified of *me*. When they were happy to let me go, I knew I was right to leave. And so here I am. While I gather spells for Saint Willow in her quest for power, she keeps Scouts looking elsewhere, their eyes far from mine."

If you ask me, Saint Willow is the one who got lucky. In her desire for a full magic caster, she found the one thing that was rarer.

"But before I was her gatherer, I was—for a short time—her caster. She sent me out on squeeze jobs, and I did them. Mind wipes. Idea plants. Peeking into people's heads to look for whatever information Saint Willow wanted. I thought I could handle all that casting, no problem. But it was too much too fast."

"And that's how you went Ivor." I already knew it was working for Saint Willow that turned Nima's full magic useless, trapped inside a body too burnt out to cast it again. But I don't know exactly how it happened. I'm not sure if I need to hear another story of Saint Willow being ruthless with her power. Except I think Nima needs to tell it, so I listen.

She nods. "The last squeeze job she sent me on—I knew it was too big for me. I was always in pain, with no chance to recover between castings. But you know Saint Willow and how she can't accept failure."

I do know. She runs me the way she runs the sector—no mistakes are overlooked, no debts forgiven. I'll only be reminded of this with each fight she makes me enter. With each time I'm ordered to cast. As Nima's words turn over and over in my mind—*I was always in pain, with no chance to recover*—I shudder. The image of an Ivor's display cage, its bars gleaming beneath the gray sky, forms. I shove it away.

"So what kind of job was it?" I ask, hoping my voice sounds normal.

"Saint Willow comes from a big family. Branches that run long, with some growing past Tea's borders. After she was entrusted to run the gang, a long-gone cousin came back into the picture, claiming the right to be leader. He wasn't wrong—he *was* blood, and older—but because he was away from the sector for so long, the family promised Saint Willow the vote wouldn't go his way. And it didn't. But that wasn't enough for her. I was to make him disappear. Him, and everyone else who voted for him. All at once."

I rub goose bumps from my arms. I'm chilled to the bone. To cast so strongly while still hurting—no wonder Nima turned.

Jihen should be nothing but grateful that his cousin sees him as no threat.

"After I woke up from casting," Nima says, "my magic had changed on me. I no longer had it to cast. But it let me see other magic in the air. Magic I could collect."

"The magic of gathered spells."

"Yes." She stares at me. "And now *you're* her caster, Aza. You're in danger. Saint Willow owning both of us makes her the strongest person in all of Lotusland. Maybe the world. How long do you think it'll be before she'll make full use of us?"

A shiver rolls along my spine. Saint Willow has already started up her own tournament. It's too easy to imagine her going even further. Ordering Nima to gather spells and then me to cast at every whim. The world, seeping with plague. The sun, snuffed out like a candle.

I get to my feet, unable to stay still anymore. Anger turns me hot now instead of cold. "What do you want me to do? She has complete control over me. She holds my family's lives in her hands. And this magic I have isn't my own. I can't even cast the right spells anymore."

It stings to admit this. It always will. How I no longer control magic as much as it controls me.

"I want you to help me," Nima says. "To help *us*."

I walk over to the piano and sit down next to her on the bench. The sensation of having done this already—sitting here with the Ivor, making plans and spinning secrets, the feeling of everything being on the line—makes the world waver.

"How?" I ask.

She starts to play again. The light notes are a poor match for this grim turn of our conversation.

"Right now, you're keeping Saint Willow busy. She's spending a lot of time thinking about you fighting in her tournament. I know you hate it, but we can make it work for us. Only when she's deeply preoccupied does she let her attention slip a bit. If you can keep her busy worrying about you, it'll let me plan on the side without her noticing."

I narrow my eyes. "I don't want her on me any more than she already is."

"It's the only way to keep her focus away from me. I saw you fight last night. I know you lost. We both know Saint Willow won't be happy about it. Give her reason to keep her mind on you and the tournament. Make her believe you need all her focus in order for you to cast as she wants."

"What are you planning?"

Her fingers pause on the keys once more for just a fraction of a second. "I need to make things right. To fix everything I've done. Which means that if you do your part, I can do mine. Then the both of us will be free of her forever."

"How would I be free of her?"

"Because for your help, I'll get you back the one thing you miss most."

I wait, barely daring to breathe.

"You want your own magic back, don't you?" Nima smiles. "Magic you can actually control?"

To get my magic back.

To have to cast the gathered spell once more.

To repeat what happened that night—

Revulsion turns me to ice.

"Nima, I can't do it again." My voice is jagged with barely stifled panic. With the slipping away of a dream I thought I had given up already.

She shakes her head. "That night—it wasn't supposed to happen that way, Aza. It was an accident. Bad luck with bad consequences."

A part of me clings to that. I know better than anyone how out of control the magic we called for actually was—havoc is its nature. And how if we do it again, it will be my own magic this time. Magic I know how to control completely.

But I also know gathered spells always carry a risk. Small or big. No matter what.

"It was still our fault," I whisper. "We still did it."

She plays more notes, music from her fingers like a casting of her own.

"No," Nima says, "not our fault. It was Saint Willow's. For making us do it in the first place. But this time will be different. I promise. So—we'll get you your own magic back. Just the way it was. And then this other magic stuck inside of you will finally be gone."

TWENTY

For a second, hope runs wild. Huge. I feel nothing else.

But what Nima is talking about—it can't be done.

"Don't lie," I say. Disappointment is crashing down. A gatherer can retrieve loosed magic, but it's always mixed up with other magic. Ether, essence—it moves as it wants. "You know it can't be done."

"Do I?"

Doubt trickles in. It's true I don't know much about gathering. But she's asking me to trust what she says now. Even though that's never worked out in the past.

I shrug, feeling terse and on edge. Trying to tamp down the hope that keeps flaring. "Otherwise why didn't you just gather my own to give back to me the first time? Instead of strange magic I can't really use?"

"Because I had no time." Nima runs her fingers along the piano keys, not playing a song, just filling the silence of the lounge. "I *was* gathering back yours—magic is identifiable, distinct to a caster the way a print is to a finger. But Saint Willow said I wasn't working fast enough. She wanted magic returned to you and didn't care whose it was. I tried to explain, but it made no difference to her. All she could see was power."

So much for learning to see beyond what she wanted. To think of looking for more.

My heart pounds, hungrier than ever. Desperation is a pain of its own kind.

My own magic.

"How much time would it take?" I can't stop my voice from trembling.

"Two days."

None of this seems entirely real. Her answer is too simple. "How can you be sure?"

"Because I've already started gathering it. I'd explain the process to you, if I thought it'd make you believe me. But you'll never be able to see it the way I do. I can't talk enough to make you taste light or smell the dark. You'll just have to trust me."

I glance at the blue beads of her necklace. There's magic in them, all of it strange. I think of Shire's lost magic and what Nima might say if I asked her to gather *that*. Just so I could have a piece of my sister back.

Or what about Oliver? If all magic has a print, his is still out there, waiting to be seen, to be found. How would he feel if I told him he could have it back? Would he still prefer it gone?

I listen to the gatherer play, Nima's fingers dancing across the keys, and am still torn. "You're asking me to trust you—even after what happened."

"Just as all magic has a cost, Aza, so does escape. I need this, and so do you. Everything is at risk with us both under her control. Staying with Saint Willow while she plots all the ways she can use us—we can't let her do that. This is the only way out."

Two days.

Then this unwanted magic will be gone from me. I'll have my

own back again, where it belongs. And all I have to do is keep Saint Willow's eyes on me. On the tournament.

But two more days means two more fights with this magic that fights me as much as I fight it. Each so full of risk, where anything can go wrong. The target of being a champion on my back like a bull's-eye. The Founders with their inconsistent skill. None of us truly safe.

And then images from that night rebloom bright in my mind. My chest goes tight with the reminder that it can always be worse. If the gathered spell goes wrong again, I'll have crossed a line once more. I'll be more monster than human.

Still, to not have to worry about casting Nima's gathered magic on a whim from Saint Willow . . .

I have to keep fighting for the gang leader anyway. If I work with Nima, at least there's a chance for something more. Something else. To see what might exist behind the smog.

I know I have to try. Nima's right that working for Saint Willow makes us dangerous. Just as it's made me hate magic, hate being a Wu. For that, I will hate Saint Willow forever.

But I can give her some of that pain back.

"So do we have a deal?" Nima's playing the same song from earlier. The one saved for celebrations. The places where you get to be free.

My stomach is still in knots, tied up by equal parts worry and relief.

But I nod. "Deal."

A flash of a grin as she stops playing. It changes her face and reminds me we're nearly the same age. Not so different. It makes me feel better and worse. "Good. Meet me here in two days. At noon."

"Two days." I get up to go.

"Trust me, Aza."

"Fine." I move away, still unsure. I don't say the rest before walking out of the lounge. How trust—and these deals—have yet to work out for me.

TWENTY-ONE

It's my own fault that Jihen catches me before I get all the way home. I left the Tea Chest, but my mind was still in the hotel lounge, listening to the piano and imagining escape.

"Ah, good morning, beauty." He pops up next to me on the sidewalk, as suddenly as though he had been dropped from the sky. For an instant, the world wavers, and I'm back in a bright green forest, in danger of being crushed by falling bamboo. I smell their stalks instead of the sector. The sky is sunshine and wispy clouds instead of smog and gray.

I stumble to a stop on the sidewalk, gone stiff. I'm terrified that my conversation with Nima shows on my face, in my eyes. Why can't smog masks cover everything?

Jihen can't find out. He would run and tell everything to Saint Willow, and that would be the end of this new plan.

His smile is as smug as it was last night in the ring. "Sorry, but you're needed. Genji-wei—come with me now. Boss wants to see you."

The knot in my stomach from earlier comes back. I have no doubt what Saint Willow means to talk to me about. Jihen would have been sure to tell her every single detail of my loss last night.

"I know where headquarters is," I tell him. "I can get there myself."

He clasps my arm. "Not this time."

On edge, I cast instead of trying to squirm away. I press my palm against my shirt—a starter of cotton fibers for the most minor skin spell, no stronger than a static shock. Just leftover magic, because the last thing I need is a Scout's attention. Or more pain.

Jihen jumps and lets go. He scowls, shaking out his hand. "So brave with casting now, are we? Not so long ago, you were sweating with worry about a squeeze job."

I make myself laugh. "That was just *leftover* magic. Or couldn't you tell? Aren't you a big-time show host now?"

His expression darkens, goes sulky and stubborn. "And just yesterday, I saw you *lose*. Saw you eliminate *no one*. Are you still in pain? All that magic being cast, and that's all you have to show for it, no? Sai-zai."

What a waste.

I tug my mask higher. "The notecards were an interesting touch. I'm sure no other tournament host will ever be able to take those bragging rights from you."

He squints and his mouth purses, and I'm reminded this is Jihen's look of power now. He must like how it feels. "The car parked at the corner—get inside. She's there, waiting."

I turn around to look and sense myself shrinking.

Shiny black paint, tinted side windows. The front seat is empty. But there's Seb and his suit, standing on the sidewalk, pretending to be on his cell. And Luna, white shirtsleeves bright against the dinginess of the buildings. He's standing by the car's back door, clearly waiting for someone. Me.

"Hurry up," Jihen says to the back of my head, his tone now as sour as the set of his mouth. "Fai-nay."

I walk over, hoping I appear steady. Stuck in a small space with Saint Willow, surrounded by men who are quick to do her bidding—making an exit when I want won't be possible.

Without a word, Luna opens the back door. I slide inside the car.

Saint Willow is in the back seat. She's wearing a wide-brimmed cream silk hat, sprigs of green berries tucked into the band. The hat covers her black hair, and the wide brim is pulled low even in here. She's dressed in one of her elegant blouses, a snake with scales of silk.

Sitting down beside her, I do a quick scan of the inside of the car. Nothing weird about any of it, aside from the fact that it's being guarded from outside.

Luna shuts the door. The light inside the vehicle falls to a dark and murky gray.

"You lost last night." Saint Willow's voice is wintry, her fury spiking through like icicles. "And embarrassingly so. You're the big draw to my tournament. A supposed champion and the caster who is ordered to do as I want. What do you not understand?"

Heat rushes along my neck. "I told you I don't have full control over the magic."

"Then get it. By tonight. You've already made a mistake. Don't do it again."

Or your parents will pay. You'll pay. The Wus will never recover.

I choke back frustration. "It's not that easy."

"Make it so." She smiles, and her teeth are sharp and foxlike in the half light, her eyes glinting like the hardest of diamonds. "You will do this, Aza. I won't let you go. Power doesn't grow from allowing weakness—it grows from demanding it be something better."

"You can't force magic." Will she ever see that she'll destroy everything in trying?

"Can't I? That's what magic *is*—pure force. It *wants* you to cast." Another cold smile. "We made a deal, and now you have your magic back. So use it."

"It's *not* my magic!" I want to leap at her. Instead, I force my hands to unclench. "That makes all the difference."

"You promised you would cast for me. I gave magic back to you. That's the deal, Aza. It's really very simple, and I'm done debating this with you." She opens the sleek handbag at her side and takes out an envelope. She holds it out to me.

"Your cut from last night." A withering glare. "A truly pathetic amount, but a deal is a deal. As we both know."

I grab the envelope from her, shocked there's anything at all. From its weight, Saint Willow is right that I didn't make a lot. But I still made something. And something is always good enough to put toward the future.

From the shadows, her eyes narrow as she watches my face. "Don't forget that bets can also be placed on casters to *lose*, Aza. Your cut isn't entirely from technique-style wagers."

Heat climbs the back of my neck as I process the truth. How some of the crowd decided from the start that I wouldn't win. Why? Were they just lucky guesses? Something they saw in me? I'm supposed to be a winner. I *need* to be.

"How does it feel knowing some of the crowd is *expecting* you to be beaten?" Saint Willow asks.

More heat climbs, burning my cheeks. I stay silent and will her to finish.

She laughs softly, the sound sharp as it digs beneath my skin. One more smiling gleam of teeth as she gestures to the envelope in my hand. "Well, I suppose it's nice how even when we lose, we're still winning. You made marks for me. But you *will* fight as I want you to fight. Exactly as I say."

Her self-satisfaction is suffocating. Her corruption sucks up all the air in the car like poison eating away at flesh.

I shove the envelope of marks into my bag, more desperate than ever to get out.

"No more mistakes, Aza," Saint Willow says, still smiling.

I yank at the door handle and stumble out of the car.

Luna is a blur as I stalk past. Jihen and Seb, too. I don't turn to see if they're following me. I just keep going, needing to leave the gang leader behind me.

Nima, don't make me regret trusting you.

TWENTY-TWO

I'm still trembling when I get to the teahouse.

It's not busy inside.

The tables are mostly empty, and only a couple of customers are looking at the shelves of merchandise.

I slip off my smog mask, my stomach sinking. I don't know why the sight is so difficult to accept. All my life, Wu Teas has struggled, so I should be used to it. But this hushed kind of quiet in the shop—it's a reminder of how easily things can change back.

My parents are behind the counter, appearing vaguely shell-shocked, and my stomach sinks further. I've never seen them more carefree than this past month.

Them changing back is worst of all.

"What's going on?" I ask. This morning—promising to return quickly so I could help with the shop—feels so long ago.

Dad gives me a pained look. "It'll be fine, honey. The shop's been through worse."

"Tell me."

"A few of our larger deliveries never arrived today." Mom seems on the verge of tears as she whispers this to me. "We had to turn away dozens of customers who came looking for what should have been here. Some were understanding, but not all. And they had a right to be mad—what teahouse runs out of all their top-selling blends at once?"

"We called the distribution center," Dad says, as grim as Mom is upset. "The accounts show the trucks were loaded and ready to go. But somewhere along the way, the drivers got orders to delay the deliveries. They can't seem to trace back to how it all got started. So the whole thing is still a mess."

"I have no one to blame but myself," Mom says, sighing. "I knew we were low on stock, and I waited until the last minute before ordering more supplies. But we've never had such a problem with deliveries before."

"No, it's no one's fault," Dad argues. "It's just bad luck. I've reordered and asked them to do a rush delivery for tomorrow, but they've already said they can't guarantee anything. For now, all we can do is hope everything actually arrives sooner rather than later . . ."

"And trust that customers will care to come back to check. And that no one will remember this ever happened at Wu Teas."

You've already made a mistake. Don't do it again.

The timing of this isn't bad luck. I know it's intentional. I was warned, I lost, and now this is the cost.

The inside of the teahouse somehow grows small. Everything about it leans in close—the scents of tea, the freshly painted walls, the uneasy quiet—so that it's hard to take a deep breath. Like I'm still stuck in the car with Saint Willow. And however I might run, there she'll be.

"Just when everything was going so well, too." Mom sighs again and looks out over the uncrowded shop.

"It'll be fine," Dad says. "This will all be fixed before we know it. You'll see."

"Dad's right," I add. "Everything will be fine."

And it will be.

Once I'm free of Saint Willow for good.

Later, in my bedroom, I take out the starter holder from my desk drawer. I replace the ones I used last night—which was hardly any—and attach the holder to my belt loop.

I find both silk ribbons and tie them around my upper arm, peonies first and then willow trees.

It's an hour before midnight when I climb out of my bedroom.

I push my way through the snowball bushes and turn east. I take alleys and side streets, doing all I can to stay out of sight. Soon the smells of the sector go dry, the sign I've left Tea behind and am entering Government. The faint yelling of a display Ivor somewhere nearby in the dark encourages me to keep moving. I cross the courtyard with its looming statues of the Guild of Then, already certain Saint Willow envisions the same for her Founders. A statue of each of them, with the tallest, most majestic one of herself. One more way for her to make her mark on the city.

Then I reach Tower. With its dozens of high-rise buildings, the sector is business central, all offices and convention centers and conference lounges. Which means that this late at night, whole blocks are dark, everyone having commuted home. No one lives here.

I head downtown, going deeper into the high-rises, and I'm reminded of Lotusland's nicknames for Tower at night—Ghost City, Dead Zone, Graveyard Shift.

The Founders can almost be applauded for choosing this sector to cast their ring tonight. It means they won't have to worry about people getting hurt directly.

But housed within all these corporate skyscrapers are the thousands of businesses that keep Lotusland running—wipe out enough, and the city will come to a standstill.

I guess Saint Willow hasn't thought that far. Or simply doesn't care.

I keep walking, looking all around, and the past wraps itself around me.

Shire died in one of these buildings. Fighting Finch.

My chest pulls and pinches as memories of my lost sister wash over me. Fresh grief, like she's just died instead of being gone for more than a year now. I find myself carefully examining each building as I pass. As though I should just be able to tell which one it was. Like I'm gathering the same way Nima does, except instead of gathering the essences of spells, I'm gathering the essence of Shire's last moments.

Was it this one, Shire? Maybe this one?

She'd want me to focus on the fight tonight instead of the past. To find a way to rise above the constant pain, to embrace the hum that's already building in my veins. To believe I can control it instead of being scared.

Did you know about gatherers? I wish I could ask. *What would you say to me about this other magic now inside me? Would you hate me for what I did to get it?*

Only the address painted onto its glass front door tells me I've reached 717 Endeavor Way. Otherwise it's just one more darkened office tower, smooth glass anonymous in the night.

I peer upward, counting fifteen floors.

This one, Shire?

Will it also be where I die tonight?

Mouth dry behind my smog mask, I walk up to the glass wall and peer inside.

It's the typical lobby of an office tower. Faux-leather benches scattered around in groups. A security desk and a line of elevators behind it. Lots of open space around everything.

I take a few steps back and begin scanning the walls of the building for it.

A blue sphere.

I spot it a minute later. The image is graffitied onto a part of the wall that's at the opposite end from the entrance. The black box starter of the last ring didn't need a proper door to work, either. The Founders, continuing to show off.

Removing my smog mask, I move closer to the spray-painted blue sphere. I draw on my palm. Bracing myself, I cover the starter on the wall with my hand.

I cast.

Heat, from earth through pavement into flesh. My veins sing and my palm burns and the world shimmers. Magic shapes in my mind, and I drive it forward.

A curved line forms in the wall like the tip of a knife arcing through butter.

Glass *peels* down. A door. Sphere-shaped.

And casting pain is a heavy fist to my face.

I utter a short scream, then swear out loud in the dark. At this intrusive magic for hurting more than it should. At the Founders for not being better so they could help. When the nosebleed starts for real, I pinch my nose hard enough to leave a bruise.

Two more days. Less than that, really. And then I'll never have to worry about this again.

I step through the round doorway in the glass wall.

Cool canned air brushes my cheeks as I walk into the lobby. The benches and security desk are shadows in the dark. My sneakers are soundless as I head for the line of elevators and punch the button for one.

When nothing happens, I realize they've been shut off for the night. Not wanting to risk casting again to start up a motor, I let go of my nose and turn toward the back stairs.

Fifteen floors. I'll have to hurry.

I start climbing. My pulse hammers at my temples. It's a drum deep in my ears. By the time I get to the fifteenth floor, I'm wheezing for breath. The pain I was already carrying is cranked up a notch. I'm feeling low-key feverish. Aches everywhere.

I pull open the door and stagger out of the stairwell.

A single vast room, broken up only by weight-bearing posts that hold up the ceiling. Huge framed paintings cover most of the plain white walls. Their style is abstract, bright modern splashes of colors that are supposed to convey something. The Founders' cast-lit bulbs hover midair, a line of light that wavers.

One bulb goes out as I watch. Instead of staying to see if it comes back on, I keep moving toward the registration counter. I didn't count on the time for the stairs.

The place is an art lounge meant to impress visiting conference guests. But right now, no one's looking at the paintings at all.

Instead, casters are finishing getting ready for the fight, and spectators are crowded around the bets counter, calling out wagers.

"Twenty marks on Vetta to cast three shield spells!"

"Ten on Mack to bow out."

"Eighty on the winner to win again!"

For a second, I think it's me they're betting on, and I'm confused because I lost last night. But then I realize it's Indy they're talking about. Indy the winner.

Before I hear my name said for real—and likely not in a good way—I hurry past, swiping at the last of the blood from my nose.

The lady at the registration counter is the same one as last time, and she pulls out her clipboard as I approach. Her expression says I've cut it close again.

"Aza, right? I remember." She writes down my name on the paper on her clipboard, then uncaps a marker. She's just finishing drawing the zero on my cheek when the noise of the crowd shifts. A series of cheers.

Indy.

She's in the crowd, her cap of short black hair gleaming beneath the bulbs. She doesn't look shocked anymore. Or shy. Just prepared. Ready to fight.

Someone's with her.

The swoosh of a violet gown. The shine of square-cut gems along an arm. A handbag encrusted with more of those square gems.

It's when I spot the red curls that my heart sinks.

Piper.

TWENTY-THREE

Indy and Piper.

A team.

I watch, numb except for the dart flying around inside my chest, as my former backer ties a sleek black ribbon around her new fighter's arm.

The registration lady recaps her marker. "Done. Better go get your starters before it's—"

I stumble away.

It makes sense, this new partnership. Indy would want someone backing her on a regular basis—who better than the backer of another champion? As for Piper, she's a businesswoman at heart, and Indy's already proven herself a solid investment.

Just as I did. Once.

It stings. Badly. Eyes blurred, I make my way through the crowd to stand with the rest of the fighters. Bardem and Pav, Tau and Vetta. Questions for them rattle around in my brain, even as spectators collect around us in a loose circle.

Who else thinks we're in danger here? Anyone but me starting to wonder just how strong these Founders are? Are you also still in pain from casting?

Jihen emerges from the crowd and begins to make his way over. He waves his stack of notecards to make sure no one can miss him. He's feeling adventurous tonight, spicing up his usual black suit with a sequined ivory jacket. White shoes polished until immaculate. Again there's a peek of silver from his chest pocket—the silk fan full of the fortunes that will shape how we fight tonight.

Magic-cast light winks off of Jihen's wide grin, and the room changes.

Gone are the huge, too-bright paintings, the ceiling of bulbs.

Instead, everywhere you turn is porcelain.

Walls and floor of cream porcelain tile, each inch a perfect and shining square. A soaring domed ceiling that's also crafted of porcelain, the blue of a sky that is no longer seen from anywhere on earth. Pale, crystalline, so clear that your heart aches to look at it.

Porcelain teacups and teapots, dishes and saucers. They sit on floor-to-ceiling porcelain shelves and on porcelain racks just as tall. Vases and figurines—birds, animals, tiny buildings—fill up the insides of wide glass-fronted porcelain cabinets. Hundreds of decorative plates are displayed on the tile walls, an art exhibit in the form of color and clay and texture. Fine porcelain busts of nameless people stare down at us from their perches just below the ceiling, their fired-clay expressions impassive.

Lotusland has lots of porcelain shops, some of them famous family businesses that go back two or three hundred years. But nothing they make can compare to any of the pieces here. No modern handlers of clay can shape such forms; no kiln is so delicate with its fire.

Everything here is only made possible by magic.

A vase that gains the luster of now-extinct pearls when filled with water.

A mandarin duck figurine, each of its thousands of feathers a distinct and perfect sliver of treated clay.

A teapot that flowers into a lotus when the steeping brew inside is ready.

All the magic it must take to cast and hold together every part of this ring—it seems impossible. Beyond understanding. Just as I can't tell yet if it's this new magic that makes me hurt from casting or if every fighter hurts because of the Founders. Too much about this tournament is a question.

"Eighteen hundred years ago," Jihen reads from the top card, "when the world's porcelain first came into being, all of it was made in the ancient land of Rosetta. Local clay artists made it by casting full magic. These artists were allowed to cast to their hearts' content, so eventually there was a lot of art floating around. There was so much that people had to start classifying all the pieces from worthless to valuable. After a while, whether you were seen as rich or poor came to depend on what kind of porcelain you had in your house. And so the richest families began to hire artists to make pieces just for them."

A momentary furrowing of his brow as he reads some more. I watch him mouth the word *demonstration*.

He picks up a teacup from a nearby shelf. The white of the clay reddens at the touch of his hand, and the crowd oohs. He puts the cup back, satisfaction on his face, and the porcelain returns to white. Everyone aahs. Once more looking at his notecards, Jihen starts reading again. In my dreams, I'm casting to burn up his notes, just to see him flail.

"But it was private collections that held the rarest and most valuable pieces, and the biggest collector of all was Rosetta's Empress Ziyi. What this lady couldn't buy, she stole, and what she couldn't steal, she had made, even if that meant blackmail or torture. Turns out a lot of the wealthiest families had their artists kidnapped by the empress and got imprisoned for complaining about it."

As Jihen drones on, I lift my gaze toward the ceiling. My eyes catch on the busts perched right beneath it. I count them: fourteen altogether. I'm about to look away but stop when I recognize the features on one.

Wilson.

Fourteen busts. Fourteen Founders. Twice as many as the Guild members for twice the show. I stare hard at them, wishing their faces alone would assure me of the quality of their magic.

Jihen flips to a new card, and I drag my eyes back to him.

"All of this stuff here is Empress Ziyi's personal porcelain collection, and this is the room in her palace where she stored it all. She kept it locked to servants and family, so only she could enter. A decade into her reign, a great flood came and washed across the entire plain, submerging everything for more than a year. After the place dried out, they went to collect the porcelain. But not a piece could be found." Jihen presses his finger to the front of a koi-painted platter mounted on the wall. The koi start to swim, shimmers of red and orange on blue-green porcelain.

"Legend says that the flood was cast by all of Empress Ziyi's kidnapped artists together. That it was their magic that then made the collection mysteriously disappear."

He lifts his finger, and the koi stop swimming. More oohs and aahs from the spectators.

With a flourish, he tucks his cards away and pulls the silk fan from his chest pocket. A low chuckle as he holds it out. "Volunteers? To pick the twist for tonight's fight?"

Dozens of hands shoot up. This time I keep from snickering as Jihen scans the crowd. Still he smirks as his gaze meets mine, and then he points to Vetta. "You, then."

Vetta reaches out, touches silk, and Jihen goes to read.

The pulse in my veins begins to race—this hated magic getting ready, like it knows it will be cast, whether I control it or not. Something inside me *wanting* to cast, as much as I also dread it.

"For tonight's fight," Jihen calls out, a slick grin in his voice, "instead of a flood for the empress's palace, how about we remake a kiln?"

In the next second, the sky of a ceiling goes transparent. Jihen and the spectators are looking at us from the other side of it.

And I start to burn.

TWENTY-FOUR

Fire blazes around the room. Flames lick at corners and along walls, dancing on the tops of shelves. Cabinets are now ovens and fire-places, packed to the brim with heat. Everything appears orange, the shade of apocalypse.

I stagger back, trying to get away. The world's glowing with light, set to burn. Nothing but terror fills me. My own fever of pain spikes and crawls up my throat.

The temperature in the room climbs. Higher and higher.

My skin feels as thin as paper, about to spark, to crisp and turn to ash. Breathing is like inhaling the air from the world's hottest desert, air that's known nothing but sun for centuries. Sweat stings my eyes.

Hundreds of pieces of porcelain shimmer and shine, as hot to the touch as fire itself—nearly impossible to pick up or hold. A room full of potential starters turned useless.

Then the room explodes—into shouts, the blurs of limbs, magic itself—as fighters begin turning on one another. Casting through flame.

I duck low to the ground and start to jaggedly draw my finger along my palm. It's hard to think. Heat presses in like an unending and suffocating dark. I tear off a silver starter to cast a shield when the first pieces of porcelain crash down.

Vases and figurines fall to the ground. They tumble from their high displays and shelves. Porcelain dust covers the floor, plumes blowing wide. Fighters slip and fall onto shards of cups and dishes.

The level of noise in the room turns thunderous.

Ceiling tiles begin to fall.

A new fear comes, a sliver of ice that cuts through the heat.

When does porcelain *melt*?

I peer up through a room so hot everything appears to be shimmering, no longer quite solid.

Hundreds of faces stare back at me through the still-intact transparent ceiling, mouths open and cheering.

Their enjoyment—I both hate it and understand it. I also want it for myself; I hope some of that cheering is just for me.

I cast, silently begging this strange other magic to cooperate.

Shield spell.

Heat comes from the ground—even hotter than the room. It streams up through my feet and fills my mind, a hazy red cloud. I shape it into a cape of flowers—bright vivid blooms of jasmine and orchids, peonies and chrysanthemums—and wrap it around me.

The sounds of porcelain smashing soften. Fighters no longer yell but whisper. The world slows, becomes wispy and lazy smears of color. A body swims close—a fighter, looking. They cast on me.

I feel nothing.

Even the surrounding heat somehow feels cooler.

Spell in place, I let the depleted silver coin drift from my hand.

Then, in a deluge, the pain of casting.

It comes down like an ocean wave—too huge, beyond scale, unfair. It is a blast of lightning rippling through my skull. I can't hold my spell through it, and my shield instantly dissolves.

My body is incompatible with this magic. To it, this magic is an infection to be rid of. Not something put inside me to help, but an invader. Nothing but danger.

I fall back to the floor as a scream gurgles from my mouth. Heated porcelain digs through my clothes, cut into the backs of my legs, and I scream for real as the shards burn me. I smell blood, a scent that reminds me of burning meat.

The other fighter—the one whose spell my shield absorbed—stands over me, young and floppy haired and confident. One sleeve of his jacket is singed—he must have gotten too close to the fire in the room. Founders' ink flashes on his cheeks—ring name Trey, five eliminations. He casts again, and there's a flash of gold from his palm.

My throat closes up. That arid desert air, gone. An invisible weight sits on my chest. Grows.

I scrabble at my hip, spells running through my mind. Red to make him bleed. White to break his bones. But my starters are gone. Somewhere out of reach.

My starters—*where*?

There. The lump I'm lying on.

Panic sweeps in as I keep trying to reach my starters and still can't. From above, the shadow of a trembling shelf looms. The flicker of flame along the wall, held back by the Founders so their ring is kept kiln-hot, not instantly scorching everything to dust.

I run my hand along the tile floor—it's gone hot, too—desperate for a shard of porcelain, for its dust, for anything. I'll burn my hands to hold something, as long as I can *breathe*. My heart shouts from inside my chest.

Trey, still standing over me, reaches for another starter. His eyes narrow slightly as casting pain comes.

The shelf above him trembles once more—hard. A vase comes down. It smashes him on the head.

He tips over, unconscious. Then he becomes jade stone.

The weight lifts from my chest, and I'm gasping, coughing. I stagger to my feet, my skin blistered and burning wherever porcelain has touched it. There's the dull smack of hands against tile, and I glance upward. Spectators are calling my name. I see the shape of it on their lips:

Azaaaaa! Aza the Champion!

I lift a hand to my cheek, knowing I won't feel the change just as I'm sure it's there. No longer a zero but a one. Finally.

I start to cast another shield spell, the earlier pain from casting still reverberating through me. Breaths that feel as hot as glowing embers rasp along my throat.

I can try to go invisible. I used to be able to cast that spell. Anything to hide my way through these next matches. Not even two more days of surviving this magic, with my body wanting it out like a disease.

But to go from Aza the Champion to Aza the Coward? With magic that won't listen? What if I disappear forever?

The risk is too great.

Vetta stumbles into my line of sight.

I draw before I can stop myself. Eight points scratched out on my palm. I reach down and drag my hand along the searing tile floor. Smoking porcelain dust—good for a bone spell.

I cast—not thinking, not caring, only *feeling*. Vetta is Saint

Willow, she is Jihen, she is Indy, who gets to have Piper as her backer.

Heat. My palm on fire. A red mist within my skull that I form into an image.

A skeletal tree, twisting in a winter wind.

Vetta crashes backward to the floor. Her entire body starts shaking, like some kind of current is roaring through her. She stares at me as I get closer, her eyes huge, mouth trying to work. The number nine is on her cheek.

"No— D-don't— I—"

So hot in here. I feel overwhelmingly sick from the heat, from the pain. The air shimmers orange, too bright against my eyes.

Suddenly, against my will, the magic surges again. Shock makes me go dead still even as liquid fire fills my veins. It runs fast and violent—beyond stopping.

Vetta is convulsing harder now, the floor burning through her clothes just as it burned through mine. Her body shakes and shakes. Her eyes roll.

More magic, running faster still. Growing the spell, making it bigger.

Stop it, Aza! The yell is huge inside my head. *Break the spell!*

I don't know how to break the spell.

If the Founders don't knock her out soon, this magic will kill her.

Just as I killed Kylin.

Panic slams into me. I stare down at Vetta, fear rising to sting my throat.

And then my own bones are under attack—casting pain. A wrenching as if invisible hands are twisting every limb from the inside. I fall to my knees, onto jagged porcelain that cuts into my skin. The tile of the floor singes and sears. Pain yanks and threatens to drag me into darkness.

The entire room spins, and Vetta turns into jade stone.

I bend over, crying. My throat is on fire, just as my skin is. The number two forms on my cheek.

Too close.

Kylin, this *is why the world hates full magic. Because our power is not just about what it can create, but what it can take away.*

A shadow nears through the glow of fire, and fresh pain hits me. A spell of thin needled heat, like teeth gnashing away. Blood begins to gush from all the places where I'm already hurt, the cuts and scrapes and burns. The stink of copper in the air thickens, as much a haze hanging in the room as porcelain dust.

The shadow is Bardem, pants and shirt singed in spots. He drops a red coin from his hand.

My hand reaches out and finds a tile—hot, jagged, the blue of an impossible sky—that has fallen from the ceiling. I put it in my palm and begin to draw around it. Five points. My bloodied finger shakes so hard I have to start over, retrace. Everything hurts; everything is agony.

"Bow out, Aza." His gray eyes are wide and no longer sleepy-looking, telling me it's over. The number six glows on his skin. "It's too late."

"It . . . isn't." Saint Willow is in my brain, screaming at me.

A faint bruise spreads along one of his arms as I watch—his price for the five-pointed spell he just cast on me. I wish I could believe he'll really feel that.

"Bow out," he says. "C'mon."

The crowd overhead smells my defeat. They slap at transparent ceiling tiles as they cheer. I watch their mouths. *Bar-dem! Bar-dem!*

My gaze slips, catches on the Founders and the porcelain busts they've cast themselves into. Whether it's the orange light that's everywhere or something else, Wilson's even easier to make out now, his face more human than porcelain. The effort of keeping the ring cast shows—in the grimace of his mouth, a paleness to his dark skin.

I don't even care that he hurts, too.

"Aza, bow out," Bardem says again.

I keep trying to draw, but my finger does nothing but shake. There's a vise around my brain, shutting me off.

He takes a fresh starter out of his pocket. "You should have quit."

I'm still trying to draw when he casts.

The cold nothingness of jade stone.

TWENTY-FIVE

I open my eyes, and every piece of porcelain once owned by a mad empress has disappeared. The walls of tile are just white paint, and nothing hangs on them but abstract paintings. Only the faintest swirl of porcelain dust in the air tells me I was just inside a ring cast by magic.

The winner is Indy again. Her expression is still humble.

Jihen makes the official announcement. Then he shouts out the address for tomorrow night's location—*496 Cloche Road, midnight, don't be late. Look for a scarlet flower.*

Then Piper's with Indy, and I have to turn away. That same dart in my chest from earlier comes back, even sharper this time. Piper is a reminder of who is actually in my corner. Indy is a reminder of who I used to be.

I turn to leave, making my way through the crowd and toward the exit. I need to escape, to be alone and nurse my wounds and convince myself I can do this all over again tomorrow. I take off my silk ribbons and stuff them into my starter bag. I put my smog mask back on and pretend I'm unrecognizable now. I walk, trying to block out all the voices that come at me as I pass through the mass of people.

Indy's the winner, but I'm being whispered about just as much. As soon as the last bit of porcelain dust faded away, my name rose from where it was, my loss the thing that won't die.

Aza the Loser, right?

More like Aza the Cruel. You saw her last spell.

I bet on her to lose!

The words burn as hot as the flames in the ring. They work their way through my ears, into my brain, becoming a memory I will never forget. Like everyone else here, I know about Etana the Cruel. She's famous for killing to win. But to think of me that same way isn't fair. That spell on Vetta started out exactly as it was meant to. When the magic spiraled out of control at the end, it dragged me right along with it.

At the last second, I make myself stop at the bets counter to pick up my cut.

The envelope is as thin as the one from last night's fight. The weight of the marks in my hand stings, like salt on a wound.

I shove the envelope into my bag and push open the door to the stairs.

It turns out descending fifteen flights isn't any easier than going up them, especially when you're beaten down. Pain from fighting is still wrapped all around me, the newest and freshest layer. By the time I get outside, I'm limping badly, breathing in broken gasps.

Smoggy city air blows over my skin as I move along the sidewalk, cooling it after the fire and heat, washing away ancient porcelain dust. I tug my mask up higher, still careful to keep my head lowered. Others are leaving the building at the same time, barely behind me.

When the initial tremor hits, my first thought is that it's a quake.

I don't panic. With the earth slowly falling apart, quakes have long been a part of everyday life in Lotusland. Still, as everyone else around me does, I start eyeing the area for somewhere to go. All the buildings here are up to quake code, but why take chances?

Another tremor. The ground vibrates. Then, in the distance, a long, deep rumble, like something pulling up out of the earth.

People point and start running, rushing past me in their hurry to see.

The entire sector now feels like a death trap. I'm trying to decide where to go when I look up and watch as a building down the street begins to tilt.

Twenty floors, glass and concrete and rigid lines. Built not to fall.

It tips over like a drinking glass knocked on its side.

The noise is tremendous, a boom I can feel in my bones. Concrete dust billows from the building like it's in a race with itself. I'm blinking fast against grit. My throat is coated with dust all over again. The cloud builds as it winds its way into the sky, a near match for the city smog that has blotted out the shape of the sun for too many years.

I can't look away.

That too-big blast of magic I cast on Vetta, unleashed and uncontrollable as it grew—this is the result on the outside world. Breakthrough damage. From me.

"Which building was that again?" The question comes from somewhere behind me, but it takes a second for me to hear it, shock still drowning me so that it feels like I'm underwater.

"Dunno, just another office tower," someone else says. "But yeah, wow."

I tune them out and make myself walk faster.

I shiver as a night breeze lifts my hair, cuts through my clothes. More people push past me on the sidewalk to get a closer look. I let them. Concrete dust blooms, keeping everyone half disguised, hiding faces.

I shiver again as another breeze comes, swirling away the dust for the space of a single heartbeat.

Now I *do* see a face. Someone I know all too well. Someone I hoped never to see again.

Finch.

Watching me.

Waiting for me to give away the secret of reclaimed magic.

TWENTY-SIX

I hurt even before I open my eyes. The light comes into my bedroom dull and gray—not pale enough to still be early morning. I've slept late. My body, trying to heal with sleep.

The taut wire that is my pain is pulled even tighter inside me. I imagine it in there, sharp enough to cut, as honed as the edge of a blade. The physical cost of fighting with strange magic is turning out to be as uncontrollable as the magic itself—and there's nothing I can do to make it better. It's as unavoidable as casting itself.

One more day. One more fight. And tomorrow, I can go find Nima.

Scents seep in through the walls and door—fresh tea, hot rice. My parents, likely already awake for hours.

As I get up to get ready, I can't help but notice how the sounds from the teahouse are too few now. There are hardly any chimes of customers coming through the door. The murmur of chatter from the dining room is minimal and muted.

What will Saint Willow do next, now that I've failed again? What comes after sabotage?

In my head, the memories of Finch's face swarms. Appearing out of the concrete dust like something rising out of water.

I used that dust as cover to slip away and move down the street. Then the dark to get from Tower back to Tea. I knew he didn't follow, but I felt him with me anyway, his cold green eyes still everywhere I looked.

It was only a matter of time, him finding me. Just as Oliver would have discovered my secrets if I hadn't told him first.

He said Finch was no longer interested in magic, but he was wrong. And now I wonder if he knew Finch would be there last night. And what that means.

I tiptoe past Dad, busy loading the breakfast dishes in the kitchen. Out in the teahouse, Mom's in the dining area, serving the two tables of customers. She's as polite as ever, but distress pulls at the corners of her mouth. Worry in her eyes. All the good of the last month come undone. Guilt singes me, as hot as last night's fire.

I go behind the counter for Wu Teas' landline and dial the number for the Salt Lick.

"Salt Lick, how can I help you?"

I exhale quietly in relief at Oliver answering. If Finch had picked up, I'd have hung up.

"Oliver, it's Aza. Can we meet somewhere for a few minutes? I need to talk to you."

The pause on his end says how surprised he is that I'm calling, reaching out again. "Sure. Want to come over? I have to watch the shop."

Now it's my turn to pause.

"Finch isn't here," Oliver continues, reading my silence over the line. "He won't be back for a couple of hours."

"Okay. I'll be there as soon as I can."

Dad appears just as I'm hanging up.

"Good morning," he says, coming to stand behind the counter with me. The teahouse books and files he was in the middle of going over are still laid out. A flicker of worry crosses his face as he sneaks a glance out over the near-empty shop. Then he notices my starter bag over my shoulder. "Where are you off to? No breakfast first? There's a fresh pot of tea in the kitchen."

Another wave of guilt. I'm supposed to be around more with all this time off courtesy of Saint Willow. "I have to see someone really quick. Sorry, I won't be long."

"Is this the same someone you met yesterday? What is his name again? Oliver?"

"I— Yes. It's Oliver." At least this time it really is him.

Dad smiles and shuffles some papers around. "See, it doesn't have to be weird, right? I'm glad we can talk about this."

I have to smile back. It makes me happy that my parents still feel good enough to keep working on things between us, despite the sudden backslide with the teahouse. Even if Wu Teas never recovers, at least we had one good month together. Feeling like a family again.

"I'm glad, too," I say. "Anyway, I'll be back to help out."

"No rush." He sends another glum look across the teahouse.

"The shipments haven't come?" Silently I curse Saint Willow. Until she's pleased with me again, I suspect we won't be getting our supplies at all.

"No, unfortunately. I'll call at the end of the day if they still haven't come by then." Suddenly, he begins to pat his pockets. "Oh, before I forget—someone came by this morning and left you their contact information."

For a second I think he must be talking about Oliver. But that doesn't make sense, since I just talked to him on the phone.

Before I can make another guess, Dad takes a slip of paper from his chest pocket and hands it over. "About work, he said—he'd like you to call back."

I read the name. Fear mixes with confusion.

Cormac.

My eyes lower to the short message scrawled beneath a number.

Call me back—have info for you.

So the Scout is back. Still alive. Relief trickles through me—he must have escaped from Earl Kingston on his own. And now he has new information.

But . . . about what? Is he still investigating Shire's death? Is he getting close to finding out she was a caster of full magic? That I am?

The fear and confusion grow.

I shove the paper into my pocket, trying to keep my fingers steady. "Thanks. I'll call him back later."

TWENTY-SEVEN

I'm careful to look for signs of Jihen as I leave. I know Saint Willow will want to speak to me before tonight's fight. Last night's loss absolutely guarantees it.

I search for signs of Cormac, too, who's apparently come calling. Until I find out what he wants, I need to stay prepared.

But there are signs of neither. I pull on my smog mask and make my way toward the Salt Lick. Soon pain has me limping, and I regret my decision not to backtrack to the nearest train station when I had the chance. Still, the easiest way to lose anyone who might be following *is* to make a maze out of the streets, and since that's best done on foot, I trudge on.

The mild scents of grass and woods fade out, turn into sharp whiffs of pepper and cloves, salt and pungent herbs. The marks of the Spice Sector.

A few customers are just leaving the Salt Lick when I get there. I stand outside, waiting. It's not raining, but it will soon, the sky going a dark gray, the air turning heavy with incoming moisture.

"Aza."

Oliver's holding the front door open. He's watching me carefully with those always-too-serious hazel eyes of his, a curious smile on his face. I can tell he doesn't mind that I'm here—he might even be happy to see me again. Realizing I feel the same way is unnerving, like I'm slipping down a slope I can't afford to lose hold of.

"Thanks for letting me come over," I say as I step inside the shop and carefully tuck my mask into my pocket.

Oliver's smile turns wry as he shuts the door behind us. "As long as you're not going to peek into my brain this time."

"I promise I won't." I quickly glance around the shop—the barrels of salt, the shelves full of canisters and tins. We're completely alone.

I'm about to tell him why I'm here, but I hesitate. For another minute, I just want to pretend we're anyone but who we are.

I sniff the air. "Why do I smell . . . cookies? Instead of spices?"

"A fresh shipment of our cookie dough salt came in today," he says, gesturing toward the back of the shop. "I'm still in the middle of packaging it."

"Cookie dough salt? I didn't know there was such a thing."

He lifts a brow. "Wu Teas hasn't bought into the cookie trend in some way? Cookie everything was all over the city last year."

"No. But we *did* buy into the cheese trend the year before that." Our Cha-Cha-Cheese blend was one of the teahouse's desperate attempts to find new customers. "It sold, but not well enough to keep around. I don't think my parents really minded since eating cheese makes them sick anyway."

Oliver laughs. The sound of it—it's a good laugh, balancing out the seriousness of his eyes. It drifts over, sits on my skin like a balm.

"Well, we've had our cookie dough salt forever," he says. A flicker in his hazel eyes, making them darken a shade. "It was my mom's favorite."

His mother. The last time Oliver mentioned her was when he told me how his parents died. His guilt still hangs over the memory.

"Does it sell okay?" I ask. Shop talk feels safer.

His eyes go back to hazel as he grins. "Not really. Not compared to our vanilla or chocolate ones. But we'll always carry it. Finch is really careful about reordering, too. Here, come try it."

I follow him—and the scent of cookies—into the back of the shop. His words echo in my head. It startles me, the idea of a gentler Finch. Finch who loved his mom. It's hard to even imagine him in this space. To me, he will always be the ruthless fighter from the ring, determined to cast, willing to kill for a victory.

The kitchen of the Salt Lick is laid out like Wu Teas' kitchen—the expected appliances, crowded counters. Tins and paper bags are strewn all around, and dustings of sparkling light tan powder are everywhere. A large glass jar is full of grains of the same pale brown, and when Oliver lifts the lid, the smell of cookies doubles.

He pinches some of the tan-colored salt into my palm. It tastes like the cookie dough it promises—sugar and butter, hints of chocolate and milk—but also more. Heightened. That same sugar, caramelized. A twist of lemon. Vanilla from the pods.

"I like it," I tell him. "Maybe a different name will make it sell better."

He tastes it from his own palm. "Yeah, maybe. Mom never minded the name. So Finch probably won't go for changing it."

"She was your mom, too," I say quietly. "He's not the only one who deserves to be sad."

A few seconds of silence as we look at each other.

"I know you hate him," Oliver finally says, "and I don't blame you. But everything he did was because of me."

"Shire's not dead because of you."

His hazel eyes are unflinching. "She's not dead because of you, either."

I shake my head, knowing I can't agree. I guess it's how he feels about Finch, too.

"Oliver, the reason why I called is because last night, after the fight, I saw Finch. He was there, outside of the ring."

His features flicker, emotions crashing together. "You saw someone else. He doesn't care about magic or casting anymore."

"It *was* him. I think he's trying to find out how I got magic back. And Finch with magic again—" I fight back a shudder, the memory of that green gaze washing over me. "You know we can't let him."

Silence hangs between us. The presence of our siblings. I wait for Oliver to speak first, wanting to know what he's thinking. I can go after Finch on my own if I need to. But Oliver telling me he understands would make it easier.

"He's used a gatherer before," he says, the words flat. Listlessly, he pinches at more tan-colored salt and lets it fall to the floor. "If he wants magic back badly enough, he'll find one again."

"He has nothing left to offer as payment, though."

"There's always something else to give up." Desperation in his eyes. "I don't know if I can stop him."

"*I* can stop him, though."

A haunted look that I can barely meet. "You'd cast on Finch."

"Only if I had to." I watch his face as I tell him this, hoping he'll see how much I don't want to do it. Not just because casting hurts or because everything is at risk every time I do it. But because, in the end, Finch is still his brother. "But with your help, I'm hoping it won't come to that."

"What can I do?" Oliver's voice is brittle.

"Keep him away from the fights for now." One more day, and Finch will never be a problem again.

"I can try. I'll do my best."

"He doesn't know we're friends. Maybe he'll tell you if he has a plan, like he told you last time. And then you can tell me."

I'm expecting him to get mad because I've asked him to betray his brother, but instead a small, shy smile lurks around his lips. "Are we friends, then, Aza Wu?"

Was he always standing so close? Scents swirl heavily—salt, sugar, *him*. I'm suddenly more than aware of my own pulse, fast in my veins. My own heat, outside of magic. For the first time in days, there's something more visceral than pain, and in a good way.

"I *hope* we're friends," I say. I swipe at the salt left on my palm, nervous with him again.

"Can I ask you something, then?"

"Sure."

"Promise if you're in trouble, you'll cast on him without thinking about me?"

Something in my chest twists. I'm not the only one still riddled with guilt. Does he remember that the last time he asked for a promise—that I wouldn't kill Finch in the ring—I kept it?

"Oliver—"

His expression is raw. "Promise, okay?"

I breathe out slowly, as though doing even that has the potential to be painful. I give him the answer he both wants and fears. I wish it gave me more pause. "Okay."

He blinks like he's waking up, all dazed hazel eyes and soft features. "Okay, then."

"I should go," I say. The scents of butter and sugar, making my head spin.

I move before I can wonder too much about it. Before it's like an apology instead of the thing I most want to do.

I lean in and kiss him.

He tastes like salt and an intense sweetness beneath it that surprises me.

"I'm glad we're friends," I say, leaning away.

He pulls me back. "Me, too."

TWENTY-EIGHT

Once I cross into Tea, I focus on getting myself together. It's hard to concentrate, the feel of Oliver's lips still pressed into mine. It's hard *not* to want to think of that.

But I can't.

By the time I'm a block away from the teahouse, the rain has finally started. I'm also back to limping, that low-fever feeling once again with me. It's getting difficult to remember what it's like not to hurt at all.

The fight is twelve hours away.

It isn't like Saint Willow to just let last night's loss go.

So where is Jihen?

When I see Wu Teas from across the street, I know he's already come and gone.

The just-painted storefront window of the teahouse is smashed. Thin gray daylight reflects off the sidewalk in front, gone brilliant with its carpet of glass shards. A half dozen people are standing around, craning to see into the shop. Just off to the side, a cop is interviewing some bystanders, witnesses to what happened. The words *robbery* and *vandalism* float over. *Masked men.*

Terror fills me as I rush over, panic like a sharp knife scoring my entire body. My parents were at the shop for the entire morning—they would have been here. They would never leave it unattended. They don't know how.

This is my punishment for losing last night's fight—I did this to my parents.

I get closer and stand in front of the gaping window. I take in the knocked-over dining tables, the tipped-over shelves. There's merchandise littered all over the new floor: piles of loose leaves, dented tins, smashed cups. Tea smells blanket the air—toasty, grasslike, all shades of green. I know that scent better than anything. But right now I can't find any comfort in it at all.

The till is missing from where it always sits on the front counter.

Inside the shop, another cop is talking to my parents. I'm so relieved to see them I nearly stumble. It hurts to take in their stunned faces, their visible fear. The carefree feeling from just days ago has completely disappeared.

Saint Willow hasn't left her fingerprints on Wu Teas this time, but outright holes in the shapes of punches.

This is a message. Another sign of her displeasure. It might be exactly what Nima meant about keeping Saint Willow preoccupied. But it's way too risky doing it this way, putting my parents and the teahouse in danger again and again.

I'll have to keep the gang leader busy by keeping her happy. And only happy. Until Nima is ready.

"Hello, Aza."

A familiar voice interrupts my thoughts. I pause to place it, because it doesn't belong anywhere near here.

I glance up, rain dripping into my eyes.

Embry. In one of his classy suits, with a cop's silver armband tied around his sleeve. It's nearly as shiny as the broken glass at our feet.

"Hello," I say stupidly, slowly tugging down my rain-dampened mask. It's almost surreal how he's right here, seemingly to bring more trouble into my life, as if I didn't have quite enough already. I haven't seen him since the end of the annual tournament last month. I can't imagine why he's come.

"I think we need to talk," he says. "Walk with me, please. I'm interviewing you about the robbery, all right?"

The cool demand in his teal gaze tells me I can't argue.

We turn the corner.

"I thought being head Scout would have saved you from dealing with this kind of stuff," I tell him, feeling half-numb. "I mean, robberies happen all over the city."

"They do. I don't need to be here. But then I heard this was at Wu Teas."

"You came looking for me?" My head's clouded, and my words come slow, thick. It's the pain in my bones. It's Saint Willow's message to me. It's talking to Embry out here, in this part of the world that is not supposed to know anything about fighting rings.

"Yes, but not about the robbery," he says. "Which I *am* sorry about, by the way. Don't worry about your parents and the tea-house. I'm sure the department will find out who did this."

Not this time, I think. Saint Willow is beyond normal cop business. It's how Lotusland works. How it always will.

"Aza, this new casting tournament that's just started," Embry continues. "Can you tell me about it?"

I never thought I'd ever see the Speaker of the Guild in action as a Scout, but here we are. I try to hedge, unsure of what he wants to hear, what he might already know. I know I can't risk making Saint Willow angry anymore. Which means that as much as I'd like to give her up to Embry right now, I can't. Not without any kind of guarantee she'll never again be a problem.

"What have you already heard?" I ask.

"Rumors." Embry frowns. "Some truly troubling things. The Guild is looking into them."

So he's here on behalf of the Guild. Not as a Scout.

"I don't know anything about the new tournament," I say. "I've just heard rumors, too. But they don't add up to anything."

"The lightning storm in the Spice Sector the other night." He wipes rain from his face. "The building that just fell in Tower. We know both are breakthrough damage and that it lines up with the timing of this new tournament. We're concerned about further damage. About how much worse it might get."

Images of Lotusland finally being swallowed up by a crumbling earth flash across my mind. Of the city sliding into the Pacifik, then sinking out of sight. Both scenarios leave me cold, fill me with a dread that curls along my spine.

I glance more closely at Embry, whose own gaze is distant. "It sounds like you already know plenty."

"I'm a Scout, Aza. It's my job to investigate anything that hints of full magic. And if disasters keep happening every night, it won't be long before other Scouts begin to dig harder. And I won't be able to stop them."

"What then?"

He shakes his head. "I don't know. We've managed to keep the tournament secret for as long as it's existed. But magic has limits.

There's always a cost. If this new tournament doesn't understand that . . ." A long exhale, full of frustration.

"Then maybe it's best if all the tournaments come to an end." I can't believe I'm saying this. The part of me that needs to cast wants me to shut up. And to say this to Embry, of all people. Embry, who has spent his life in the Guild.

But the images of Lotusland falling away won't fully fade.

His eyes narrow. "You really don't know who's running this new tournament?"

"I don't."

"Strange. Because I know you're fighting in it. I know you have your magic back."

I wake up like I've dunked my head in ice water.

Embry can never know I'm casting magic that isn't mine. He's a Scout, truly worried about the state of the earth. He can't let a caster who has no control over their magic walk free.

"I . . . found a gatherer to get it back for me," I tell him, my mind racing now, rain making me blink fast. I'll take the blame. Less complicated this way with no one else to chase down.

His eyes narrow another fraction. "The same one you used to get the spell to take away Finch's magic, I'm presuming."

I nod. I'll give him that.

"All right." A hard smile. There's an edge to it that nearly makes me flinch. "Now that we've established you actually know more than just rumors, who is running this tournament?"

"The ones who cast the fighting rings don't ever show themselves," I say. I'm not lying. Everything I'm telling him has truth sprinkled in.

Telling Embry the truth might bring an end to this tournament of Saint Willow's. But it also might set her off in other ways. Worse ways. And after seeing what just happened to the teahouse . . .

And then there's my own magic. If Embry goes after Saint Willow, Nima might be found out, too. She won't be able to gather. I'll be stuck with this strange magic forever.

If I can just hold on for one more day, then everything will be fixed for good.

Embry watches me for another long moment. Rain drips down my face, but I ignore it. He's an Ivor, but still his power emanates.

"You know I can't let this tournament continue, Aza. For many reasons. But it needs to be done carefully. The Guild has no interest in forcing their way in." His smile stays hard. "But if I have more questions, I hope you don't mind if I come find you again?"

Another question that really isn't one. "Sure."

He nods. "Thank you."

"Can I ask you something now?" Embry's right here, and it seems as good a time as any to finally know. The note is still in my pocket, urging me to find out. "What happened when I asked you to go help that Scout named Cormac? Earl Kingston got hold of him, remember?"

"There was no sign of him anywhere within Kingston territory by the time I got there. My assumption then—as it is now—is that he managed to extricate himself before I arrived."

"Have you seen him back at work?"

"I don't know what he looks like, Aza. But his name isn't one I hear around the station. If you're not sure where he was assigned, he could be anywhere in the city."

"Isn't there some kind of internal system where you can, you know, punch in his name?"

"Sure, I can do that. I'll tell you what I find out—if anything—once I do."

"Thanks." I wanted to find out more *now*, but there's nothing to be done about it.

He adjusts the silver armband, preparing to leave. "Why the continued interest in a Scout who was giving you a hard time?"

"Just—I like tying up loose ends."

"I know you better than to believe that." He frowns again, more deeply this time. "Be careful, won't you, Aza?"

"Of course."

Embry slips away.

I head back to help pick up the shattered pieces of the teahouse.

TWENTY-NINE

It took until dark to get the teahouse back into shape. Despite the brave faces they put on for me, I could tell it would be some time before my parents would feel safe again.

We boarded up the broken window as best we could, swept up glass and ceramic and tea, and righted the furniture. My parents cast their leftover magic to help. I only cast leftover, too—I didn't want to attempt anything stronger.

The teahouse will be closed to customers for at least a day or two. Repair people, insurance companies, and suppliers all need time and space to calculate the damage done. There will be a cost to make everything right again.

My parents believe they can pay in marks, but I know the truth: That what we owe goes beyond marks and signatures on paper.

Nima, will this plan of ours really work?

An hour before midnight, I step out of my bedroom and stand in the darkened hall, making sure my parents are asleep. As quietly as possible, I tiptoe to the front of the teahouse, guiding the way with my fingers along the walls. There's less light than usual with the front window all boarded up.

I click on the lone lamp in the dining room that's not smashed. Again, I see everything that got damaged and all that is still broken. The whole room feels wrong and unfamiliar. Fresh hatred for Saint Willow turns my skin hot.

Behind the front counter, I reach for the landline. From my pocket, I take out the piece of paper with Cormac's number on it and smooth out the creases.

Call me back—have info for you.

I dial, the pattering of rain against plywood loud behind me. Uneasiness lies in my stomach on top of all the other aches inside me. I wonder about tipping points, about points of no return. The skyscraper the other night had stood tall, absolutely sturdy—but enough force, and it was gone. Toppled over and turned into nothing but dust and debris.

The phone rings and rings, but no one picks up. Not even an answering service.

I hang up, unsure what to do next.

Asking Embry didn't reveal anything new. I already assumed he didn't find Cormac at Earl Kingston's.

But it's too late now to try to guess where Cormac could be right this moment. It's time to go.

I click off the lamp and go back to my bedroom, making sure to shut the door behind me. I fold up the paper and hide it in my desk drawer.

I refill my starters and attach the holder to my belt loop.

Carefully, I wrap silk ribbons around my arm, peonies first and then willows.

I can't help but think about an alternate version of my life where I might be getting dressed for something like a dance instead of a fight. An occasion that has nothing to do with danger or debts to pay.

Shire would be here, still giving me sisterly advice. And Kylin, legs swinging as she sat at the foot of my bed. Maybe even Rudy as chaperone. That would be something.

There's a soft knock at my bedroom door.

Instantly, the daydream comes to end. Like the curtain's come crashing down.

I picture the teahouse's boarded-up front window. Secure, but *not* that secure. I imagine Saint Willow's men here earlier today, their hands smashing things as ordered, instructed to leave behind a message.

What if she decided it wasn't enough of one?

My pulse skipping fast, I open my bedroom door.

Mom.

She's in her robe, hands tucked deep into its pockets. Without her makeup, she looks older than she really is. Dark shadows line her eyes.

"Aza, I saw your light beneath the door. Is everything okay? You don't always stay up this late, do you?"

It takes me a second to react to her being here right now. She's supposed to be asleep, and I have to leave. "Everything's fine. It's not that late, is it?"

"Well, maybe not. Maybe it's just been a very long day and that's all. I've been trying to sleep, but . . ."

Of course. It makes sense that the robbery would be on her mind.

Mom peers more closely at me. Her eyes scan my clothes. "You're still dressed? You should probably get to bed soon. It's going to be noisy here in the morning. Everything needs to be properly assessed, so we've arranged for a lot of people to come through."

"Okay, I'll go get ready." I tug at my shirt, making sure the hem is still covering up the starter holder at my hip. I could never explain it away. "Sorry if my light kept you up."

"No, it's fine. Oh—this is pretty, Aza." She touches the silk ribbons tied around my arm.

My stomach clenches, a fist going tight. My parents can't find out about the tournament. They've learned to trust me about magic, but this would be too much. Everything we've fixed between us would fall apart.

"Where did you get this?" Mom asks.

The innocence of her question catches me off guard, and my answer slips out before I can stop it.

"The Mothery in Textile."

"I like the material." She drops her hand. "All right, I'll leave you alone now. I'm going to try again to get some sleep—I'll be more than happy to leave this day behind. You get some sleep, too."

"I will. Good night, Mom."

"Good night, Aza."

I shut my door. Still unnerved, I stay still and listen. When I hear the sound of Mom shutting the door to her bedroom, I let out a long, shaky exhale.

I grab a fresh smog mask, then tug it on and head for my window. I've already got my hands on the frame to push it up when I catch my reflection in the glass.

This time, my face shimmers, and I see a version of myself that looks more like Shire. She was the pretty one, the beauty in the family—something Jihen never lets me forget. But now I can see the ways we are the same. A longing for her catches in my throat, a silent sob.

Shire, tell me how to do this. How do I control magic that won't be controlled? I can't lose again tonight. Can't make Mom and Dad pay anymore.

But my sister can't answer me now.

I shove the window open and climb out.

THIRTY

On the train ride into the Bakery Sector, I doze on and off, trying to rest my body before the fight. Each time the train hits a bit of warped track, my head smacks into the window I'm leaning against, startling me half-awake.

Still groggy by the time I get to my stop, I stiffly climb off and head toward the address of the ring.

It's a building on the far side of the sector, its exterior all red brick and wide-paned windows. The brick is dusty and the windows cloudy. There's also graffiti all over the place, and I wonder how hard it'll be to pick out the image of the starter. The sidewalk in front is pocked with weeds, the small parking lot the same.

Everything about the pizza restaurant—converted from an old flour mill—points to it being long shut down. From where I'm standing across the street, the sign on the entrance announcing a new gourmet sandwich bar "coming soon" is also clearly faded.

All of it only makes the shimmer of light coming through the windows more noticeable. Enough to attract the attention of anyone walking by.

It's supposed to be a secret location.

Embry would be furious.

I step off the curb to cross the street when someone approaches from around the corner.

Heart thumping, I quickly step back, ducking behind a tree. Through low-lying branches, I get broken glimpses of a figure moving along the sidewalk. They turn into the lot of the pizza place, go around the side of the building, and disappear from view.

I wait for a few more minutes, but the person doesn't appear again. I finally move, crossing the street for real, and follow where they went.

From the side of the restaurant, I can see the back of the lot. There's a fence marking where it ends, and on the other side is the rear of a bakery. Unless the person had reason to climb fifteen feet of wire just to get to a closed bakery, I bet they came here to find the ring, too.

It's understandable that it's taken me until now to run into someone else headed to a fight. Most people like arriving early when it's an event they're excited about. It's no accident that I always cut it close.

I go up to the building and lay a hand on the brick.

A clear vibration zips up my arm—the effect of hundreds of people being inside, moving and talking.

Through the clouds on the window, there's the dance of light, the clear shift of bodies.

Wilson, how can you and the Founders call this protective magic?

I back up to look at the building once more. I nearly stumble doing it, slightly dizzy. The restaurant butts up against the west side of Flower, and scents of night-blooming plants—jasmine, flowering tobacco, phlox—are tangled up in my nose with the yeasty bread smells of Bakery. The effect is disorienting, like I'm stuck between places.

Considering all the graffiti on the walls, I'm lucky it only takes a couple of minutes—no longer than it took that other person, anyway—to find the scarlet flower. The small image is somehow separate from the rest despite being surrounded by other graffiti. Or maybe it just feels that way, since I know what to look for.

I move toward the building again, drawing on my palm. I rest my hand over the red graffiti flower.

I cast.

A line appears between bricks on the wall. It follows along the mortar, tracing out the rough shape of a giant flower—if flowers were made of squares instead of curves. Bricks instead of petals.

The bricks inside the line roll up like a blind being drawn. Darkness directly behind the flower-shaped doorway, then light farther along.

One second. Two. Three. Then casting pain. A series of blows to my ribs, because this magic—disobedient, wild—just doesn't care.

I'm still breathing away the impact when I step through the doorway and into the restaurant.

Once again, it's the familiar golden light from magic-cast bulbs. It glows off red brick interior walls and the long stretches of dark wood that make up the floor. The peaked ceiling is formed of sheets of hammered tin. The restaurant's tables and chairs—also made of dark wood—are still here, pushed to the sides of the room. Everything seems lightly powdered, streaked with white. Baking flour.

People are moving in streams, registering, buying starters, and placing bets, everything happening around the three tables lined up along the wall. Shouts of how time is running out to bet rise over the noise of the crowd, stirring urgency into a space that already feels spiked and frenzied with anticipation.

"Get your bets in, counter's closing in five, fight starts in ten!"

"Winner of the last two nights is Indy! She's at twenty-one eliminations—how many more will she get tonight?"

"Aza is at two eliminations! She hasn't won in this tournament yet, but take your chances and maybe win big! Five minutes, every-one, get your bets in!"

My face burns.

But none of it's a lie.

Maybe—despite how badly I want to believe otherwise—Indy *is* the better caster in this tournament. Smarter, tougher, stron-ger. Maybe being a fighter to save my family was never meant to work.

Something close to fury hits me. It rides over the pain that's pulling at already-overwrought muscles. It shocks me back to what I need to do:

Win one last fight with this magic.

Get my own back.

Only then will I be free.

I tug down my smog mask and turn toward the registration counter to get my name and number. Founders' ink still drying on my cheeks, I cut through the center of the room, where the rest of the fighters are already waiting. I avoid eye contact as I move, pretending I'm a stranger. That no one here means anything.

She stops me mid-step.

Indy.

Up close, without the immediate frenzy of the ring around us, she's younger than I first thought. Smaller, too.

It's easy to tell myself she not as strong as she's appeared. That all of it's been luck, which can swing back my way. But even if all of that is true, it doesn't matter. Not when casting uncontrollable magic means everything can change in an instant.

Indy's eyes are close to nervous as she looks at me. Clear dark skin with a hint of a flush. Beneath the lights, her short black hair shines, as does her ribbon of black silk that's wound around her upper arm. The Mothery—Piper—in her corner. Just as they were calling out at the bets counter, the number twenty-one is displayed on her cheek.

"Um, hi," she says. "I'm Indy."

I don't want to do this at all. I'm way too aware of where we are, of everyone around who might make too much of us talking. But . . . "Hi. I'm Aza."

"I watched you in the last tournament. I was cheering for you to win."

I'm surprised enough that it takes me a second to react. Not because Indy was there—I still remember how many spectators there were, the roar of them as they watched us fight—but to hear someone say those words again. That I *won*. It's a reminder that I didn't just survive the tournament—didn't just survive Finch. I beat him.

"Thanks," I finally manage. "I know who you are, too. You've been winning."

The flush deepens across her cheekbones. "It's always close."

"Maybe. You still won."

She just nods, and I'm glad she doesn't say thank you.

"So, I know Piper was once your backer," she says. "I just wanted to say that she wasn't looking for a new fighter after you. I was the one who convinced her to sponsor me."

I stiffen, wishing she was less sincere. And that I didn't understand why she did it, though I do. I did the same thing with Piper after my first fight. "I'm glad Piper's helping you. You're both lucky to be working together."

"Yes, we are. Thanks. Sorry, I just didn't want you to think she was looking to replace you."

The memory of Piper telling me never to be sorry for winning comes back.

"You don't need to be sorry for having a good backer," I say to Indy. "It's like saying sorry for casting the right spell in the ring."

A smile crosses her lips. "Okay, I won't be sorry anymore, then."

I smile back. "Good luck."

"Thanks. Same to you."

She moves away first, and I turn to leave, too, pretending that Indy and I aren't headed for the same exact place.

But it's too late. The crowd's caught on, watching us with curious eyes. A conversation between the champion of another tournament and the current winner of this one. Speculation builds like a fire, and not too gently.

The whispers fill my ears.

Indy's better, anyway.

Maybe Vetta will get revenge tonight and there'll be some kind of showdown.

I hope the Founders will be ready. It wasn't a coincidence that building in Tower fell last night.

Cold sweat washes over my skin at this last part. I think about tonight's location being barely hidden, the sloppy carelessness of it. I think back to Wilson's face, straining to hold the illusion of the last ring. The dangers of this tournament sit in my stomach, a hard lump of panic.

One more fight.

Jihen makes his entrance.

He's grinning as he approaches, his arms raised over his head like he's already the victor tonight. His black suit is overlaid with a pattern of shiny black diamonds. Tucked in his chest pocket is his now-familiar silver fortune-teller fan.

He stops, encircled by fighters. He doesn't fit in here. His cheeks are plump and unmarred while ours gleam with ink. We stand around him as though he's some kind of savior, but it'd be smarter for us to back away.

Jihen bends down and runs his hand along the floor. He gets back up and shows us his fingers, which are dusted with flour.

I blink, and the flour is snow.

I blink again, and the restaurant is gone.

THIRTY-ONE

Snow, everywhere.

Miles of it. An endless expanse spreading in every direction, broken only by the rise and fall of low, sloping hills. Beneath a purple-tinged, cloud-filled sky, the white of the snow flashes mauve and lavender, the shades of faint bruises. The scene is both beautiful and harsh, at odds with itself.

Snow starts falling heavily. Bits of ice feel like pinpricks on my skin.

"This is the Syook Valley of Haneh." Jihen lets snow tip out of his hand as he reads off his notecards.

We're still surrounding him in a loose circle. But the snowy plain of this ring is much larger than the restaurant, so that spectators have fallen farther back, more shadows through the snow than people.

"This place no longer exists, of course," Jihen continues. "When Haneh fell into the Great Yellow Sea twelve hundred years ago, Syook Valley went right along with it. But back when it *did* exist, the valley was one of the few places on Earth that stayed frozen year-round. And because no plant life survived here, no wildlife did, either. It's also said that its three-day crossing was so treacherous that every single hill was actually built out of human bones. That means right now, we're standing in a valley that is more grave than ground."

I still think it's ridiculous how Jihen keeps reading from

notecards, but the ominousness of his words can't be ignored. I shudder as they replay in my mind. A wind cuts through my clothes, and I shiver when I glance down at my feet and realize I'm standing on a rise.

Who died here? How many? Whose bones am I now perched on?

My breath comes in hard white plumes, cold through my teeth.

Jihen flips a card, looking chilled himself. He swipes at snow that keeps him from reading his notes easily.

"The valley came to be well known as a testing ground for endurance, and casters saw crossing it as a kind of training. They came over in groups, and everyone practiced casting, even though it never stopped snowing. Because the valley was so cold, their fingers kept losing feeling. They would grow drowsy from the loss of body heat. At night, they went to sleep knowing there was always a chance they wouldn't wake up in the morning to train more. It turned out that most didn't."

The wind is howling now. My teeth won't stop chattering. I flex my half-numb fingers, wondering if I'm imagining that they're moving a fraction more slowly than just a moment ago.

The cold has buried most of my pain, but to not be able to move in exchange isn't a trade I'd make willingly.

Through falling snow, I scan the faces of nearby fighters. Tau, pulling her baseball cap lower over her face. Pav and Bardem, pale in the purple light as they listen. Everyone's numbers on their cheeks glow a ghostly white, somehow too bright against the delicate lavender landscape.

Vetta is watching me with narrowed eyes, her bright pink hair turning a pastel shade as snow begins to cover it.

Indy, her gaze calmly roaming the hills of corpses.

I have to beat every one of these casters tonight. Somehow.

The snow starts coming down even harder, faster, flakes like mini daggers of ice. My sneakers have disappeared, and snow is now building up to my ankles.

I look around, wondering where the Founders have cast themselves. It seems useless to try to find them, with the snow thickening by the minute. But then I remember where I spotted Wilson in the bamboo forest and in the room of porcelain, and I look higher. At the snow-painted sky.

Before I can make out Wilson's familiar features, I see someone else's.

The glint of glasses over a face I know. Snow catches on her frame like a bend in the light.

Nola.

Nola, who was always so methodical about taking care of her glasses in the ring. Who I once nearly drowned in order to advance.

Wilson must be up there, too. Just completely hidden this time.

I clumsily kick my shoes clean, trepidation climbing as fast as the snow. And it's getting hard to see Jihen as he reads off his cards.

Actually, it's hard to see much of anyone. The world is nothing but a dense blanket of violet-tinged snow being shaken into the air. From the edge of the group of fighters, a few muffled yells float through:

"Hey, we can't see anything!"

"Someone tell the Founders to dial back on the snow!"

Jihen speaks again. I can't see him. I can only imagine him frantically brushing snow off his cards, lips pulled into a scowl.

"I need a volunteer, someone to pick tonight's twist," he calls out.

"And how are you going to read it?" The faceless fighter saying this sounds annoyed. "How can anyone cast in this?"

"Maybe instead of another parlor trick, they should focus on not destroying any more of the city," someone else grumbles from within the snowscape.

Unease flutters at this last comment. I wasn't sure if I was the only one wondering about the Founders and their magic, though it didn't seem likely. But this is the first time it's being said right in the ring, and I'm curious how Jihen might react.

He snorts. It's not hard to imagine him flicking away the suggestion as he would a fly—bothersome and pointless. "Like I said, who wants to pick?"

"I'll do it." A different faceless fighter, sounding so cold he probably just wants the fight to start already.

We wait.

I can pinpoint where Jihen is supposed to be, but it's mostly blurs within the snow as the fighter finds him. Jihen holds out the silk fan.

Gauzy distant cheers from the shadowy fringe of spectators.

I drag my iced-over hand to the starters at my hip, convincing myself I'm ready. My teeth are chattering even harder now so that I hear their echo in my brain.

"The twist tonight," Jihen declares, my ears snatching at the words in order to process them, "is that *no coin starters will be allowed*. The Founders will now cast magic to make them useless. Only elements from the fighting ring itself will work as starters."

My already-cold breaths go icy with shock. Confusion swirls as thick as the snow.

No coin starters?

My hand falls limply to my side, bumping against the metal holder. My skin is so numb I barely feel it.

Heckling and boos.

"Are you kidding me?" Another fighter, disbelief in her voice. Her teeth are chattering, too. "There's nothing out here but *snow*. You really want us to fight by making each other *cold*?"

Jihen snorts again. "If you can't use your imagination, then you don't deserve to win."

Snow. My only weapon tonight. *Everyone's* only weapon.

The magic inside me begins to thrum, sensing release. It's the only bit of warmth I feel at the moment. Burning heat against a glacier.

Jihen's voice, coming from the purple-tinged dark:

"As always, last caster standing wins."

THIRTY-TWO

I fall stiffly to my knees and drag my hands through snow. My breath comes in gasps as the wind blows around me. I can't think of anything outside of the cold, my mind sinking deep within it, imprisoned.

Only snow.

Only snow.

ONLY SNOW.

My finger shakes—from the cold, from nerves—as I make it scratch out a star on my palm. I see nothing but the storm. Do it all only by feel. Five points to start. To test.

The yells of other fighters poke through the veil of the world, broken and garbled and sounding far away. The ground trembles as dozens of feet run across its snow-covered surface.

A fighter stumbles past, just the blur of a shadow.

I lunge.

I have no clue who they are or if I've ever fought them before. It doesn't matter here in the ring. It can't. Not knowing will make it easiest, always.

We both fall. Our thuds onto the ground are soundless, like cotton onto cloud. Snow fills my mouth and stings my face. I'm coughing, sputtering.

The other fighter—now on top of me—is coughing just as hard.

I cast first.

A sensation of warmth comes from deep inside the earth. It rises, meets me, becomes me just as I become it. For a second, the snow at my feet thins, and I can see my sneakers again.

Magic rises and I push.

Snow collects midair, like angry white mutant bees from some other dimension. The mass forms into a giant fist of cold and punches the other fighter in the side of the head.

They tip over, half collapsing on me.

I shove them all the way off and roll to my side. Just as the Founders turn them into jade stone—knockout—casting pain comes.

A surge of an ache. It hits me between the eyes from the inside of my brain. A hammer starts to pound against my skull.

Nausea rolls in, and I stagger to my feet. Still, my veins are burning, the magic in them *needing* to come out. I draw another star, this one six-pointed.

It wants more. *I* want more.

A body comes flying at me, silent as a missile.

They knock me backward to the ground, and my breath leaves me like my lungs have been punctured. All their weight, a grunting, writhing mass. Their knees pin my arms—I can't move. I begin to sink downward into the cold.

Snow—into my ears, up along my cheeks, closing in around my eyes.

Panic pounds.

I can't breathe to scream.

Against the valley's strange purple light, I make out the fighter on top of me.

Once-bright pink hair, now paled to pastel.

Vetta's eyes are inches away, the only things I can really see, and they burn down into mine. They are wild, filled with the memory of my bone spell that took her out of the fight last night. Wind hollers and spins.

"Hey, champ," she says. Her voice is a damp blur through the snow all around us. Her knees grind my arms into the ground. Snow clenched in her fist. "My turn."

She casts.

A wide sweep of snow glides across my face like the wing of a giant bird, and everything goes black.

Panic.

I struggle for air as snow fills me, pushing into my nose and mouth and across my eyes. A vise squeezes my chest, tighter and tighter. My heart thunders, deep beats of protest. I try to twist an arm free, but her knees press down with the weight of the determined. With the desire for revenge.

I can bow out right now, if I want. Just slam an elbow into the ground and call for the Founders to save me. And then at least I could *breathe*—

Is this it, then? The thought—the *yell*—flashes across my brain. *Is it already over?*

Then, from inside all that icy darkness, I feel Vetta stiffen, the motion abrupt. I hear her swear.

Casting pain from her spell on me.

Her body shifts a half inch as she shakes off the sensation. And it's just enough—one knee slips on one arm.

I scrape my hand along the snow on the ground. Flakes swarm over the spell star I've already drawn on my palm.

The thin edge of a scream as snow charges at Vetta's face. She heaves herself backward and lands on the snow-covered ground.

The vise inside my chest loosens, and I struggle to my feet. I cough out snow and breathe in huge lungfuls of air. The sound is a rasp against the wind, nearly lost within it. It reminds me of how close I came to being eliminated.

Because of Vetta.

I draw, picturing a wide river of flame, coursing as fast as an incoming tide. And I cast.

Heat bubbles in my veins, liquid and eager. I direct the tide of it toward my hand, shuddering as the burning sensation builds and builds. An invisible torch of fire sitting in my palm.

I draw a line into the snow-covered ground around Vetta's head, and the heat from my hand pours in, filling the line even as it forms. No starter to alter the magic's form. Nothing but its most basic state. A simple release.

I'm only vaguely aware of other fighters around, shadows in the nearby deep that mean nothing, the cheering of spectators barely heard. All that matters right now is Vetta, who brought me to this edge, who gave this magic inside me no choice.

Along the line of drawn heat, snow sizzles and melts. It turns liquid and begins to swell, a built-up wave about to crash. Melted snow floods over Vetta's face, over her body.

In the next instant, the cascade of water freezes solid. The coldest entombment.

Vetta's trapped. Unable to move. Through the curve of ice over her face, her mouth is frozen open. She meant to scream.

Before I've looked away, casting pain hits.

It's huge, engulfing. Like something ripping free inside me, pieces now unmoored and crashing around. I shake, dry-retch into the snow. I force my finger across my palm, preparing for the next fighter. Seven points.

In the next second, a sharp crack booms through the air. Vetta's icy tomb shatters into pieces.

I rear back, blocking my face from flying shards.

When I look again, Vetta is green jade stone against the white snow.

Someone else steps through the storm.

THIRTY-THREE

Snow in the air, thick and enveloping—whoever the other fighter is, I can't see. And they can't see who I am.

They move closer, a blur inside the storm. Just a half dozen steps away.

It doesn't matter.

The magic in my veins has grown ravenous, roaring to get out. It senses the waiting spell on my palm. It wants, and I can no longer tell where the line is between it and me. If I'm in control or it is.

That doesn't matter, either.

Because I know I want, too.

The fighter moves closer yet. The world spins. This part of Lotusland—of *earth*—no longer feels solid. It's now just a passage of wind and cold, of storm and ice. And I'm here inside it, as powerful as all of that combined.

I drop low and press the spell on my palm to the snow-covered ground. I cast.

Heat climbs through the earth, fills me. I release it out through my hand so that it dives back into the earth. I push the heat forward beneath the surface of the ground, a hot and unseen river of magic.

When it reaches the other fighter, I claw the magic still. Push it upward into the snow beneath their feet.

In an instant, the patch of ground thaws, and the snow liquefies into slush. The fighter stumbles, the snow-covered valley floor giving out beneath them.

My spell ends.

A second later, the slush freezes, encasing the fighter's feet inside it. They're stuck.

Before they can cast themself free, I draw again.

Eight points this time. I cast, gasping as pain from the effort of guiding the magic through the ground slams into me.

Through the haze, the outline of the fighter tells me they've freed themself. I watch the shapes of their hands come together. About to cast.

My next spell is ready first. A storm of magic builds in my mind, as furious as the one gripping this valley. I force it to move, like a conductor commanding a tired orchestra, demanding it play once more.

I grab at the falling snow. The flakes melt against my palm. Re-form into dozens of tiny icicles. Their points are as sharp as darts.

I hurl them at the other fighter.

I hear the icicles make contact. Shouts of pain as they lodge into skin like thorns stabbed into fingertips.

More casting pain comes. It is a dozen punches and a thousand fists. Everything hurts.

The fighter is pawing at their face, pulling at bits of ice.

Already needing to cast again, I draw a messy, jagged spell star on my palm with an icy finger.

This magic I hate, now the conductor of *me*.

Ten points.

Bigger than the last. More powerful, more fulfilling. I'm the most powerful fighter here, and for a second, I understand Saint Willow more than I ever have before.

The other fighter casts before I can.

Hard slashes of ice tear at me. They cut into my side like tiny frozen spurs, into my head like ice-cold barbs. Through their frenzy, I see the other fighter still dragging their hands across their face. They used the ice bits there to cast, my weapon turned into their starter.

I push through the flurry, trying to see, to breathe. The ice is blades on skin, knives on flesh, and I can tell I'm cut, beginning to bleed. The smell of blood wafts into my nose, feels nearly as hot as the magic coursing within me.

Rage whips through me.

I want to see this fighter's face now. I want to know who they are so they can see who *I* am. It's all I can think about. Pain, the state of the outside world—they fade from my mind, swallowed up by the storm, by this heat in my veins.

The other fighter's hands blur as they go to cast again.

I do it first.

Heat from beneath my feet.

A torpedo of needlelike cold shoots forward. The other fighter falls, a motion of gray within the storm.

I cast again, before the pain comes. Twelve. No, thirteen. *Fifteen points.* Magic, bounding forward, stretching.

More heat from the ground, from inside the earth. Snow falling down melts away before it can land.

And the landscape of the Syook Valley of Haneh changes.

The season turns.

And for the first time since stepping into the ring, the ground beneath the snow is visible.

It is a vast space of soil the colors of roots and brick, sand and stone. Snow keeps receding, my heat forcing it away as I draw more magic from the earth. In the back of my mind, I think about how this might be destroying everything I've ever known. Then, just as quickly, I think about how the magic doesn't care.

The sounds of the valley compress, turn into a mere hush. The storm around me has pushed outward, revealing the other fighter, now scrambling to get to their feet. Farther out, there's movement within the snow—the last fighters still in the game. Past them, I know jade stone is everywhere, all its parcels of green already half-buried.

Agony hits. The built-up pain of a double cast, melding together before crashing into me. The taut wire of pain running through me shakes wildly. I nearly convulse.

But a fifteen-point star.

The magic isn't spent yet.

It shakes apart the ground even as it is drawn from it. Rumbles come from the deep. A long, thin crack appears at my feet, spearing across the surface of the earth. Smaller cracks break away from it and keep going. The snow around me pulls back more and more, swaths of it curling over onto themselves, sea foam falling back into the matter that formed it.

And then the first of the bones appear. Grayed by age and lack of light, they emerge from the cracks in the ground like fingers digging their way out. They sit at my feet and call to my magic. Casters of the past—they want to know me, too.

I draw—fifteen points once more. I bend over and grab at bones. I cast. The magic billows in my mind, forms its cloud.

And I see the face of the other fighter now. I'm not even surprised. Who else could it be?

Indy.

She charges, already casting her own spell, the number twenty-six on her cheek. Snow is caked across her palm as she propels magic my way.

But nothing happens. No blow comes; no snow suffocates me.

I watch Indy falter. She's just as confused, staring down at where the snow had been in her hand.

It's gone.

All the things this can mean—all the dangers—run through my head.

Then the cloud of magic swarms, and my fifteen-point bone spell hits.

Indy's scream fills the air as she flies backward from the force.

She's jade stone before she even hits the ground.

I'm already turning away, already looking for the next fighter, when I realize it's over. The storm is dying back, the snow no longer falling. The clouds thin and drift away. Lumps of green pop up across the breadth of the valley, the whole scene like an eerie mock-up of a graveyard.

I turn in circles, my eyes crazed and wild as they dart around for more.

But I see no more fighters.

Just me.

I've won.

THIRTY-FOUR

The valley disappears.

Snow drifts away. Soil and bones dissolve. The strange purple light becomes golden yellow. In an instant, we're standing once more in the closed-up pizza restaurant in the Bakery Sector. White powder lies everywhere, on top of the tables and across the floor, tucked along wood grain, no longer snow; it's back to flour.

The pain from casting that last spell finally comes, jagged claws of great beasts reaching deep. It's my ever-growing price for casting with ill-fitting magic, something I'm alone in during every single fight. Even if the Founders' protective magic is actually as strong as the Guild's, it won't work on me. The room wavers, going black at the corners.

I'm blinking the inside of the restaurant back into focus when my eyes catch sight of it. It takes me a second to realize that it doesn't belong.

At my feet, a long, thin crack has split the wood flooring.

It's the same crack from the valley.

Now I *am* cold again, and my thoughts start to spiral. Breakthrough damage, with a real remnant left behind from a fighting ring.

That's never happened before.

Just as starters have never failed before.

My mind races as I think back to Indy's spell. Did I actually cast enough heat through the valley that it made her starter disappear? Or did the Founders fail to hold the ring together?

I stare down at the crack in the floor and fight back a shudder, the slow pound of a headache. A bitter and wild amusement stings the back of my throat.

A year-round event? *Really?*

I worried before that none of this would matter to Saint Willow—not the ring crumbling around us, not the damage to the outside world—as long as she stayed safe. Alive to do it all over again if needed.

This far into the tournament, with everything I've seen when it comes to the Founders and their protective magic, I know I'm right. Just like she won't care *how* I won tonight, only that I did.

I can't care, either, it turns out. All of this will have to be enough to keep her occupied and focused on me, just as Nima wanted.

I touch my fingers to my cheek. There's a four there now. Even if the number wasn't there to show it, I'd still know. For better or worse, I'll likely never forget any one of those eliminations.

Who did I become in the ring? I feel like I left myself behind at some point without even meaning to. As though the hated magic stepped in and took control.

That heat—that level of power—it scares me.

Jihen claps for attention then and announces me as the night's winner. He says, "Congratulations, Aza" like the words physically pain his lips to form. His less-than-enthusiastic delivery is missed by most of the crowd, though, since everyone's whispering about my last spell instead. Not all of it is good, but the derision doesn't bother me for once—it's been too long since I won.

What *does* alarm me is that I hear no whispers about how *Indy's* spell didn't work. All anyone could see was her not casting in time. I bet even Indy is still uncertain of what happened. I have a suspicion, of course, though it's one I can never share.

Still, however it worked out, I needed the win tonight. Saint Willow will leave my family alone now. Until tomorrow, anyway. And by then, Nima will be ready.

The idea of freedom has never felt closer.

My face gets warm when I catch sight of bright red hair among the crowd. Piper, making her way toward Indy.

What might have she been thinking as she watched me cast that last spell on her fighter? I don't know if I ever want to find out.

I avert my eyes when Piper reaches Indy, hoping they don't glance my way. I didn't miss how Indy was the last fighter to get to her feet after being turned into jade stone. Her healing time was the longest.

My fault.

I twist my hands behind my back, as though not seeing them will let me forget how I lost control in the ring. When I feel a sting along my palm, I bring it closer to inspect, sure it's just a cut or scratch from the fight.

But it's neither of those. Instead, it's a burn. Dark red lines, puffed the way fresh blisters are. The lines are in the shape of a spell star. Fifteen points. That last spell.

It'll leave a scar, most likely. The permanent mark of my losing control. Of casting magic that isn't mine and letting it control me instead.

I let out a weary sigh and drop my hand. It'll hurt to draw on it during tomorrow's fight. But it's a very small price to pay if I can put it toward escape. Like Saint Willow said, I have to learn to see past the obvious, the expected. To remember the long game.

I forget about my burn as Jihen announces the location for tomorrow night's ring.

Gunpowder Way, midnight, a yellow diamond.

Goose bumps lift on my skin, and there's a hollow kind of rush in my ears. It's almost enough to convince me I just heard wrong. Almost.

Gunpowder Way is the Tea Sector's southern border, just past gang headquarters. It's not a mistake that Jihen doesn't mention a specific address—the only thing out there is the pink woods. Tomorrow night's ring is going to be cast from a place where two-hundred-year-old magic still exists within its turned trees.

It's closer to Wu Teas than I like.

I go by the bets counter to pick up my cut for the evening. The envelope is thick with marks. Enough to help fill the void of customers at the teahouse. At least for a while.

Cutting through the crowd, I keep my hand tucked against my side to hide the burn. I also try to hide how I'm limping, the pain from fighting still strong. When the whispers that trail me turn into a surreal mix of cheers and boos, I pull on my smog mask, fiercely glad that Oliver isn't here to witness this. He wouldn't be able to hide his discomfort for me, or his pity. Finch would love every bit of it.

I doze off on the train ride home. It's broken sleep, both uneasy and anticipatory with thoughts of tomorrow. Through the windows, the city smog is cool and gray, an unseeing murk that doesn't judge.

Soon the last of the pastry shops and bakeries are replaced by teahouses and cafés. I get out at the station nearest to the teahouse and hobble along. My search for signs of Cormac along the streets is half-hearted. I'm wary thinking of why he wants to find me, but I'm also too exhausted to fully care.

I push through the hedge at the back of the house and crawl in my bedroom window. From my desk, I get the cop's number, and in the dark make my way to the front of the teahouse. I call the number, my skin clammy as it rings on the other end.

A minute later it's still ringing, and still no answering service. I hang up, both irritated and scared.

Where could Cormac be, and what does he know? What does he *want*?

In the unlit kitchen, I cast on the television. With my heart in my throat, I find the all-news-all-the-time station.

It doesn't take long for it to show up on the ticker.

Guilt threads itself through me as I read.

City agriculturists are calling it blight, but only because the event is so bizarre it's the only term they can agree on. No one has ever seen anything hit this quickly, or this thoroughly, across so many different types of vegetation at once.

It happened in the span of hours—nearly all of the Bakery Sector's agricultural lands have turned sour. Plants going black at the roots and then soft with mold, beyond salvaging. Wheat, oat, barley, millet, maize, and rye—all lost. Produce grown in those fields would have supplied hundreds of the sector's businesses. Thousands of people's food supply will be interrupted. It will take years for the soil to fully recover and then years more for things to start growing again.

Only disease in the meantime.

Bleakness sits in the pit of my stomach. There's no doubt that the breakthrough magic is getting worse with each fight. I need to get my parents out of the sector during tomorrow's fight—to be nearby is too risky. The Founders' protection is full of holes. As unreliable as my control.

I cast the television off and stumble to my bedroom. Trying to keep my burned hand from getting jostled, I fall asleep. My dreams that night are of food crumbling to dust whenever I try to hold it. The blistered spell star on my palm bleeding its shape into that dust. I shake the dust free, and the ground keeps crumbling away beneath me.

THIRTY-FIVE

Instead of the sound of customers filling the teahouse the next morning, it's that of repairs—just as Mom warned. Workers are installing a new window while a fine mist of droplets comes through the open frame. Others are repairing the crooked shelving and fixing the lights.

There's a fancy-looking new till on the front counter. Dad's there, going over the machine with a guy who has more patience than everyone else in Lotusland combined.

I step farther into the room, eyes gritty from not enough sleep. Hammers and saws and too many voices force their way into my skull. I want to tell them they all need to leave, the headache inside there already taking up too much room. Every part of me hurts.

Knowing that I'll be fighting again tonight makes my stomach sink. I'll have my own magic by then, but it won't keep me from going in already in pain.

Nima, you better be ready. Today's the day.

My own magic. Back in my veins.

I'm cold at the memory of what happened last time. At the thought of paying that kind of cost once more. Only Nima promising that was a mistake—that it won't be like that again—keeps me believing. Lets me hope I can finally be back in control. To be free of this other magic has come to mean being free of Saint Willow.

I can't let this chance go by.

"Aza, you're awake. Good." It's Mom, coming over with papers in her hand. The robbery has left its mark, worry and a kind a dazed bewilderment stamped all over her. And exhaustion. This kind of busyness in the teahouse isn't the good kind. "We need you to get something for the shop."

My stomach sinks. The day is already too full. I don't have to meet Nima until noon, but there's somewhere else I have to be first. I need to make sure my parents will be safe tonight. It's why I have an envelope full of marks inside my starter bag.

"Can I do it when I get back?" I ask, unable to consider what I will do if she says no. I don't want to have to lie my way out—I already did that last night when she nearly caught me leaving for the ring. How much can I push my parents' new trust in me before it cracks? "I made plans, since I figured you guys would be busy today with insurance people and stuff."

Mom smiles. "You know, you can always bring Oliver by, once this mess is cleaned up."

I fiddle with the strap of my bag, my eyes burning from more than lack of sleep. She wants so badly for me to be the daughter whose life is filled with things that don't mean danger. I can't blame her for that. But I can't be that daughter. Not right now. Not yet.

"Okay, maybe later," I say. Still a lie, but a necessary one. "What do you need today?"

Mom passes me marks—I make sure to take them with my unburnt hand.

"New cloth napkins," she says. "We need to replace the ones we lost. And I'm thinking of that ribbon you had around your arm last night. The quality of the material was quite good, so I'm sure napkins at the Mothery will be equally nice. I put in an order this morning."

I try to smile as I realize it's too late to avoid what's coming next. "Oh?"

Mom nods. "Choose something nice and washable when you fill out the order and pick it up? You can stop by on your way home."

"Sure." I pocket the marks, my mood falling even more at the idea of seeing Piper. I meant to avoid her for as long as possible. I don't know if I'll ever be ready to face how she must feel about me now.

"Thank you, dear." A quick one-armed hug. "And I mean it about wanting to meet Oliver."

I turn to go. I leave through the teahouse's front door, checking for signs of Jihen, and now Cormac, too. I don't know how the Scout might appear when he finally shows, or what his intentions might be. Until he tells me what information he has, I can't tell if he means to work with me or if he's out for revenge. Neither can end well.

But there is no sign of him.

Pulling a mask on, I head down the front steps and make my way to the nearest train station. From there, I take the next eastbound train to Culture. It's the sector where people go for the theater experience, for shows and dinners and nights out.

It's also on the opposite side of the city. If you need to run from Tea, you can't run any farther than Culture, out there on the east side.

The train pulls to a stop at the station, and I follow other passengers out the exit. I scan the rain-misted skyline for the peaked ivory roof of the Prestige. The hotel is considered the nicest in the sector, if not all of Lotusland—no one would turn down a free night's stay there.

The next fight is in the pink woods, just south of Wu Teas. And while I'll have my own magic back by then, it doesn't change the fact that the Founders' will still be inconsistent and weak. This tournament will happen tonight regardless, and so will the after-effects. I still haven't forgotten the smell of the Spice Sector on the night of the lightning storm. The smoke and fire in the streets as I imagined Oliver burning.

Again, I see that long crack running through the floor of the pizza restaurant.

What if tonight's ring gives way even more?

Tonight, my parents can't be anywhere near the pink woods, or anywhere near me. A surprise night out—especially while the teahouse is closed—is the perfect solution.

I walk into the lobby of the Prestige, tugging my smog mask below my chin.

The interior is as impressive as I imagined. Midnight-blue carpeting, brown-black wood on the walls, and silver chandeliers dripping with crystals. I walk past upholstered cream armchairs and go up to the front desk like I've been here a million times before.

"Two overnight guest packages," I say to the attendant behind the desk. "The best ones available."

"Will they be for yourself and a guest?"

"No, they're gifts."

"Wonderful." He enters information into a computer and gives me a polite smile. "And how would you like to pay, credit or marks?"

"Marks." I open my starter bag, take out the thick envelope, and hold it out. The guest packages are going to cost me nearly everything I've made so far working for Saint Willow. If something else happens and I need more marks, I'll be stuck. But I can't risk anything else. My parents can't pay again for my mistakes.

The attendant takes the marks and finishes punching in the transaction. He pulls open a drawer below the counter, takes out two fancy, heavy-looking envelopes, and hands them to me. "Two premium overnight guest packages, including tickets to tonight's sold-out show at Green's Theater and dinner at the Choppery. Full car service, upgraded linens, and breakfast in the hotel lounge are also included. All to showcase the very best the Prestige and the Culture Sector have to offer. We hope everything will be enjoyed."

"It will be, thank you." I take the envelopes—they're as heavy as they look—and place them in my bag. I pull my mask back up, step away from the counter, and walk across the plush blue carpeting of the lobby.

It's not time yet to meet with Nima.

I leave the hotel, bracing myself for Piper.

THIRTY-SIX

A westbound train comes, and I climb on.

Through the rain-glazed windows, the landscape of Lotusland changes. From the theaters of Culture to the bookstores of Paper to the fashion houses of Textile. I get off at the stop closest to the Mothery and walk the last two blocks.

I go slow, not wanting to hurt more than I already do.

I go slow because I'm thinking about the first time I came to Piper's shop and how scared I was. How she still intimidates me with nothing more than a lift of an immaculately penciled brow.

At the door, I take off my mask with trembling fingers. I step inside the shop.

It's late morning, and Piper's not alone. A handful of customers wait to get fabric cut. She's polished as always in her pink-and-red pantsuit, her hair brushed into a huge bun. I want to think her lavishness is exhausting, but it's not.

Because I'm still dreading her seeing me, I duck my head, pretending to be deeply interested in browsing the wall of velvet in front of me.

The bell at the door chimes as the last of the other customers leave.

"Aza, you shouldn't be here."

I spin around, fear fluttering in my throat. "Hi, Piper."

She comes to stand beside me, frowning. Disapproval is clear on her face. "You know we're not supposed to talk about the tournament outside of the underground."

She's unhappy about more than that. I can read that on her face, too.

"I'm here to shop," I say, gesturing vaguely toward the wall of fabric I was pretending to look at. I'm careful to keep my burnt palm out of sight. "The teahouse needs napkins, and my mother called in an order this morning. I'm supposed to pick out the fabric. I was just thinking this stuff seems nice . . ."

"Hmm, so she did. I didn't connect her name to Wu Teas." Still frowning, Piper narrows her gray eyes as she considers the array of velvet I'm pointing to. "But unless you really want napkins made out of velvet, you should tell me what else you're here for."

The coolness in her voice stings more than any spell. "I wanted to say I'm sorry about that spell I cast on Indy. That last one."

"Aza, I've told you before about apologizing for winning." Her expression chills, too, and I can barely keep from dropping my gaze. "Winning is winning, and regretting how you do it is a waste of time for a fighter. What happens in the ring stays in the ring, and the sooner you believe that, the better off you'll be."

My nervousness snaps, turns into desperation. It hurts that Piper, of all people, can't seem to understand.

"I want to believe that, but I can't." I blink fast, trying to push back the beginning of tears. Between Finch killing Shire and Saint Willow dragging me back as her fighter, the ring and the outside world have long been the same thing. It's too late for me to keep them apart. When I fight, I'm fighting the outside world at the same time. "You know what led me to the ring in the first place. It's never been something separate for me."

"And that's exactly why you being so reckless is dangerous." She sighs. "Of course I know why you chose to fight in the first place, Aza. But it doesn't change that you're not alone in the ring. That there are hundreds of other people in the tournament who can also be hurt."

My eyes swim. "It was a mistake. I didn't mean to cast that way."

"You've never slipped before. I'm worried."

A part of me wishes to tell her everything. How the magic inside me is all wrong, and that's why I slipped. How I'm only fighting again because I'm forced to. But how could I confess that Indy beating me bothered me more than I wanted it to? That I'm angry she's free to walk away from fighting while I can't?

That a part of me actually liked not being in control?

Piper could never forgive that.

"I promise it won't happen again," I say. At least that's one truth I can tell. It's the easiest promise I've ever made. Nima will have my magic back by now, and soon I'll have it back, too. I'll never lose control again, and I can stop worrying about how much further I can slip. I'll stay the Aza I want to be. "I don't want anyone else to get hurt."

She smooths a painted nail, a glint of gentle reprimand on her face as she lifts a brow. "*You* should not want to get hurt, either."

Her voice is warmer now, and my throat gets tight at Piper caring again. "No, I don't want to."

"I'm glad to hear that. Protective magic works best when fighters work alongside it."

It's on the tip of my tongue to ask what she thinks of the Founders' power so far, but I stop. There's no point. Piper can't change anything about the tournament, and neither can I.

"Will you be fighting tonight?" she asks.

I nod.

The coolness comes back. "Then I'm looking forward to seeing you be more careful."

It's the only way I can truly fix things between us.

The bell at the entrance chimes, and a customer comes inside the shop.

"So." Piper gives me a shopkeeper's distant smile. "What kind of napkins for your mother?"

THIRTY-SEVEN

I leave the Mothery—new napkins stuffed into my bag and smog mask back on—and head toward the train station. I climb on the first westbound train out, wishing I could walk home as I've always done. Losing this bit of control hurts, too.

The mist-like rain is over, and I crack my window open. The scents drifting in change as the city's sectors do, going from the smokiness of Tobacco as the train cuts through to the clean herbs of Tea. They wash over me as I lean against the glass, trying to sleep so I can escape from my own body.

But I'm too wired to properly rest. My thoughts are racing, and something close to hope thrums in my veins nearly as strongly as pain does, as the heat of magic does.

Meeting Nima now—it's all nearly over. A dream that once seemed impossible is finally within my grasp. I can see it for real the way I've never seen the sun.

I will the train to go faster.

I get off at the station in the sector's center, closest to the Tea Chest. The lobby of the hotel is crowded with guests checking out. I keep walking, wishing I could run ahead, drawn to the lounge by the sound of the piano, by the idea of being able to breathe again.

I round the corner to the lounge and smash back to earth.

Nima at the piano.

And Jihen at the bar.

"Hello, beauty," Jihen says to me, swishing his drink in its glass. He's already dressed for the fight tonight. His black suit is shot through with gold threads, and his silk fan of fortunes pokes out of his chest pocket like a dagger seeking ways to slice. "Nima *said* you would be here."

I go cold as I stare at him. His grin is so wide as he drinks, I wonder how he's not spilling all over himself.

"What's going on?" I drag my mask low with fingers of ice and look to Nima, bile crawling up my throat. "Why is he here?"

She's pale as she shuts the lid of the piano. Her hands tremble. Those are the hands of a *gatherer*, someone who can hold together dust—*ether*—and that they're actually unsteady only makes me colder. She's been blindsided, too.

Where is my magic? The words are a silent shout inside my head. *Tell me we're going to be okay!*

Nima gets to her feet. "Aza—"

"Not so fast." Jihen sets his glass down, cutting her off. He smacks his lips, smiles, and waves his finger at Nima. A warning to be quiet.

When he steps close, I rear back, nearly stumbling to the ground. The moment doesn't feel real. This is supposed to be escape, so why do I feel more trapped than ever?

"What do you want?" I ask. I hate how my voice shakes. That Jihen gets to hear it.

He smiles again, slimier than ever. His glee says it all.

Whatever's going on, I won't like it.

"Boss means to tell you herself. The car's outside—let's go."

No one speaks on the way to headquarters, but everything is too loud anyway. Jihen has cast the radio on and hums—badly—to all the songs. Beside him in the passenger seat, Nima's stiff, her eyes unmoving from the road ahead.

She still hasn't given a sign of what happened with Jihen before I arrived. I have no idea what he knows. Until I'm sure, I can't give anything up.

From the back seat, I watch the sector go by, a scream inside my skull. There's a taste of metal in my mouth, a mix of terror and panic. I can feel hope slipping further and further away with each second. With every block we pass, the box of Saint Willow's newest trap—whatever it is—closes in that much tighter around us.

As Jihen drives, wild ideas of how to get rid of him flash through my brain. Each of them is more than plausible, some even easy— a single second, and Nima and I can be free again, our plan back on track.

But each of them also requires me to cast this magic that won't listen.

And even if we could get away, what happens next? Where can I go that won't set Saint Willow after my parents?

Then I get a glimpse of the pink woods, and I stop thinking altogether. The front of the shut-down dim sum restaurant looms through the glass, bigger than life, wanting to swallow me up.

Saint Willow is inside. A queen spider nestled snugly on the web of her own making.

I jerk back from the window, trying to breathe, a headache circling.

The tires screech to a stop at the curb. Jihen waits for me to stagger out and then pushes me to walk ahead of him and Nima.

"Not a word," he grunts as I fall into position. "Save all your questions for Saint Willow."

"Must suck to still be on a short leash." I toss a hard smile over my shoulder that says I'm enjoying this. "Even after you told her about the tournament."

He grunts. "Moh toh-ah."

Shut up.

I'm at the entrance.

I open the door of the restaurant and slowly step inside. My fear has grown so huge it's hard to feel anything else. Like some kind of human-made eclipse.

Amber light, lotus-print carpet, and gold-papered walls. The smell of perfume, the heat of danger.

Saint Willow is sitting at her table in the center of the room.

Seated beside her is Finch.

THIRTY-EIGHT

My vision dances. The hollow boom of my heartbeat is deep in my ears. Terror surges through me, swamping me with its tide. I have to reach out and grab hold of the back of one of the restaurant chairs.

Finch. Here. In this space that Saint Willow only reveals to her own men, to the people she has control over.

But he's been here before. My thoughts are rushing, trying to make sense of everything. He came here to buy the gathered spell that he used to kill Shire.

My heartbeat, now a driving and relentless drum. In the warm-toned lighting of the room, his green eyes are somehow the iciest I've ever seen them. He stares at me, the hunger in them—for revenge, magic—grown as sharp as a blade.

The back of the chair I'm holding creaks just once, my grip like a vise. It's the only thing keeping me on my feet.

I drag my eyes from Finch, trying to surface. Luna and Seb float into clarity, standing behind Saint Willow. They're on guard, but their faces are as impassive as if they were deep in the middle of a card game.

"Aza."

Saint Willow's voice is soft. She says my name like she cares for me. Her silk blouse is the color of a blushing rose, and her black hair cascades down in waves. The expression on her face—the refinement deadly, her smile as gracious as it is barbed—reminds me that her beauty is simply a mask worn by a monster.

She gestures to Nima. Her smile turns flinty as she contemplates her gatherer, but I can't be sure what it means. How much she knows. Maybe she's simply angry that Nima and I were meeting alone.

"Play for us," the gang leader demands.

Even paler now, with her eyes carefully averted from everyone, Nima heads toward the back of the restaurant and sits down at the piano. The song she picks is meaningless to me, just notes filling the air.

"Aza," Saint Willow says, "come sit down, please."

I can't make myself move. I'm already too close to her. To Finch. Everything that's wrong is here in this room.

The sudden image of Oliver's face flashes in my mind. Oliver, who is nothing like Finch but is still, in the end, his family.

Did you know your brother planned to be here? That he was up to anything at all?

The top of the gang leader's trap slamming down on me, shutting out light and air.

Jihen pushes me from behind. "Ni mai heng kwee gwoung? Jing nee-uh. Buht poh-ah!"

You're not going to listen? She'll hurt you. Brat!

On legs I can barely feel, I move to the center of the room. I drag out the chair across from Saint Willow and sit down. There's a fist of pain inside my skull.

From the kitchen there's the sound of dishes, and my stomach rolls at the idea of Xu bringing out her cart. Asking me if I want buns or noodles. Pouring me tea while I pretend that I can live with the things that happen here. To have to eat while acting like everyone at this table isn't a threat.

"Why am I here?" I clench my hands in my lap when I see they're shaking. My palm stings. My headache roars. "I won last night. I did what you wanted. Leave me alone, and I'll keep doing it."

From across the table, Finch's eyes are unflinching—like half-buried gems winking from the dark, waiting to be unearthed.

Saint Willow smiles. "I knew you could do it, Aza. Last night, you proved your new magic is now completely within your control."

I stay quiet, knowing she's wrong. I didn't kill Indy with that last spell, but I could have. This magic is more than an intruder—it has now taken over. It runs me, not the other way around.

My hands clench tighter as I wait for the rest, as I know I'm supposed to. Still standing behind Saint Willow, Luna and Seb are statues, but I know they'd move in an instant to shield the gang leader. Jihen stands at my back, equally ready.

Saint Willow gives a low chuckle. "Will you accept my sincere congratulations? After all, the timing couldn't be better for what comes next."

I shrink in my seat. *For what comes next.* "What are you talking about?"

"We need to take advantage of how you're now back in absolute control. Tonight, you will be sure to lose."

Surprise makes me twitch. I stare at Saint Willow, confused—and suspicious. She's never been about anything *but* winning, from marks to power to controlling the entirety of Lotusland. "You want me to *lose*?"

She nods. I notice how she's flushed, her cheeks a bright, near-girlish pink. "You're going to throw the fight tonight."

"But—why? I thought you wanted me to keep winning for as long as possible." Saint Willow lives for power, but she craves applause just as much. Having her fighter lose doesn't fit.

Another low chuckle, but the glee is sharper this time. My fear comes back, and as she speaks, a kind of hollow rush fills my ears at the same time. Piano notes filter in, sour-sounding.

"Oh, Aza. I'm disappointed you're still unable to see past what's right in front of you—to see only what's presented, like a child being entertained. It's why you keep missing how I've been building toward something bigger this whole time. Yes, you being my fighter and a champion *is* part of my plan, but it's only one step of many."

I listen, unable to move, both enthralled and repulsed by her self-satisfaction. In a way, hearing this makes me feel as intrusive as the magic that's inside me. Like I'm peeking in on Saint Willow when she's most raw, real, and utterly herself. Her love of power is unmatched. Pure. Whole. I see how it leaves room for nothing else.

"The first step was making sure you got magic back, of course. Once that happened, I moved to the next, which was making you my squeezer. And not just my squeezer, but one using *magic*. That was a very important step, because it was only through casting that you would regain control. After that, my next move was to introduce you to my new tournament as my fighter and to keep reminding the audience you're a champion. Spectators *will* bet on a whim, but never as much or as often as on a fighter who will almost always make marks for them."

Saint Willow casts a curl of hair back into place. I watch as she adjusts a silk cuff, her fingers turning its pleats as sharp as knives. I imagine those fingers as shadows slowly tightening around my throat. Letting me breathe just enough as she constantly stays one step ahead.

My plan with Nima no longer feels out of reach—now it feels beyond foolish. Like something we came up with in a bizarre shared dream, and upon waking up, we didn't know any better than to figure out it wasn't real. Could never be.

Whether she succeeded in gathering back my magic before Jihen arrived at the Tea Chest no longer makes any difference. Not unless I can escape whatever the gang leader is planning for me now.

"And so we've reached the next stage—and that's why Jihen's brought you here." Saint Willow's teeth shine behind her painted mouth. Her smile is as foxlike as it was in her car, when she instructed me from the half shadows. "You becoming champion of my tournament was always a given—I knew it would happen, given how you cast and who you are. So it means I've long planned for more—why should I settle for what's expected when I can have *spectacle*?"

"'Spectacle.'" I repeat the word like it's new to me. Meanwhile, panic is blooming, wild as weeds. Saint Willow's joy is visceral. My head pounds, the pain inside a bellow.

"Spectacle is why—and *how*—I created my tournament, Aza. Every ring is brilliantly cast and perfectly crafted. More than that, it speaks of great magic—of great *power*. And people, they are drawn to it. Drawn to *me*. They come expecting the best, knowing only I can give it to them. They demand to be entertained as never before. So now this is my burden—to keep growing that spectacle. In doing that, I will also keep growing my power. It all ties together. Which means tonight will have to be the biggest fight yet. And what could be bigger than the rekindling of a past rivalry? Not just any rivalry, but a rivalry between two past champions?"

Stunned, I look over at Finch. Caught in the spell of hearing Saint Willow's plans, I managed to stop thinking of him.

His gaze meets mine—still cold and flat. Still hungry for magic.

And that's when the panic wraps itself around me wholly. Threatens to smother me.

Saint Willow is going to force new magic on him, too.

She takes my shocked silence for understanding and smiles again. Still foxlike in its cunning.

"Now that you've gained the confidence of the crowd, they'll bet on you to win. And you've beaten Finch before, of course—why wouldn't they bet on you again? But instead, you will lose, while *I* will be betting on the winner. We'll all win, actually—your family will stay safe, Finch will be back in the ring, and I'll make more marks than anyone else there."

To fight Finch in the ring again. This caster who I beat only by giving up my own magic. Who took away his own brother's. Who killed my sister. The two of us, casting magic we can't control.

"It's nothing personal," he says, shrugging. The lie of that is in the icy gleam of revenge in his eyes. "Though obviously I'll enjoy beating you in the ring."

"But you can't fight tonight," I say, shaking my head. The pain in there is brittle, like glass wanting to break. Saint Willow might have been planning this all along, but she doesn't know that Nima's been too busy to work for her as she normally would. "The spell for new magic—it always takes time to gather."

Saint Willow's face lights up. "Not necessarily. Isn't that so, Nima?"

The piano falls quiet. A dish clatters in the kitchen.

I slowly turn to face the gatherer, everything inside me a shout, in complete denial.

One look at Nima's face, and I know it's true.

"I'm sorry, Aza," she says. Her carefully concealed eyes finally reveal something, and it is pure guilt. "Your magic—it was ready."

THIRTY-NINE

My mind reels. Spins back in time.

It was that night. Just over a month ago. The night magic became mine once more. Magic that ended up being wrong, having no right to be stuck inside me.

I stood at the corner of the intersection and waited. It was raining. Cold despite it being summer.

I came alone, as instructed. I searched the crowd for Nima, still too nervous to be excited. To have full magic again. To once again be able to cast. None of it seemed quite real.

The day after I agreed to get magic back, Saint Willow's instructions came to the teahouse. A simple letter sent by courier, with the Tea Sector gang's willow mark on the envelope so my parents would assume it was about my job.

The note was written as I expected Saint Willow would've explained it to me in person. I heard her voice in my head as I read it, the terse businesslike tone that said I had made this deal with her and now it was time to fulfill my end of things. I was getting magic back, but only with the agreement that I would use that magic to serve Saint Willow.

Then as I kept reading, her tone changed. I heard the threat there. The dark promise of what would happen if Nima and I failed.

Tonight, 9:00 p.m. The corner of Fannings and Estate in Tea—you will meet Nima there. My gatherer will be fully prepared to restore magic for you. I would attend, but Luna and Seb have reminded me—and rightly so—of my long-standing decision to remain in the shadows whenever possible.

Neither of you is to leave until the spell has been cast. Attempt another double cross, and Wu Teas will pay. Come to headquarters tomorrow morning. To show me.

Only sections of the Tea Sector were busy that late at night, and the corner of Fannings and Estate happened to be one of them. The location was at an intersection flanked by Tea's latest-running train station and all-night teatini bars and cafés. Dozens of people filled the adjacent sidewalks. Even more were streaming across the intersection, where the crowds would take minutes to cross, there were so many people. Cars lined up at the lights, waiting their turn to go. The whole place was a hub of activity.

It would have taken me hours to find Nima there if she hadn't found me first. She stepped onto the corner and walked up to me through the rain, her eyes wide. Dark blue contacts that night.

"Where is Saint Willow?" She glanced around, seemingly as nervous as I was. "She said she meant to see this happen with her own eyes."

"She's not coming. She said as gang leader, she should stay out of sight as much as possible."

"What?" Surprise pulled her brows together. She swiped rain from her face. "But this shouldn't be done without her. She's the one who's making me do this."

"It's what she told me. And technically, she doesn't need to be here. She'd only be watching us, anyway."

Nima shut her eyes hard and breathed out deeply. When she looked at me again, her face was flushed and she was biting her lip. "We should wait. I can talk to her, make her come to see it for herself. What happens if she doesn't believe we did it?"

I understood her sudden fear. Saint Willow would make us pay if something went wrong. But now that Nima was finally here, I was impatient to get it done. Still nervous, but also finally excited.

To have magic again.

"It'll be fine," I said to Nima. "She's already ordered me to go down to headquarters tomorrow to show her that it's been done. We're covered. So what do we do?"

Nima shook her head. Distress was still written all over her. "You don't understand—"

My own fear bubbled over. I knew I was cornered with only one way out—and so did Nima. So why was she now the one blocking it?

"No, *you* don't understand," I snapped. I was drenched, tired of waiting. "*You're* her gatherer. Without *you* gathering this magic for her, Saint Willow wouldn't have the power to do this. If I don't get magic back tonight, she's coming after me. My family. Everything. I have to do this no matter what."

The gatherer seemed frozen. Her eyes glittered, suddenly hard. "No matter what. Are you sure you mean that?"

"I have no choice."

"Choice is like cost. There is always more than you assume."

I sighed. Cost no longer made a difference. I was already stuck. "Nima. It's going to be tonight. *So what do we do?*"

A long moment of silence between us. So that the only sounds in my ears were those of the city. Of the busy street. So many people. All of them talking about nice, everyday things. Instead of magic, and power, and the ugliness that always came with them.

Finally Nima gave a slow, reluctant nod. Her shoulders slumped an inch. She held out the blue bead. "This is a self-starting spell. Since you once had full magic, all you need to do is hold the starter and it will cast the spell for you."

The blue bead was heavy in my palm. The weight of the magic of strangers. Magic that would soon be mine. "Can we go somewhere else? It's too crowded here. I don't want anyone to notice anything."

"It . . . has to be done where there are a lot of people gathered. Just as it took force to strip your magic from you, it's going to take force to put it back. There's nothing but leftover magic out here, but taken all together, it should just be enough."

Rain streamed down into my eyes, but instead of everything blurring, there was a kind of heightened sharpness to all that was around me. Details never to be forgotten. I tried not to think about the casting pain. "This is going to hurt, won't it?"

A small, thin smile. It left me more uneasy than assured, and I shivered, chilled.

Still wondering, I stepped forward when the light changed and began to cross the street.

I kept going straight as people flowed along with me. As they came from the other direction and brushed right past. I clutched the blue starter bead in my hand so tightly my fingers lost all feeling.

Dread and anticipation and a knife-edged kind of eagerness that was nearly ugly in its greedy desperation—I tasted them all.

Magic—I *longed* for it.

Then all that feeling fell away. For a single heartbeat, the world hitched before smoothing back out. I staggered mid-step, barely catching myself before I was able to start walking again.

Nima hadn't told me the entire truth about getting magic back.

She hadn't told me it was the very *opposite* of hurting.

An onslaught of delicious sensations, like being enveloped in washes of light, in color. Then, in the next instant, magic *pushed* into my blood. It was new and strange and wholly unfamiliar, the pleasure of its presence nearly painful. In my mind, it was an ocean of water flooding vast desert plains that had never known such relief could exist. I was those plains, and I drank and drank and drank. Until I felt I was made up of nothing but power.

I blinked, and the world knitted back together. Just Lotusland again. And Nima was somewhere, watching closely to see how I might have changed.

I was sure nothing had, on the outside. As I finished crossing the street, everything felt the same, my arms and legs and hands.

But about what was *inside*—I would know the next time I cast. If I still felt like Aza.

Then I heard the cry for help.

I turned around, confused.

Someone in the crowd behind me had fallen. The intersection was at a standstill as people stopped to see what was happening.

Another yell as someone else went down, and my blood ran colder than the rain.

This was my fault. The real cost of my getting magic back. Those people, their lives.

The price was their deaths, just so I could cast magic.

Nima came close. Her eyes glowed faintly orange beneath their contacts, full of regret.

"No matter what, you said," she whispered before turning and disappearing into the streets.

Another person fell. More screams. Cars honked their horns as the light changed back; drivers couldn't see what was happening. Then as drivers began to slump down in their cars.

I ran, knowing there was nowhere to go.

FORTY

Chaotic streets disappear, and I'm back in the dim sum restaurant.

I stare at Finch across the table, a knot in my throat.

My magic. In *him*.

In Finch's veins, for him to cast as he wants. Or doesn't want, if my magic won't let him control it. The same way this unwanted magic doesn't let me.

If he decides he *likes* the lack of control.

Oliver, did you know your brother meant to do this?

I lunge clumsily across the table, reaching for Finch, for Saint Willow, wanting both gone from my life. A strange sound comes from me. I'm an animal, steel claws digging into me so that I need someone else to feel that pain as well. Saint Willow's name comes from my throat in the form of a growl.

Luna and Seb step forward, moving as one as they always do.

From behind, Jihen's hand comes down hard onto my shoulder, forcing me back. Pain reverberates as I hit the chair, rocketing throughout my head.

"Sit," Jihen says. "Or I'll tell you again what will happen."

"Go ahead, since it makes you feel good." I practically spit out my words as I glare across the table. My headache is inescapable, muddying everything other than this moment and this scene. My hate for everyone here. "I've heard it all before."

"But you haven't, Aza." Saint Willow's smile hasn't faltered one bit despite my near-attack. If anything, it's grown even more confident. "I predicted that you might not react well to my news about Finch and your magic. And so I've set a safeguard in place to ensure that you keep seeing the bigger picture, as it were. From this point onward, should anything happen to me, my men here have been instructed that Wu Teas—and your parents, naturally—should also come to an end."

"No." My voice is a hoarse whisper. The room's amber lighting swells and shimmers, leaving me dizzy. Great fists of panic press down on my chest so I'm struggling to breathe. "You can't."

"I did." Saint Willow suddenly scowls and calls over to Nima. "Start playing again—I never said you could stop."

The silence in the restaurant continues for another heartbeat before Nima begins to play again. The notes are heavy, uneven—full of shock.

I feel their thick beat in my pulse. Wanting to explode. I can't keep up with Saint Willow and her ugly surprises. Always one step ahead. Just as she said.

How long has she known about Nima's and my plan?

The gang leader nods, like she's watching all my thoughts play out on my face.

"I notice everything under my watch," she says. "Instead of showing my hand, I held it close. I knew giving your magic to Finch would be perfect for the spectacle I wanted to present."

It's nice how even when we lose, we're still winning.

I sway in my seat, sure I'm going to be sick.

Nima and I never had a chance. *I* never had a chance. I stripped Finch's magic to stop him from ever casting again, and here he is.

I did it to avenge Shire, but she'll always stay dead. If she were here, she'd be furious that I did any of this.

"It's okay, Aza," Finch says softly. He winks. "I'll let you lose with dignity."

"You have no idea what it'll be like." A sob threatens to tear free as sounds of people dying fill my head again. The screaming. My guilt, threaded through it all. "Paying the cost for stolen magic."

He leans toward me over the table. Face as cold as the Pacifik in midwinter.

"I don't care," he says, his voice still soft. "In fact, I can't *wait*."

"Losing will be *easy*, Aza," Saint Willow soothes. Like she hasn't just told me about laying another death trap for my family. "Compared to winning, it will be like doing nothing at all."

I'd scream at her that her Founders might not be as strong as she believes them be, if I thought she'd listen. That they're lesser, weaker than the Guild. Their magic-cast bulbs flickering out, Indy and the snow that failed her, that long crack in the wooden floor of the bakery that never got erased—

I don't want to be around to see what all of that might lead to.

"You don't get it, do you?" I say. "I *can't* control this magic yet, no matter what you think. I've been lucky to get away with what I have so far."

"Then you'll learn soon enough with Finch casting your own magic at you." Saint Willow's expression goes hard. A flash of petulance puckers her lips. "Really, Aza, why do you refuse to learn after everything I've done for you? You only beat him because of me, remember? You're still only casting because of me. You owe everything to *me*."

Hatred floods me, fast and thick and unstoppable. I taste the breadth and depth of it on my tongue. Bitter and smoky. There's a hint of fresh blood in there, too. Something else giving way inside me. As magic has limits, so do casters—I'm getting much too close to mine. Getting pushed to the brink.

I see nothing but red.

I draw because I can't stop myself.

Fifteen points slashed across my palm. My finger scrapes at the burn. The sting is nothing.

I slam my hand on the table, and the dream forms.

Heat. The flowers of bruises around Saint Willow's neck. Her fingers, reaching up as if she can claw in breath. I see the plea in her dark bulging eyes, and all I do is laugh.

A hand comes down on mine. The skin is smooth and cool.

The red haze of the dream fades.

Saint Willow's hand.

Nothing but cold understanding on her face.

"I know what you want, and I'm sorry I can't give it to you. You know what will happen if you cast on me. But perhaps one day you'll realize how I'm only saving you from the worst of yourself, Aza. Because your parents, Wu Teas—I am as creative as I am powerful, and that's not a combination you want to test."

She slides her hand away.

I pull mine back, feeling half-wild. Sure I'm hysterical. Everything has gone wrong. Nothing fits, even my skin—pulled so tight around me it's hard to breathe.

"Tonight," Saint Willow says, "stay in the fight until it's just you and Finch. Give them a show they'll never forget. Only then will you lose."

Pressure, grinding me small. My heart races, like it's got someplace else it needs to be. I think of the train ride here and how for that tiny, glorious pocket of time, I was nearly the old Aza again, and not a single thing felt wrong. The idea of freedom nearly within reach was the best magic I was ever able to cast.

Now, to lose tonight on purpose, using magic I paid for with death?

How can anything be right again?

A near-peaceful numbness overtakes me, and it's terrifying.

Acceptance.

"You're going to restore deliveries to the teahouse," I say dully. "You're going to make sure there are no more delays. Ever."

Saint Willow smiles, and her beauty strikes me once more. "I'll have Luna and Seb get it done tomorrow."

"Do it before the fight. Or no deal. And no more robberies, either. No attacks. Nothing."

"Of course. And this fire I'm seeing right now, Aza? The one your eyes say you want to burn me with? Make sure you bring it to the ring tonight."

"See you soon," Finch says to me. The small ways he looks so much like Oliver—they unnerve me to my core.

Unable to stay here for another second, I push away from the table. No one stops me. I glance over at Nima on my way out. Dismay and fear are on her face, hands frozen on the keys.

I stumble to the door, then outside. I keep moving, going as fast as I can. I need to get away. I squint against the bright gray light of day. Pain in my skull spreads outward, the bursting of some dark star.

Finch, casting *my* magic—

I bend over at the waist, breathing deep, willing myself to not pass out. The sob finally comes. It's such a pathetic sound that I heave myself back into motion. Finch knows how much I hate this—but better to be angry than broken.

With trembling fingers, I yank up my mask. I keep moving north, heading back to the teahouse. In my haze of hatred, I lose track of time. Everything inside me that was already hurting when Jihen found me only hurts more now, like heat on a stove turned up to its limit. The scents of the sector cling to my skin—grass, hay, clover—and I wish they were stronger so they could cloud my mind entirely.

I'm three blocks from home when I spot a sector display Ivor. Its cage hangs from the lamppost on the corner. As I get closer, the Ivor begins to shout, to shake the immovable steel bars. The crowd passing by beneath slows down to watch for a second, then continues onward, reminding themselves how lucky they are to have only leftover magic now.

"Youuu . . . oh, I know *you*."

I freeze at the Ivor's voice coming from overhead.

Because I know it, too.

Shocked, I look up.

Wilson.

He's changed so much, in every way possible. His shriveled form, back hunched over. His eyes say I'm familiar, but he has no clue why.

My mind circles back to the last time I saw him in the ring, casting as part of the Founders.

I didn't see his face in the snow of the valley. Only in the bamboo and then among the porcelain, where his complexion was oddly pale, his expression pained as he helped cast the ring—

I shiver in the late-afternoon warmth, unable to look away from Wilson in his new shattered form.

This is the price you pay to cast for Saint Willow.

"You." He stares at me, all eyes and confused madness. He shakes the bars. "*You.*"

I lower my head and walk away, my eyes hot with tears.

"Not so fast."

Someone's blocking my way on the sidewalk. A steely voice that says he has questions for me.

I glance up, mind going blank again.

Embry's bright teal eyes, cold as an iced-over sea.

FORTY-ONE

"We need to talk, Aza."

I take a step backward. Embry wouldn't hurt me, but his expression says something's happened, and he thinks it's my fault.

I can't forget he's still a Scout here in the outside world. And I'm still a full magic caster. His job is to hunt me down. Lock me up. Hang me up as a warning like Wilson in his display cage. Whatever our relationship is in the underground, it will never matter up here.

"How did you find me?" I tug my mask down and glance around. The sidewalk is crowded, and I keep my voice low. I still taste blood. The pounding of my headache continues.

Embry's expression is withering. "Call it cop intuition. That, and we're less than three blocks from Wu Teas. Where you *live*."

"I have to go," I say, trying to swerve around him on the sidewalk. Envelopes from the Prestige and napkins from the Mothery shift inside my bag.

This is a bad time for Embry to find me. Half of me remains at headquarters, still absorbing the promise of Finch casting with my magic. The other half is in that cage with Wilson, wishing he never came across Saint Willow and her tournament.

"Aza." Embry stops me with a single pointed look. "Do I need to bring you in on official business to make you speak to me? Or would you prefer to give me five minutes of your time right now? *Un*officially?"

I go hollow at the idea of having to walk into a building full of Scouts. I'll never figure out how Embry does it every day, working beside people who would put *him* away if they knew.

"Okay, five minutes," I say. "Where?"

Embry frowns as people brush past us. "Just not out here."

I lead him to the Guz-n-Go on the corner.

The scene inside is typical: people playing the lotto, paying for gas or cigarettes, little kids crowded around the candy shelves. The air smells of old hot dogs and cheese. The clerk's expression lets us know we're supposed to actually buy something. Our shoes stick to the floor as we move over to the slush machine.

Embry grabs a paper cup, shoves it beneath the spout for cola-flavored, and begins to fill it.

"You walked past that Ivor on display," he says softly—so softly that it tells me just how angry he is. "Did you recognize him? I did. The second I had to put him in that cage."

I slide my eyes away, my throat clenching up. The sound of kids arguing over candy filters into my ears, the innocence of it jarring against what Embry's talking about.

He finishes filling the cup. "Was Wilson involved in that tournament I was asking you about yesterday?"

Now my mind races, and I'm back on guard. "Yes. He . . . cast too strongly. You know how that can happen."

"You have to stop fighting in it. Or tell me you've already stopped, and I'll apologize for not thinking better of you."

"I haven't stopped." I struggle to think of a good reason that will make sense to him. But there's nothing. Even if I could tell him about being forced to, it wouldn't make a difference to him. None of it can be changed. Bad, uncontrollable magic. The Founders being weak.

"Mind telling me why not?" He fits a lid onto the top of the cup. "Wilson going Ivor isn't enough?"

Heat climbs up my neck. "I just have to fight."

"And if you shatter this entire city apart?" His voice is as chilled as the slush in the cup, but I read the disappointment in his eyes. "To the point of no repair?"

I want to tell him that hurting Lotusland does scare me, but that what scares me more is Saint Willow hurting my parents. How she could erase the Wus with a single order.

The unfairness of her power—I can't pay for all of it.

"You think I *want* to fight?" is what I finally end up saying.

Embry passes me the cup of slush. "I'm not sure what to think anymore. Nothing you've said is exactly reassuring."

Another flush washes over me, so I feel fevered not just from pain but also from shame. I take a drink of the too-sweet slush to try to find relief.

"I could stop you from fighting, Aza." His voice is back to soft. "As a Scout, I *can* stop you. I can take you in right now and let you be questioned until you lead us right to the tournament."

"You can't do that." I say this just as quietly, despising myself even as I say the rest. "I'll tell them about the Guild if you do."

Embry's teal eyes go sharp.

"Here is what's going to happen." Fury is the velvet lining his words. "You're going to stop fighting in this tournament, and for that, I'll let you go. Because once we're asked to look into it as official Scouts—and we *will* be, if more lightning storms, falling office buildings, and mysterious blights keep happening—then I can't help you if you're still a part of it. Deal?"

I make myself shake my head. "I have to keep fighting. I can't tell you why. I wish I could."

"Then you should know that I'm going to do everything I can to shut down this tournament," he says. "Either as a Scout or member of the Guild. It'd be irresponsible of me to do anything else. I've seen enough to know just how dangerous it is—and still can be."

I can tell he's hoping that will do the trick. That he won't have to look back and wonder if he tried hard enough with me.

"Would you believe me if I told you I do hope you get it shut down?" My hands are clenched around the cup. I press my still-healing burn hard against its coldness, but the heat continues to cling. "Like I said, I'm not there because I want to be."

He's grim as he peers down at me. "This doesn't help you."

I only nod.

The kids in the store head out the door. The sudden silence seems loud in comparison.

"I guess we're done here, right?" I ask.

Embry gives me another long look. I can barely keep from backing up.

When he goes to the till to pay for the slush, I let him. I don't say a word as I follow him outside.

"I'm sorry," I finally manage. My hands squeeze the paper cup even harder, hard enough that a bit of slush leaks through the edge of the lid.

"I am, too, Aza," he says as he walks away, leaving me to wonder what his next step will be.

FORTY-TWO

Stiff and tired, I get home minutes later. The inside of the teahouse looks nearly back to normal. The window is fully installed, and all the repair people are gone.

My parents are sitting at one of the tables in the dining area, tea and pastries in front of them.

"Aza, you're back." Mom motions me over. "How was your day?"

She doesn't need to say the rest because it's written in her smile: *How was your day with Oliver?*

The thought of Oliver makes me restless, uneasy. I want to talk to him, to ask him about Finch and his loyalty. But I also don't want to know. The truth can't be excused away.

I leave my still-mostly-full slush on the front counter and walk over. I sit down beside my parents, pretending I could eat.

All I can think about is tonight's fight. It was supposed to be so different. Having everything go wrong at the last minute has shaken me. Knots of worry are tight in my stomach.

I look at the plate set out in front of them. "Wow, sweets? Isn't it nearly dinner? Are we celebrating something?"

"We're celebrating getting the teahouse back in order." Dad pours me tea and pushes the pastries in my direction.

"*And* our supplies finally arriving," Mom adds, smiling. "About an hour ago. Can you believe it? Two days of phone calls and excuses, and then they just show up at the door without further explanation."

I pull up my lips, trying to smile back. "That's good to hear. Hopefully it won't happen again."

"They promised it wouldn't, but I suppose we'll see."

Dad nods and gestures—not entirely kindly—toward the front counter. "Now I just have to get the hang of using that new till."

"When are we reopening?" I ask.

"First thing in the morning," Mom says.

I take the napkins from the Mothery out of my starter bag and hand them over. "How do these look?"

"Perfect."

I place the two envelopes from the Prestige on the table between them. "These are for you guys—from me."

Dad picks up one of the envelopes and reads the logo on the front. His brows lift. "The Prestige?"

"It's a mini getaway to the Culture Sector. One night's stay in the Prestige's premium suites, tickets to tonight's show at Green's Theater, and dinner at the Choppery. Breakfast at the hotel in the morning, too."

"Aza." Mom watches Dad open the envelopes and pull out certificates. "You can't afford these working as a courier for Saint Willow."

"I've been saving up. And it's as good a time as any; you should get a break before the teahouse reopens. There's car service included, too, which means you won't have to take the train at all. You'd better go pack—the driver's getting here at seven."

My parents exchange a long glance that says they're unsure about leaving me alone for the night. They haven't gone away since Shire died. My sister was always the one to watch over the teahouse.

"This place will be fine," I say. "I'm pretty sure there's a statistic out there that says the same place never gets robbed twice. Not twice in the same week, anyway."

"It's not the teahouse we're worried about." Mom squeezes my arm. "We know you're more than capable of watching it."

"I'll even open in the morning so you don't have to hurry back."

Dad's expression tells me he's still far from convinced. "I don't know, Aza. We still have some loose ends to tie up before reopening. I'd hate to leave you with that."

"I can do it, no problem." Panic strains—I need them gone. "I promise I'll be fine."

My parents exchange one more look.

Mom asks, "You sure?"

I nod.

"Well, it's one night, right?" Dad smiles at me. "What can happen in one night?"

Everything.

I smile back, hoping it reaches my eyes. "Have fun."

FORTY-THREE

Two hours later, there's a knock at the front entrance of the teahouse.

It startles me from sleep.

I open my eyes, stare up at my bedroom ceiling. It takes me a few seconds to place where I am. Why I'm in bed. Why everything still hurts.

Then I remember.

My parents have left for their night away. The driver was five minutes late. By the time he pulled up outside the teahouse, my nerves were rubbed raw. After the car disappeared around the corner, I limped my way back inside the shop, locked the front door, and fell asleep in my bed. A two-hour nap before the fight as a final bout of recovery time.

Because I don't have my magic back. Because it's going to be Finch's. And he'll never return it to me.

The knock comes again, more insistent, and now I'm fully awake. The shop's long closed, but what if I forgot to flip the OPEN sign on the door?

I get out of bed and make my way to the front of the teahouse.

It's dark outside. Tiny rays of light from the streetlamps stream in through the blinds over the window. The person at the door is nothing but shadow, their face hidden.

The sign *is* flipped to CLOSED, and I frown. It's at eye level—impossible to miss.

Which means they saw it and ignored it.

There's a twinge along the skin at the back of my neck.

I get closer to the door.

The guy is in his late twenties, small and thin, with delicate features and curly brown hair.

I walk up and mouth at him through the glass, *We're closed, sorry.* Then I point to the sign just to make sure he gets it.

He smiles almost shyly and presses a business card to the glass for me to read.

EARL KINGSTON

I take a slow step back, as uncertain as I am fearful.

This is Earl Kingston? Feared Tobacco Sector leader who has lined the murky waters of the Sturgeon River with those who have supposedly double-crossed him? Members of his own family included.

I shouldn't be surprised that he doesn't look how I imagined him. After all, for years I thought Saint Willow was a man.

What can he want?

This is the Tea Sector—not his territory. Technically, I don't have to let him in. I work for Saint Willow. He has no power over me or anything else that she controls.

But he's still Earl Kingston. Still a gang leader, and dangerous. I doubt the bodies that now live in the Sturgeon have much to say about technicalities anymore.

I move toward the door. Everything in the room seems off-kilter somehow, from the angle of the light shining in to how my fingers feel on the lock of the door. My pulse has kicked up a notch to go along with my pounding headache.

The last thing I want is Earl Kingston in my parents' teahouse. But perhaps what I want even less is to have Earl Kingston *outside* my parents' teahouse. At least if he's inside, I can find out what he wants and then finally get rid of him.

I unlock the door and open it just enough for us to talk. "Can I help you?"

"Yes, you can." Another smile and a voice like honey. Big brown eyes. Plain tee beneath a bomber jacket, basic jeans, and sneakers. The unassumingness of it all only adds to the off-kilter feeling.

He holds up his card again, as if I can have possibly forgotten who he is. "But from inside the shop, if you don't mind?"

The flash of a weak and final protest in my mind—*No, Aza, don't*—and I open the door wider.

He steps inside. He casts leftover magic to shut the door behind him.

"Now, Aza Wu, you're going to tell me everything you know about a cop named Cormac."

FORTY-FOUR

I stare at the gang leader, my thoughts pure chaos as I try to remember what Earl Kingston might know about Cormac and me.

I should have tried harder to get in touch with him.

Cormac, is the info you have for me about Earl Kingston? Something you meant to tell me before he got here first? What exactly did you tell him when his gang was holding you?

Earl Kingston steps farther into the teahouse. He's no taller than I am, but his reputation eclipses everything. The shop around him fades, pulls away. There's nowhere else for me to look.

"So this is Wu Teas." His gaze sweeps the room. "It's less ... grand than I pictured it. I've heard about the legacy of your family's teahouse—serving royalty and fancy bloodlines and all that. Though all those people and their families are long dead now, of course."

"Why are you here?" I want to remind him that he's in the Tea Sector now, that Saint Willow might have something to say about him coming into her territory. But Saint Willow finding out about this won't help me in the least.

"Exactly what I said at the door," he says. "We have unfinished business between us, and it goes by the name of Cormac."

"All I know is that last month, one of your men came here to ask me about him. I told him everything I know. Nothing's changed."

Earl Kingston walks over to a rack of tinned teas. Lifts the lid of one—it's our Lotusland Fog blend, smoke and earth and musk—and sniffs.

I catch a glimpse of silver inside his sleeve, just against his wrist. A blade like his man carried.

I attempt to swallow, remembering the feeling of a sharp point pressed to my neck. I taste fresh blood as one more thing inside me falls apart.

"Tell me," Earl Kingston says, "do you recall what you told him?" He digs his fingers into the tea tin and pulls out loose leaves.

It's like walking along the edge of a cliff, figuring out what he already knows so I can decide what else to tell him.

"I told him how I overheard Cormac and a guy named Diego talking about Milo Kingston," I say. Milo's name being mentioned is why Earl Kingston is here. No one can talk about Earl Kingston's cousin unless Earl Kingston says it's okay to talk about his cousin. I've never missed the irony of it being the gang leader himself who had Milo killed after he discovered his cousin's double cross. Betrayal of blood is the worst sin.

He digs into the tin for more leaves. "You said Cormac and Diego's conversation took place right here, didn't it? In this teahouse."

My eyes follow his as he glances over at the darkened dining area. I see him imagining the scene, just as I imagined it to describe it to his henchman.

"Yes, it was right here," I say. "I told your man everything, and then he told me you already had Cormac. That you were going to make him tell you everything he knew."

Earl Kingston's face gives away nothing as he watches me speak. "Have you talked to him since then?"

"No."

"Cormac said you made it all up. That you were covering up something, and he was your scapegoat."

I shake my head. The edge of the cliff, so close. "Not true. Cormac's the one who lied."

Earl Kingston lets tea leaves slip from his fingers to the floor of the shop. His smile is as sweet as his voice is honeyed. "I think he's right. I think *you're* the liar."

My skin ripples with goose bumps. The room tilts more and more.

"And the reason why I think that," he continues, "is because I'm the one who left Cormac's number for you to call. You trying to reach him just proves there's more you're not saying."

I fall back a step, wanting to get out of reach, but there is no escape.

Here I was, calling Cormac, worrying he'd found out something about Shire. It was all a trap.

The gang leader picks up another tin of tea from the shelf— Dragon blend, an oolong. He breaks the seal and lifts the lid, sniffing. His smile over the tin is still sweet while his brown eyes go as sharp as that blade against his arm. "I'm waiting, Aza. I'm sure you have thoughts on what I just said? On Cormac accusing *you* of lying?"

Everything's happening too fast. I'm slipping down the cliff, grabbing at bushes along the way like they can keep me steady, keep me from falling farther.

"Then you know I never actually spoke to him," I say. "I called the number, but no one ever answered. I haven't spoken to

Cormac since *you* spoke to him. And that's the truth. I don't know anything else."

"Then why the eagerness to reach him?"

"He's a Scout. Was I not supposed to call him back?"

"Like I said, Cormac swears he's never met a Diego. We looked into it, and we have nothing but dead ends to show for it. You're the last link. So, I'll ask you one last time about this Diego. And before you answer," he continues, digging his fingers into the leaves, "consider how upsetting it would be if your family's teahouse mysteriously went up in flames one day. Or if I had to come back and ask *your parents* if they've heard anything about my cousin."

"Fine, I'll tell you." My voice is a strangled whisper. I take a deep breath and begin the slow, trap-ridden climb back up to the surface.

"No more lies." His smile has fallen away. He's the Earl Kingston I once imagined, a hawk circling its field, maintaining its rule over its territory. He snaps the tin shut and places it back on the shelf. "Start."

"Cormac and Diego weren't ever in here. Someone I know—a friend—was the one who overheard Cormac and Diego talking about Milo. When Cormac found out my friend knew, he started panicking that my friend would start talking about it. That the news would eventually circle back to you. After Cormac saw my friend and me together, he decided to use me as leverage to make sure my friend never talked. He dropped my name around to make it look like I was connected to the conversation from the start. After your man came here last month to question me, I knew he'd never believe I wasn't involved. So I told him what I'd heard about the conversation. I figured it wouldn't make a difference who overheard it, whether it was me or my friend."

Earl Kingston narrows his eyes. "Who's your 'friend'?"

"His name is Finch." I can barely get the words out. I wrap my arms around myself, revealing that I'm feeling vulnerable.

"Why did you cover for him?"

I squeeze my upper arm, hard.

The muscles scream, and pain makes me flush like I'm blushing. Tears come to my eyes as I hurt. "Because I liked him. He was cute—green eyes like emeralds, hair like the sun before the smog came." This seemed like the exact kind of thing Earl Kingston would believe about me. "I knew he was in over his head. I didn't want him getting in trouble."

"Eyes like emeralds, huh." Earl Kingston laughs. "This Finch will never know just how lucky he was."

I shrug, let a small, shy smile escape. I squeeze my other arm, trying to bring a fresh flush.

Earl Kingston takes a step closer. His curly brown hair is soft-looking. Wolves can look soft, too, before they tear you to pieces. "How do I know you're finally telling me the truth, Aza?"

Black at the edges of my vision. "You're here right now, talking to me face-to-face. This is where I live. There's nowhere else for me to run, and we both know it. So why would I lie when you'll just come back and find me here?"

A sweet grin, all honey. "Smart girl. Where is Finch now? Where can I find him?"

Pressure to think—it's a vise at my temples. I need more time.

Earl Kingston and his gang can't find Finch where Oliver might be. Oliver has nothing to do with any of this and never will.

I know I'm running out of options. I've been toying with danger ever since I first lied to Earl Kingston's man, and if Earl Kingston digs just a little bit deeper, I have no doubt he'll find out my real relationship with Finch. The game will be up for me, sooner or later.

But I need to get out of this right now. Earl Kingston is waiting to hear something, and I have a fight I need to get to.

If Earl Kingston finds Finch tonight, at least there's a chance Finch won't get my magic.

If he finds him later, most likely Finch will cast on the gang leader to defend himself.

Either way, both of those options get Earl Kingston out of my face.

My game has a bit of life in it yet.

"I don't know where Finch lives," I say. "I never found out. And after everything, he got together with my best friend, so I hope I never see him again."

"Then find out," Earl Kingston says. His voice is too gentle, poison delivered with a kiss. "I'll be back. And I'll expect an answer, all right? Please don't make me . . . redecorate this place. It's gained a certain kind of charm for me."

I nod, going hot under my skin. "Can you tell me what happened to Cormac after you questioned him?"

Earl Kingston only smiles once more, says nothing, and leaves.

FORTY-FIVE

The second Earl Kingston is gone from the teahouse, I rush forward and lock the door. I'm breathing hard, half gasping. My headache is a battering ram inside my skull while panic swirls in all directions, touching every part of me.

Cormac might be dead.

I swear out an apology to the missing cop, my eyes filling. He was trouble for me, but he was doing his job. I never meant for him to disappear.

Where's the line, Aza?

Nausea rises. I lean my head against the glass of the door, wondering who I've become and who I want to be. Is it too late to pick? Maybe I've gone back and forth over the line so many times that it's disappeared for me entirely.

Shire. Rudy. Kylin. Wilson. All those people unlucky enough to come across my magic. So much cost.

But then Earl Kingston's honeyed voice is back in my ears, full of threat. I hear Finch talking about casting my magic. About taking one more thing from me.

Setting the gang leader's sights on Finch, hoping one will take out the other—I don't regret it. A lot of people are gone because of me. But I've lost so much, too. It makes me cling to survival because it's the only thing left. The only way out.

I pull myself upright and head toward my bedroom. It's time to get ready.

I don't have far to go—it's still early, and Gunpowder Way is right here in Tea. But I can't move as quickly as I want. Everything is stiff, sore. Laborious. Is this what it feels like to be old? Powerless?

From my desk, I take out the metal starter holder and attach it to the belt loop at my hip.

I pull out both ribbons and start wrapping the first one—pink peonies on cream—around my arm. But then I stop. I look closely at the ribbon. I feel the raised stiffness of the dried blood and mud that I still haven't washed off.

This is a piece of the past.

Indy is Piper's fighter now, not me, no matter how much I wish it weren't so.

I refold the ribbon and tuck it into the corner of my starter bag.

I wrap just the willow one around my arm, noticing the print hasn't held up. Blood and dirt from the ring are smeared everywhere, nearly obliterating the willow trees. I don't mind in the least.

I hang my starter bag across my chest, breathing deep as my ribs squeak in protest. Pulling on a fresh mask, I go to open my window.

My reflection in the glass again—only me this time. No Shire tonight.

I shove my bedroom window open and drag my leg over the sill.

An hour until midnight. The air is cool on my skin, the smog-covered sky the gray of steel. I smell dead snowball bush blossoms, earth, the tea fragrance that lingers in every inch of the sector. The sound of nearby traffic is a low roar.

I jump to the ground, pull the window shut, and squeeze through the hedge.

I turn south and begin to walk. At this time of night, it would take me nearly as long to walk to a station where the trains are still running as it would to go directly to the ring. But every step on the pavement is jarring. The taste of blood comes and goes. My breath is a series of fast, shallow wheezes.

Even in the dark, you can't miss the pink woods. The stretch of forest is thickest at its west end here in Tea, its hue richest, before gradually thinning as it runs eastward. By the time the woods reach their end there and meet the blighted lands, the wide carpet of trees has narrowed to a single line, its hue gone a pale blush.

I stand on the curb, gang headquarters at my back. The outside of the restaurant is completely dark, but I know that means little. I wonder if they're all inside right now or if there's someplace else they go at night and the only reason why I haven't seen it yet is because Saint Willow has yet to drag me there, too. Jihen once told me they're always moving, to keep everyone guessing. It makes them harder to catch.

In front of me, the pink woods loom. Aside from the street and the small strip of the Tobacco Sector that trails lazily into this part of Tea, there's nothing between me and the next fight. Nothing between me and Finch. My magic—my own—feels so close and yet so far away. As I gaze into the red-tinged darkness, I'm over-come with the sense that the world's about to tilt off its axis, to tip over like a spinning top sent flying with a touch—and that it's my hand doing the tipping.

Shivering as the wind picks up, I cross over into the pink woods.

Right away, I notice how my home sector actually smells different here, so close to this part of the city that's held on to magic for
hundreds of years. The usual tea scents are gone. All I can smell is
sugar. Inhaling the scent too deeply makes my stomach spin like
I've eaten too much candy. I envision sugar crystals forming on the
edges of my smog mask with every breath, crystals shining in my
hair and eyelashes.

No one knows for sure what exactly those casters were thinking,
or dreaming, or wishing when they drove their full magic into this
place. The only thing most people agree on is that those casters
died with sweetness in their mouths, and that's why the woods
smell so sweet.

This thought leads to another, so that now Oliver is on my mind,
Oliver and his kiss and how I still need to find him. Part of me hopes
he *does* confess to knowing what it was that Finch was planning,
because then I won't care when he hates me for setting Earl Kingston
on his brother.

I turn eastward and follow the line of crimson-hued trees,
searching for the entrance to the ring.

Yellow diamond.

There are no walls here, no concrete or glass or brick.

But leaves and branches can be painted on just the same. I brush
my hands along them as I walk, letting their sweet scent waft over
my palms, through my fingers the way hair runs through a comb.

I hold out my still-sore hand with its burnt palm over the trees,
telling myself all the sweetness drifting along it must come to
mean something. If not redemption, then maybe the burn will finish healing faster, at least.

I also keep my eye out for signs of leaked magic. For gaps where hints of the underground might peek through—anything that might be the forest equivalent of light in the windows of a long-closed pizza restaurant. The Founders have been sloppy before, so it could easily happen again.

A night breeze comes, swirling the scent of sugar into the air. Trees shake and shimmer.

There.

Against the line of crimson growth, a glimpse of a color that's *not* crimson. Like a single buttercup in a field of bloodred roses.

I head over and peer at the spot more carefully.

The painted yellow diamond covers a single leaf.

If not for that perfectly timed breeze, I probably would have missed seeing the starter altogether.

The trees are also somehow *warm* here.

It's like I'm standing in front of an invisible furnace. The change in temperature—I can feel it through my clothes, through my *skin*—is impossible to miss. As real as the pink woods are real. From cool night air to the kind of dry daytime heat Lotusland almost never sees.

Leaked magic.

An angry exasperation fills me. I hate the Founders for agreeing to work for Saint Willow. They need to be stopped before the city's destroyed, but I also want to see them crash and burn for their egos.

More than anything, I wish I didn't understand them so well. But I do.

The pure need to cast.

I draw on my palm, trying to avoid the worst of the burn. I reach out toward the painted leaf. As I brace for pain, a strange thrill runs through me at the same time. The effect is bewildering, like something falling into place even as it means to shake me apart.

This magic inside me—I can't deny it, but can I control it? Do I *want* to? I shudder.

"Aza!"

The voice comes from the dark.

I spin, pink trees blur, and it's Oliver.

FORTY-SIX

He runs up to me, out of breath.

I'm so surprised he's here that I can't speak right away. I drop my hand from the starter and turn to him.

"I saw you from a block over," he manages between half gasps. "We need to talk."

My heart twists. The last time he came chasing after me through the dark was to tell me what his brother was capable of.

I pull my mask off. "You knew about Finch, didn't you?"

Oliver runs his hand through his hair. "I just found out this morning. He couldn't resist telling me. I've been looking for you."

Just this morning.

Relief is sweet, like a pink leaf from one of the trees has brushed my lips. Then immediately I'm ashamed.

I shouldn't have doubted him. I should have remembered how being brothers hasn't kept Oliver from seeing all the ways Finch has already failed him. More than once, he's come to me looking to help instead of to lie.

"I said it wasn't too late to change his mind," Oliver says. "That if he actually goes through with it, we can never go back. I thought saying that would mean something, but . . ."

Something in my throat goes tight at seeing him so hurt. I can't imagine being able to walk away from Shire for good, no matter how much we argued.

But Shire would never do what Finch means to.

"What did he tell you?" I ask Oliver. "Did he say where he's going to do it? Or when?"

He shakes his head. "He wouldn't say. Only that it hasn't happened yet. I haven't seen him since he told me, though. Maybe it *is* too late."

Maybe. Finch didn't have my magic yet at the dim sum restaurant this afternoon, and right now it's nearly midnight. More than enough time to have done it sometime in between.

But my gut says Saint Willow will want him to wait.

For the spectacle.

Which means I bet it'll happen tonight at the ring. He won't be able to wait any longer. And he'll need the crowd to help with the spell.

The memory of that night looms again. All those people dying. All because I got magic back.

Fighting back a chill, I glance at Oliver. He seems stunned still. Finch's betrayal is all over him.

"I'm sorry," I say. "I know he's your brother. The brother you've been wanting back so badly."

"He's also the brother who's been lying about giving up magic. And now, taking yours." Oliver's expression goes grim, defeated. "I'm sorry, too. I wish I could have made him listen. I wanted to believe that deep down, a part of him still wanted to hear me."

There's a broken note in his voice. I know exactly what it means. I knew the second I saw Finch watching me through the dust of concrete, his eyes hungry for what I took from him.

"It's not up to you," I say to Oliver. "It's not your fault."

His features go pained at hearing that last part.

"Finch is never going to forgive me for our parents. I can be sorry about that forever, but it won't be enough. Having full magic is the only thing that matters to him now."

Full magic and its limits. Its costs.

Trepidation crawls back—I have to tell him about Earl Kingston.

"I have to tell you something," I say. There's a fresh wind rustling through the trees, and even as the air sweetens, I brace myself. "Something I'm sorry about. That I did to you."

He goes still. "Is this about us? Or about Finch?"

"I guess all three."

"Okay. I'm ready."

"It's Earl Kingston," I blurt out before I can change my mind. "He'll be looking for Finch soon."

"Earl King—wait, what?" Oliver's shock changes to fear. He knows of Earl Kingston. "Why?"

"I needed him off my back. He came by looking for someone to blame. I gave him the idea that it was Finch."

Confusion cuts into the fear. "I don't get it."

"I know. It's"—I rub a hand over my face—"a *really* long story. Can I promise to tell you all of it as soon as I can?"

"If I say I don't believe you, would you tell me now?"

The fight, about to start. But—

"Yeah, I would," I say.

A long minute goes by without him saying anything. He just keeps studying me, his hazel eyes dark in the night. I return his stare, wondering what he's thinking, if our kiss is suddenly on his mind again the way it is on mine. If it's been ruined for him. "Then, fine, I'll wait."

I exhale. "Thanks. And I *am* sorry."

"I am, too, if the stories I've heard about Earl Kingston are even half true." There's a bitterness to his words. "But now that my brother has full magic back, I'm probably worried about the wrong person."

"Your brother having magic is the danger I've been trying to prevent all along."

Oliver reaches out and touches my arm. "You can't fight him tonight. He wants revenge against you for what happened last time. I have no clue how far he'll go to win."

His hand is warm through my sleeve. For a second, the pain in my head lessens, if only because I'm distracted from it. "I have to fight. You know that."

"I do." His eyes flash. "But I'm still saying it, even if it makes no difference."

"You shouldn't be here." My need for him to be away from the ring is as strong as my need to get my parents away from the sector. I think of light bulbs burning out early. Wilson as an Ivor, caged forever because he pushed his magic too far. "I'm supposed to lose the fight tonight, okay? Maybe I'd rather you not watch."

"Saint Willow wants you to lose?" His bewilderment is an echo of mine when she first told me.

"The fight is rigged. It's just another way to collect as many marks from bets on the fight."

"The fight won't be any more dangerous?"

"I'm only worth anything to Saint Willow if I can keep fighting. Same for Finch. He can't do anything to me. It's just another fight."

A shadow in his gaze. His reluctance to leave is nearly palpable.

"If you want," I say, not wholly sure this is smart of me but unable to stop, "I can come see you tomorrow and tell you how much I hated having to lose."

His slow smile—I feel it somewhere in my chest. "Sure, okay. But still be careful, even if nothing's going to happen?"

"I'll be careful." I take a step closer.

He steps closer, too. "Can I—"

"Yeah, you can."

His lips are sugary from the air, but the salt I still taste there is all him.

FORTY-SEVEN

I wait until he's out of sight, his form swallowed up by the night as he walks back toward the Spice Sector, before turning to look for the painted yellow diamond again.

The dash of gold from within the trees, a leafy gleam in the night.

I reach through the invisible heat emanating from it and curl my hand over the bit of graffiti.

I cast.

A tremor deep in the ground, and heat climbs through my feet and up my body until it's in my mind. I direct it toward the wall of pink trees in front of me.

Branches start to shake. Leaves tremble and begin to fly off in every direction. The air turns pink with them, a wild blush of a storm.

When everything's still again, I see a slim gap between the trees.

A doorway. Shaped—of course—like a diamond.

Instead of stepping through or guessing what part of the planet I've just destroyed, I shut my eyes and wait for new pain.

It comes just a second later. A sharp, razor-edged sting behind my eyes that rolls downward to sit as a throbbing knot deep inside my nose.

Soon the worst of it passes, and I go up to the doorway and squeeze through.

Pink leaves on pink branches growing from pink trunks inches from my face. The scent of sugar intensifies as I lean forward, thick as an invisible cloud.

The thought of Oliver comes, and I imagine him already far away from here, safer with each step he takes.

I push through pink branches as neatly as though I were squeezing through the snowball bushes outside my bedroom window. I keep going, night its own paintbrush so that all the pink around me turns into a kind of muted crimson. The blood of long ago.

The path begins to open up. There's the growing sound of voices, and the pink-hued darkness starts to lift.

I step into a large clearing.

At a quick glance, the scene could pass for a campsite. The woods setting, the night sky, the golden light of lanterns—it all fits. But everything else screams of underground magic. A battle tournament. And how tonight, a fight will take place.

Three tables are set up along the edges of the clearing. Dozens of light bulbs hover overhead—a bunch flicker even as I watch—their glow shining down on the crowds of people already here. Fighters are getting registered, ring names and elimination tallies slashed across their cheeks in bright white Founders' ink.

There are people in front of the bets counter, too.

Same as always.

And yet there's a hungry and frenzied energy to this ring that I haven't felt in a while. It plucks at my nerves, makes anxiety twitch to life. The last time a fight was this charged was the championship match. Finch and me.

I gaze out at the ring, stomach in nervous knots.

The crowd is much larger than normal, hundreds upon hundreds. The level of excitement in the air is amplified, growing by the minute. When the sound of the bets being called reaches my ears, I know for sure Saint Willow has once again gotten what she wants.

"The return of Finch! Don't let the zero on his cheek fool you; he's a past champion of the Guild's official Tournament of Casters! Get your bets in!"

"Marquee matchup tonight! The War in the Woods, and it's going to happen right here! Big bets in the works, don't miss out! Place yours at the bets counter!"

"Five minutes to get your bets in! Aza, Finch, Indy—who's going to be the last fighter standing tonight? Five minutes, folks, get them in!"

The War in the Woods.

The most memorable event in all of the underground.

I have to lose in front of all these people, I think dully. They'll get to see Finch beat me with my own magic and never know the truth. Saint Willow wants a spectacle, and here it is.

I scan the crowd for Finch, my eyes feeling hot in their sockets. If he's already here, does it also mean he's already taken my magic? The crowd's gathered, here for the taking. There are more than enough people here to help Finch finish setting the spell into motion.

But there's no panic. Just excitement.

It hasn't happened yet, then.

But when it does, how bad will it be? How many people here won't ever get to see the outside world again? Shouldn't there be a limit on the cost, too?

No sign of Finch, either—yet.

I tug my mask up and head toward the registration counter, my thoughts still stuck on all the different ways we're paying for Saint Willow to have her tournament. Soon people will die from a gathered spell, and some part of the world might crumble away, and Saint Willow won't care, because all she'll feel is power. I see Wilson in his display cage, gone Ivor from casting a level of magic his body couldn't handle.

Has she replaced him? Does she realize yet the limits of her Founders? Do *they*? I can't imagine any replacement being the key to finally making their rings safe.

And this other magic inside me, running hotter, faster. It takes my breath away, this wild desire to cast.

I get in line. I keep my head down, not wanting to see anyone who might want to talk to me—Piper, Indy, Nima, *Finch*. Every muscle and bone shrieks with each movement, and my headache doesn't mind shrieking back. I just want the night done. And tomorrow, I'll see Oliver.

When I get to the front of the line, they write on my face—ring name on one cheek and the number four on the other. The ink is still drying as I weave my way into the center of the clearing. I don't look at the other fighters already waiting there, not wanting to make conversation with them, either.

A rustle goes through the crowd. It's Jihen, grin slicked across his face.

His black suit from earlier is practically iridescent beneath the lit bulbs overhead, its gold threads winking and flashing with each movement. From his chest pocket, his silk fan pokes out. As he strides over, he proudly flashes his go-to notecards.

Badly tempted to roll my eyes, I chance a closer look at the other fighters now that everyone's watching Jihen.

Indy, black silk wound around her arm, the number twenty-six on her cheek. She catches me looking and blatantly stares back. Her expression—while not outright cold—is undeniably on the cool side.

I turn my head, uncomfortable, and make a show of slowly scanning more of the room. Like I'm as cool as she is.

Finch.

Our gazes lock.

My breath goes shallow. An aching flutter in my throat, the tiniest taste of fresh blood. The air in the clearing goes thin, becomes a shrill whistle ringing deep in my ears. His eyes hold mine the same way claws lift prey.

I've never seen such calm hatred before. Such flat and unwavering determination for the hunt. I feel it somewhere in the pit of my stomach, full of teeth and blades.

Finch doesn't mean to just beat me in the ring tonight. He means to destroy me.

Frantically, I search the flat depths of his green gaze for signs of my magic. For signs of the power I was born with.

Have you taken my magic yet?

Where am I in you?

My hunger to feel whole again—it goes beyond the hunger I saw on his face when we faced each other across a restaurant table.

He longs for magic, for power.

But I long for myself.

I stare, desperation a vise around my heart, wishing I knew what to look for.

To see the unseeable is beyond casters. Beyond me.

Finch and I break eye contact at the same time.

When I glance back a half second later, he is still slowly turning away. I get a childish satisfaction at the large zero on his cheek. At the way the magic-cast light gleaming off his blond hair reminds me of the last time he was in the ring. When I was the one who stole from him.

Jihen gets closer. He's still waving his cards. He motions for applause. As people begin to play along, his entire body seems to inflate.

Unable to watch, I let my eyes fall on the crowd again. Once more, light catches on Finch's blond hair as he turns to look at someone across the clearing.

My gaze follows his.

A woman. Wearing a hat despite the dark, its brim pulled low over her face. The hat is cream silk. Sprigs of green berries are tucked into the band.

The shock makes me gasp.

Saint Willow.

She's finally come. A spider beyond her web.

It makes sense for her to finally appear. Tonight will be the peak of the spectacle she's worked so hard for. When the ring fills with applause as Finch is re-crowned, her sense of power will be unmatched. Every mark she makes will be well deserved. Never again will anyone in her family doubt their choice of sector gang leader.

Nobody here knows her secret, though—who she is, what she looks like. She's an anonymous face in a crowd of many.

I watch as she meets Finch's eyes. As she nods once.

Aza, this is it.

Dark understanding explodes. It builds like a slow scream in my mind as the clearing fades from around Saint Willow and Finch. Until they're all I can see. My magic lies between them like some kind of invisible chain, a tether uniting my biggest enemies.

Finch takes something out of his pocket.

In my mind's eye, a blue plastic bead sits on the palm of my hand. It's colder than the rain that has drenched me through. My hand clenches around it as I step off the sidewalk. The mass of the crowd, swelling against me as I walk.

The clearing here—just as crowded.

Who's going to die tonight for you, Finch? I'm suddenly full of panic as heavy as a weight. *For you, Saint Willow? For me and my part in this?*

Jihen reaches the middle of the clearing.

Finch clenches a fist. Begins to slide into the thickest part of the crowd.

Panic floods me. The memory of a cry for help in the night from the middle of an intersection.

I go to draw.

Too late.

A bright flash of light that washes out the world. A boom of sound that shakes the ground.

When the ring comes back, I'm in a part of Lotusland that now exists only as ash.

Chinatown.

FORTY-EIGHT

A long, paved street.

High arched gates are at both ends, and brass statues of ancient notables sit at their bases. Half of the buildings lining the street are shops and restaurants, and the other half are brick-front restaurants and offices. Their facades all jumble wildly together, everything wanting attention at the same time. Painted store signs. Menus hanging up in windows. Sun-faded awnings. The zigzag of black metal fire escapes.

My mind feels just as jumbled and wild as I try to see all of it at once. As I also keep watching the cheering crowd, terror a cold stone in my chest as I wait for people to start falling. To die in order for us to cast magic.

Any second now.

With feverish eyes, I skim the dozens of lanterns strung back and forth across the street. Each one is painted with a Chinese character, is as red and fat as cartoon hearts.

Some of their lights are already flickering.

The raw thrill of fear, now stacked on top of terror so my insides are amped too high.

I search for Finch.

He sees me first.

The second our gazes lock, I have no doubt it's done. I didn't see my magic earlier, but I see it in him now—in his utter self-satisfaction, the ugly pleasure and glee that line it like thorns along a stem.

A pained cry crawls up my throat. The wrongness of what he's done comes at me like fists.

But haven't I done the same? I have the magic of strangers inside me. Not by choice, but it doesn't change the fact that I'm still casting with it.

I make myself look away from him. I don't want to think about how soon I'll have to let him beat me. Worse is how my magic is so close yet might as well be halfway across the planet for all the good its nearness does me. It remains as untouchable and unreachable as ether and essence, adrift in the air.

I scan the crowd again, mouth gone dry with my fear. I'm still waiting for the first scream. It's dusk out, the sky a deep orange red. Shadow-filled light washes across hundreds of faces. Everyone's still cheering, and Jihen is taking his time basking in the attention.

It should have happened by now. Crossing the street that night— it only took me seconds. Only seconds before dozens of people began to die one by one, like puppets collapsing after being methodically cut from their strings.

But nothing.

Relief leaves me weak at the knees. My pulse spins out fast like something wound too tight and finally released.

Still, the relief doesn't last. Terror crowds back in, reminding me of the truth.

Magic always has a cost.

If Finch taking my magic doesn't demand the price of death, it'll demand a different kind of price.

But what? How and when?

Air dances, and the scents of Chinatown waft over me—if I close my eyes, I could be back in the Tea Sector. But the familiar scents are somehow *more*. Both deeper and untouched, like my childhood come back to life. The smell of blood and culture, if that has a scent—tea and rice and lotus flowers, bamboo leaves and jade and gold.

Lotusland's Chinatown used to make up a part of the Tea Sector. But just over two hundred years ago, the Great West Coast Quake hit. A lot of the city was affected, but only one neighborhood was too devastated to ever recover. In Chinatown, not a single building was left standing. With nothing left, survivors walked away and never came back.

The area was still roped off a couple of years later when a group of restless casters decided to enter anyway, intending to mark the world with full magic. And so the pink woods came to be, rose-hued growth borne on dust and bone.

I have no doubt the heart of Chinatown used to be right here, exactly where we're standing. From all the empty stores to the eerie glow of the red lanterns, this place feels nothing but haunted. It's the past brought back to a kind of half life. It's Finch having my magic so I'll never be free of him.

Jihen clears his throat and begins to read off his notecards.

"A thousand years ago," he starts, "a bunch of Lotusland's most talented casters also happened to have huge egos. They thought it would be such a shame for their talent ever to be forgotten. So they got together and decided to create a new neighborhood for the city. The plan was that when Chinatown eventually became legendary, everyone would know it was their magic that had created it in the first place. Centuries passed, and those casters would have been happy to know that their plan worked—except that maybe it worked too well. Chinatown *was* famous—but more for the casters who created it than the magic they did it with."

A single long crack appears in the middle of the street. The crowd murmurs, uncertain.

Unease creeps inward as I look at the fissure. Is this a part of the ring? The falling bamboo and changing paths in the Maze of Daiyu, the kiln heat of an empress's porcelain palace, the blinding snowstorm of Syook Valley—all of that was the Founders being creative. Pushing their magic to the brink to do it. Letting that edge begin to crumble away.

I glance up, searching for signs of the Founders. It doesn't take me long now that I've figured out where to look. The brass statues at the base of the arched gates. I count. There are fourteen altogether.

Wilson's been replaced.

I scan the faces, trying to recognize who's new. If they might be someone I know.

"Then the Great West Coast Quake hit, destroying Chinatown forever," Jihen reads on. "And the rest of Lotusland all got together and decided there were two reasons why Chinatown was the only neighborhood to go completely belly-up. The first was that way too many people had drawn full magic from the ground there."

Another crack appears in the street, and this time the crowd splits up to keep away from it. Spectators move back onto the sidewalks, pushing right up against the shops. We stay loosely circled around Jihen, not looking at one another, thinking about ancient earthquakes and how a whole neighborhood could be wiped out of existence.

Jihen peers into the crack, gives the crowd a wink, and flips to a new card.

So the fissure *is* a part of the ring. For us to fight while the ground's falling apart will be the biggest spectacle yet.

"As for the second reason," Jihen continues, "people in Lotusland believed that the earth, by shaking itself, was actually sending a message. To remind everyone that it was magic that kept the earth going and not its casters. And so the Great West Coast Quake was their wake-up call."

Another crack along the street, this one the longest yet. A few seconds of silence as a bunch of fighters glance over at Jihen, frowning. As though he should be asking the Founders to take it easy on the showboating. As though he'd even want to.

Instead, he neatens his stack of notecards. Telling us we're stuck.

The same unease from earlier blooms wide, and I glance away from the crack and into the crowd.

How to fight without falling? How deep do the cracks go?

My heart stutters at who I see.

Oliver, standing near the back of the spectators. He meets my gaze through the crowd between us and gives me a sheepish grin.

Caught.

Dread is an oversized fist in my stomach.

What are you doing here? The words are a silent shout in my head, as angry as they are fearful, at odds with the flare of happiness that comes with seeing him.

I *do* know why he's here. He wants to see with his own eyes if Finch is really going to betray him so hugely. Maybe he's still hoping that when Finch sees him, he'll change his mind—one final chance to be brothers again. Or maybe he needs to see for himself that I'm safe. It doesn't make it better. *You can't help me by being in danger.*

Just then, the cracks in the street begin to widen. A soft rumble comes from deep inside the earth. I feel it beneath my feet before the tremble peters out.

I can imagine standing here centuries ago. When the trembling kept growing, not stopping until everything was gone.

There's a low hissing sound. From inside the cracks, lava seeps forth, slow and oozing. The air now smells of fire instead of tea. As the lava moves, it begins to melt the asphalt of the street back into liquid.

The spectators move back, trying to get closer to the storefronts, while the fighters around me can't seem to tear they gazes away from where the ground is slowly opening up.

My eyes sting from the heat, my nose from the stink. Just how far can the Founders go?

Start the fight before this whole place falls apart!

But instead of pulling out his silk fan, Jihen's staring down into one of the cracks. At the lava that's bubbling up and about to touch his shoes.

There's no longer delight on his face but confusion. Surprise. The lava—he wasn't expecting it, either.

The fist of dread in my stomach clenches.

The Founders have pushed their magic too far. This ring—how much longer will it hold?

"We already fought once with heat," a fighter says, more anxiety in their voice than real indignation. "I thought the Founders were all about keeping this tournament interesting."

"Well, well—" Jihen is nearly sputtering. "That was fire, and this is lava." He's trying to show he knew the lava was coming. "They're different things."

"How?" It's that fighter named Mack, who no longer looks like he's having much fun in the ring. "They're both hot, and they both burn."

Jihen scowls. "I don't know *how* they're different, but—"

"Fire is a chemical reaction," Pav says, his eyes wide and locked on the lava peeking over the edge of one of the cracks, "while lava is melted rock. But, yeah, they both burn."

Jihen's scowl deepens as he turns to Pav. He practically shoves the silk fan in his face. "Choose."

Cornered, Pav points to a strip of silk.

Jihen takes the fan and reads from the back. A sly grin spreads across his face as he says, "*No twist tonight.* Straight-up fight. How's that for a twist?"

He melts back into the crowd as cheers break out. No gimmicks or tricks. Nothing but what they really want—to see the ultimate rematch between Finch and me. The War in the Woods. A momentous event.

I make one last frantic sweep, my gaze desperate as it searches the carved faces of the Founders again.

Why can't any of them see they need to end the fight before the ring falls apart any more? Can't they feel the lava's heat? See how fast it's already flowing?

Dusk light shifts. Finally, I get a closer look at one of the faces. A glimmer of teal. And I go still with shock.

The new Founder *is* someone I recognize. But it's also impossible. Because Embry is an Ivor. Bones of glass. Casting now will shatter him apart.

I'm going to do everything I can to shut down this tournament.

Then I let out a shaky breath, realizing I'm overreacting. Embry is absolutely determined, but he's not stupid—however he found out about tonight's match, he's only here to watch. And if getting in as a Founder can get him more information about how they work and how the tournament runs, all the better. Embry only makes them weaker by being a member, since he'll be covering up that he can't cast. But he'll know that already, and I bet he decided the risk of being discovered is one he has no choice but to take.

Then a wild war cry booms, the street erupts into motion, and fighters charge at one another.

FORTY-NINE

I spin toward the fighter at my elbow.

It's Tau.

Other fighters are in motion all around us. She's still shoving starters into her pocket.

"Hey—!" she exclaims as we crash to the ground. Her cap goes flying. Her starters, too, scattering across the pavement, just missing a stream of lava. The crowd is already shouting.

The thud jars me, too, and I bite down hard on my tongue. Fresh blood, the taste both tinny and rich.

She pushes at me. Her pink-flushed skin is much redder now. "My starters! I haven't even—!"

I draw around the white coin in my palm. The still-healing burn on my skin stings in protest. Five messy points. "Sorry."

Red flames in my mind. Their scent matches that of the air, now smelling even more strongly of fire.

Tau's hands turn into claws. She swears and twists her body, throwing me off. I land on top of her lost starters, still scattered on the ground.

Casting pain hits, batters me. It's a wave of deep prickling heat that rushes down my arms—bruises. The price for the spell I just cast.

It's still too much. This magic inside me—each time I cast is just another reminder of how it's not mine. That mine is inside Finch now.

A hard pit of fury lodges into my chest.

I let the depleted starter drop to the ground and grab one of Tau's from the pavement. I draw and cast again. Five points once more. Bone spell.

Tau shrieks as her back bows.

A voice inside my head—Shire's? Kylin's? My own?—screams that I need to slow down. That I need to pace myself or I won't last until I meet Finch. And if that happens, Saint Willow might not give me another chance.

But every other part of me doesn't want to stop at all. Everything about this fight reminds me of all the things I've tried to escape and can't seem to—Saint Willow, Finch, the loss of my magic.

The pit of fury in my chest blooms. Aching to explode.

Tau's face is contorted with pain. She gives me a final glare and slams a still-clawed hand on the ground. Three times.

The Founders hear, and one second later she's gone still at my side. Jade stone.

I crouch low and peer around, eyes scanning the street. I'm breathing hard, and each breath is like a punch to my ribs.

There are more fissures in the ground all around us now, opening up along the pavement like cracks through damaged ceramic. Orange lava seeps out. Ribbons of heat.

I look for Finch again. Everyone's moving. I spot his blond hair ahead in the crowd a second later. I watch him cast, my heart buckling painfully—as though I could still control my magic in his body. As though I still have any say at all.

When the fighter he casts on falls—Finch simply moves to cast on someone else. The ache of it hurts as much as casting pain. Someone like him shouldn't have such control over me. Is he simply a better caster, then? The same way I'm sure Indy is stronger than me?

The blast hits me from the side.

I smash hard into the ground. Everything inside my head rings. I skid along the pavement, helpless to stop. My clothes tear, and suddenly there's heat on my arm, on my legs.

Lava.

My skin starts to burn. Agony wraps itself around me, heavy and suffocating. A thin scream slips out. Tears rush from my eyes.

A fighter with short black hair bends close, her face a swimming oval. Spectators scream and cheer. *Indyyy!*

"This isn't payback for that last spell you cast on me, okay?" There's real regret on her face, despite the anger I saw earlier. Behind her, the street is chaos, a wildness made up of fighters, shaking lanterns, and smoke everywhere. "This is just the fight. This is just the *game.*"

She drops her used-up starter to the ground. She takes out a fresh one—gold, for a flesh spell—and draws. About to cast.

I shut my eyes hard, bracing, knowing it's too late for me to stop her. Her words echo in my brain. I don't know her story. Maybe she has something to fight for that I can't see just by being in the ring with her. Someone she loves preventing her from walking away. All I know is that for me, this isn't just a fight. It's not *just* the game.

Her casting pain comes, eyes fluttering wide with it. She presses a hand to her face, a grimace behind her fingers.

As Indy bleeds from her nose, my body burns. Pain grows and swells, a living, breathing thing swarming fast all over me. I'm shaking as I try to drag my unburnt arm to my starters, as I try to work my body free. A new crack opens in the sidewalk beside me. Lava seeps out like fresh juice wrung from fruit.

Indy grunts and shoves me back, her hands pinning me. She's struggling to cast while holding me down.

Before I can think about how it'll hurt, I fling my foot into the stream of fresh lava at my side. Burning liquid splashes up onto one of her arms. Onto one of mine.

The stink of burning skin—mine, hers—rushes over us, and I nearly gag. Indy pulls away with a scream, clutching at her arm. Agony of my own spirals outward as my skin starts to hiss.

Indy's starter slips from her hand and rolls just out of reach. Fighters blur by, casting on one another. The shouting of the crowd is loud, thunderous.

I lift my burnt arm—pain pushes in waves, tidal and relentless—and jaggedly draw on my palm. Eight points.

I work desperate fingers to my holder, trying to twist out a starter. Plastic catches, then slips past my hand before I can grab hold.

Panic strums at my heart. How many starters did I just lose? There's lava all over the place.

Just as Indy leaps at me, I lunge for her dropped starter. I close my fist around it on the street as Indy bangs into my side.

"This is also just the fight," I gasp. "You're just someone in my way."

I cast.

Red fire in my mind.

The jab to the throat hits Indy like a torpedo. She falls back, already knocked out. I watch her change into jade stone.

The crowd roars. One step closer to a final showdown between Finch and me. I imagine Saint Willow out there watching, satisfied with how I'm obeying—with how everything is going her way so far. My stomach churns.

I drop the depleted starter. It rolls into lava, starts to melt.

Still reeling from the fact that I just eliminated Indy, I watch as faceless fighters cast all around. Loud yelling fills the air, but it's incoherent to me. Through the noise, I realize that spectators are cheering and chanting my name—*Aaazzzaaa*.

Gratitude, rage, terror—I feel all of that, and it confuses me. I hate that I like the crowd being on my side. That I even care.

Pain from the spell I just cast barrels through me while old pain still in my head continues to unfurl, like the everlasting opening of a rose. I push all of it back as much as I can, struggle to my feet, and look out at how magic is tearing apart the ring.

Lava laces the street, a network of veins in its paved surface. Parts of the pavement have thrust outward, pushing shops askew. Cracks crawl up walls and across storefront windows. Fallen store signs and awnings are aflame.

Nearly all of the red lanterns have gone dark.

Still, spectators fill the sidewalks, confident in the Founders and their protective magic. Believing that no matter how much this ring falls apart, they'll still be safe from the costs that casting demands. That at the end of the fight, the outside world will still be there to return to.

What can Embry be thinking as he watches all of this? Is he as horrified and mesmerized as I am? As cold and clinical as I've seen him be? Once he reports to the Guild, I can't imagine them letting

this tournament go on. But that's as far as I let myself imagine—
because Saint Willow won't go down without a fight of her own.

"Aza."

The skin on the back of my neck lifts, and I turn around.

Finch.

FIFTY

He casts before I can even blink.

The flash of gold from his palm, and I'm flying back.

My own magic.

Coming at me like punches. They are like daggers piercing already-screaming wounds. I'm shaking as I hit the ground.

My back lands on a road map of lava, every single path and trail molten as they burn my clothes into my skin. A moan strangles its way out of my throat, choked away as pain engulfs me like a swirling black shawl.

The crowd is shouting and clapping from where they're standing on the sidewalks. The sound is both distant and too loud. Our names ring through the air, running together as though we're one person. We're the last two fighters left. All the others have turned into jade stone.

Fiiiinch! Azaaaa! The War in the Woods!

This. This is everything Saint Willow could have wished for. She's watching right this second, calculating just how much she's making off this fight—in marks, in power.

Finch steps closer, his presence bigger than his form, vivid against the smoke hanging in the air. His shirt is stained with dirt and smoke. The number eight is scrawled across his cheek. He moves like a hunter. There's a glow to his eyes that makes me cringe.

As he comes to stand over me, bruises blooms around his

neck—his casting pain from that flesh spell. They tell me it was just a five-point spell, but I'm already in so much pain that the impact feels more like ten, fifteen, *more*. My own magic, hurting me.

I'm in trouble.

The ground trembles, long and hard, and the street cracks open even more. As I watch, the roof of one of the stores collapses inward. An awning tears. There's the scent of smoke and ash, billowing and free.

This part of the earth is also in trouble.

My mind races to Embry, and fresh anger flares. Why can't he *do something*? So much for doing all he can to end this tournament.

But instantly, I feel guilty. Him being right here in the ring doesn't make him suddenly more able to cast. If anything, he's more frustrated than ever. He's watching the fight as a Founder, yet no closer to stopping them or Saint Willow.

"Get up, Aza," Finch says softly. Ice-cold green eyes cut me from a distance, his hatred for me as sharp as a sword. "We have to give them a show, remember? A fight to talk about."

I move back by crawling on my elbows—bruised, burned, every inch agony. I try to get up and fail because everything is spinning.

"They've got enough to talk about," I say. "You've won. So do a knockout, or I'll bow out myself."

A smile. His resemblance to Oliver shakes me.

"You think I'm going to listen to Saint Willow? I just wanted full magic back. And now that I have it, I'm going to do what I meant to do all along."

I go hot, then cold. Finally, the truth. The only way this could have ended.

A low laugh as he watches my face. As he sees me understand completely.

"There was no way I was going to let you leave this ring alive. Not after what you took from me."

I drag myself to my feet. The world is black at the edges, shadows painted there by the pounding inside my skull. A part of me wants to just let that black close in. To just not burn anymore. I'm supposed to lose, anyway...

Finch reaches for a fresh starter.

The crowd is clapping.

He isn't going to let me go. His eyes tell me that he'll never forgive how I took his magic away. How I beat him in front of those he wanted to impress most.

For all the things I hate him for, I am not so different. Full magic and its costs—I might never stop paying.

Blood suddenly trickles from Finch's mouth, and he goes still. It leaks from his nose, and something inside me clambers awake. Reminding me exactly what is inside him.

"That's *my* magic fighting you," I say, the words broken and desperate. "You won't be able to keep casting it."

He glares at me as he swipes at the blood, poppy-bright along his cheek. "I'll figure it out, now that it's mine."

"It's never going to be yours." A jagged whisper that hurts coming out. "*Never.*"

Lava creeps ever closer, seeping faster and thicker from the cracks now.

"You know exactly how it feels to need to cast, Aza. It's why you took magic back when you had the chance. So how can you blame me for doing the same?"

I'm shaking, sobs breaking free, hating him for taking so much. Knowing he's right.

The world's swimming, blazing an orange so bright it's like a sun, and I glance in the direction of the Founders again. Searching the statues for the face I know. Wishing for the impossible because it's all I can do.

Embry! Help me! Somehow!

"And the way you're crying right now?" Finch draws, and I'm frozen, unable to stop him. "Your sister cried the exact same way right before I killed her."

He casts.

FIFTY-ONE

Nothing happens.

No blow comes. Everything seems to stop. And when Finch frowns and opens his fist to look at his starter, I'm too shocked to react right away.

An instant later, relief sweeps in, nearly making me stagger.

But— How—?

My eyes are still hot with tears as I turn to look for Embry once more, the world wavering. Disbelief is wild in my throat even as I try to swallow it away.

I asked for the impossible, but it can't be true. Being saved by someone casting Finch's starter useless—it can't have been the Guild member.

Because Embry's bones—made of *glass*—

When I finally find his face among the Founders, his expression says he's in absolute agony. Mouth pulled into a grimace, teal eyes both furious and terrified. Wilson had no idea he'd go Ivor when he did. But Embry has always known what would happen to him if he cast once more. A body of delicate glass. His cost is to finally shatter to pieces.

Remorse hammers at me. Guilt like knives.

As though through thick fog, I watch Finch drop the now-useless starter to the ground and take a new one from his pocket. He casts again.

Nothing.

This can't be Embry. His magic was already pushed to the limit.

This must be the Founders. Their game magic gone weak in one more way: Their ring starters are dead. Not just Finch's but mine, too. One more hole in the tournament. One more danger for fighters to battle.

Fresh rage washes over me. Despair. If ring starters no longer work, what's left?

I tear open my starter bag. Frantically feel for silk. My fingers feel clumsy as they search.

A heartbeat later, they touch the silk of a worn ribbon—pink peonies on cream. The fabric still stiff with dried blood and old blue mud, still unwashed from the last match of the Guild's tournament.

If the Founders' ring has lost its way with its own magic, maybe magic of a different ring can make its way inside.

I close my hand over old blue mud and cast.

My blood goes as hot as the lava taking over the earth. Red flames burst to life in my mind, and Finch's hands go to his head. To his skull.

I will the flames to go higher, hotter. Because of the past. For the future.

And when casting pain comes, it's so immense that it leaves me breathless. It tears at my focus, at my *control*.

The crowd is shouting. Roaring. A wall of noise that only keeps growing.

Finch falls to his knees. His face is wrenched with the pain that's on the verge of bursting inside his head. Still, he struggles to reach for more starters, insistent on trying to cast again. That he can't see how they no longer work—that the tournament as he knew it is over—shows in his tortured eyes. His anguished expression is immortalized as he's turned into jade stone.

Everything should be over.

But the magic inside me continues to run. Too hot. Too fast. I feel it in motion in my veins, like the rapid spiking of a fever. Drawn too huge, it can no longer be contained. The red clouds of it break the constraints of my mind and push outward, wild and billowing and looking for things to change.

The Founders' magic put cracks in this world, but it's mine that will shatter it.

The world goes crimson.

The ground shakes, and lava flows, heavier now. A shop slumps, its awning crumpling, and begins to sink. Then another, and another. Red lanterns slither into a heap and begin to melt.

A deep groaning sound fills the air as the street starts to crack in half.

Screams as the crowd pushes away, as it turns and runs, trying to escape from the ring.

Bits of the street begin to drop off, leaving holes full of liquid fire. Lumps of jade stone slip downward into them. Spectators unable to swerve in time—they slip in, too.

From somewhere deep inside my brain:

People. Those are people. *Fighters you* know.

I catch sight of Jihen pushing his way through the crowd as he tries to move farther back from the street. He's swerving between buildings when he trips; a second later, he's gone from sight, a pit of lava swallowing him up.

I can barely register what this means for me. One of my biggest tormentors is gone for good—yet no part of me rejoices. Why does it feel like everything is still only falling apart?

Another deep groan from the earth, and Chinatown's gates topple to the ground. The brass statues around them tip over a second later. There's no sign of Embry, but I'm not sure what that means. Is he gone for good, then?

The faces I *do* see are morphing back into their original forms, the long-gone nobles that stood there a thousand years ago. Before they were changed for tonight's fight.

Saint Willow's Founders are fleeing from her tournament.

Scanning the chaos of the crowd, I search for signs of the gang leader, longing for her to see the disaster all her work and dreams have caused. I want to witness her defeat and then revel in it. Be as cruelly smug as she is. There's a blankness—a *hardness*—to my hate that both scares and calls to me.

Aza!

The sound of my name rises out of the noise. I hear it the way I hear an alarm while asleep, from deep within dreams. Through the red haze of magic, Oliver appears. His hazel eyes are frantic, and he's shaking me by the arms.

My stained peonies-on-cream silk ribbon falls from my hand.

Aza! Stop! You have to pull your magic back!

I— It's too late! I don't know how!

I have no clue if I'm saying this out loud or just in my head. I can't hear myself. Like most of me has disappeared the way so much of the ring has. I struggle to come back, but it's like fighting against a rip current.

"Aza." Oliver, coming closer. "You have to try."

I shut my eyes hard. The taste of blood in my mouth is steel strung around my tongue, through my teeth.

And in my mind, I stare down at all the red that is my magic. The voluminous and borderless clouds of it, grown as wide as the sky, vast and broad. In my head, I reach up and tear it away. I claw it back. Collect it—*gather* it—the way Nima might gather the invisible dust of magic. I'm not a gatherer, but maybe this comes close. Maybe this is what it means for me to do it.

When I open my eyes again, Chinatown is gone.

FIFTY-TWO

We're back in the pink woods.

No longer an orange-red dusk but the deep night of the outside world. Trees gone scarlet in the dark still stretch out far into the distance.

The light bulbs are gone. So are the tables. The Founders have run and taken those parts of the ring with them.

Just those parts, though.

The ground of the forest remains full of cracks, a scarred landscape of wide furrows and deep valleys. And in the dark, lava glows bright orange, a crisscross of streams and pools everywhere I look. The air smells exactly as the ring did—full of fire.

Breakthrough damage. But bigger and more immediate than it's ever been before.

People are shoving their way through the trees, trying to get out of the woods, to avoid the pits and the hot death that they promise.

I stare at all of this. Panic colors everything, a negative energy that pulsates like a warning light.

"Aza." Oliver is still clutching me by the arms. He's gone pale, skin as luminescent as the moon must be behind the smog. "The casters that fell into the cracks—there on the street of the ring— what's happened to them now? How do we get them back?"

He's asking about Finch. The faces of other fighters flash behind my eyes—Pav and Indy and Bardem.

The woods spin, and my stomach rolls. "I don't know—"

Then someone is approaching from the trees. They're going the wrong way, headed toward us, where there's only danger. I want to yell at them to get away, but a second later they're right here.

Earl Kingston.

My breath catches, and I go still.

Seeing him earlier tonight in the teahouse feels like an eternity ago. Like an event in someone else's life.

Two more men emerge. Earl Kingston's guys; blades glimmer in their hands. My mind leaps back—the press of steel on my neck, held there by one of Earl Kingston's men. Maybe even one of these two.

"So—this must be Finch," Earl Kingston says he looks at Oliver. "How thoughtful of you to try to warn him away from us, Aza. But I admit I'm also disappointed. I thought we had an understanding."

"This isn't Finch," I say through lips gone numb, trying to process how the gang leader's actually here. His boyish brown curls only make me want to run. Ridiculously, I wonder how bad his eyes must be—*I told you Finch has blond hair and eyes like emeralds!*

He smiles, and it's as honeyed as ever. "Stop lying. You think I wasn't going to follow you until I found him? I wasn't going to let him slip away again."

"You were watching me?" I'm not surprised, deep down. I knew my story was always going to come back around—I just didn't think it would be this soon. Another way that I've looked at everything wrong.

A modest shrug. "Of course. Having people followed is just something we do."

"I'm not Finch," Oliver says quietly. "I'm his brother."

"Then your brother's the one who's going to answer for my cousin. Where is he?"

"He's gone." Oliver goes another shade paler as reality sinks in. The loss of his brother at the hands of full magic. "He's gone. The ring—the *lava*—"

"Lava." Earl Kingston laughs, but it's cold, as sharp as carved ice. I'm reminded of Saint Willow talking about power. The hunger in her voice for everyone to know she has the most. And as Earl Kingston ignores the sight and smell of fire all around him, I also think of how power is just the flip side of madness. "I'm not going to ask you again."

Someone shouts in the dark. I can't make out exactly what they're saying, but the thinly veiled panic is clear enough—they want out. People are still pushing their way through the trees, desperate to escape. More shouts. The dark is full of chaos.

"Boss"—one of Earl Kingston's men, uneasiness in his voice—"any idea what's going on around here? Maybe we should leave and finish this—"

Earl Kingston gives him a look that instantly makes him stop talking. "All I care about is getting ahold of this Finch. So until he's right here in front of me, no one's going anywhere."

Then the world begins to break apart.

Earthquake.

FIFTY-THREE

The ground shakes—violently and deeply, with a terrible sense of purpose. As we all tumble to our knees, I know it's my fault.

This is the aftermath of my casting unwanted magic. So much stolen power—now all of it has followed me from the ring into the outside world. I can blame Saint Willow, the Founders, and Finch as much as I want. But in the end, the truth stays the same.

This is all me.

Trees creak and groan as the world shudders in long, building waves. The sound of trunks splitting as their roots tear free is as loud as thunder. The cracks in the forest floor widen even more. They are fissures that have no end in the dark, becoming gaping craters with each passing second.

I go cold all over as people tip into them. Their screams as they disappear will echo forever in my brain.

More ghosts.

I want to yell out names just as others are yelling, voices desperate and pleading and filling the air. I want to find these people in the dark and take them from this place I've destroyed. But I open my mouth, and nothing comes out.

Smells of fire and earth press close, so that the forest is smothering even as it breaks. Pain is a shroud wrapped all around me. I've never felt so dizzy.

The ground lurches hard.

Oliver grabs my arm before we can fall. Terror has reshaped the bones of his face, hollowing out his cheeks and eyes. He stares at streams of lava that are slowly converging on us. "We need to get out of here, Aza."

"*No one goes anywhere.*" Earl Kingston's low growl is as full of finality as the trees tearing from the earth. No longer the smooth-sounding boy who could so easily charm me if I didn't have reason to be scared of him. This man is what makes the boy part of him work. "Go get this Finch. *Do it now.*"

Oliver doesn't hear him. Or doesn't care. His hand tightens around my arm. "Let's go!"

Earl Kingston lunges.

In the exact same second, the earth sways. So deeply and widely that my stomach sways with it. Only Oliver's grip keeps us from crashing to the ground. We still tumble, but just to our knees. The impact thuds through me, and a fresh wave of pain rises.

Beside us, the streams of lava cascade and crash together. A molten pool forms, two thousand degrees of heat.

Momentum plunges Earl Kingston face-first into the pool.

His scream is unearthly as he sinks into the lava—I know I'll never forget the sound of it.

No more voice of honey. Or of anything.

His men run, aiming to push their way out of the trees. If they don't tumble into the earth first.

Beside me, Oliver is frozen. His eyes are locked on Earl Kingston's body. As orange light flickers across his features, I can tell he's still rehearsing that scream. Like me, he'll never unhear it.

I grab his hand and yank him to his feet. "Come on!"

We break out into a stumbling, dodging run. Cracks sprawl across the ground like roots searching for water, growing and widening with every second. Lava sears the soles of our shoes whenever we get too close—the smell of burning rubber is acrid, too distinctly unnatural here in the depths of this forest. We weave around others also trying to run, searching for the fastest way out to the road.

Every step hurts, too many parts of me wanting to collapse and give away. In the dark, I hear Oliver gasping for breath. But his hand is still around mine, and I wonder how he's able to not hate me after the things I've made him do and see.

A long, groaning tremor. The world whips back and forth. People scream as they fall.

Bodies are suddenly too close, pressing between Oliver and me, pushing us apart.

I fall.

And then my hand is empty.

In the dark, I flail, reach out.

Lost.

"Oliver!" His name is a hoarse tremble torn from my throat. The sound of it is swallowed up as more people rush past, all of them calling names, too.

Aza!

My name, coming from somewhere in the chaos. Distant-sounding.

I call for him again. Panic coats the sound of his name. "Oliver!"

More trees fall, crashing and breaking apart as they hit. The ground shakes open even more cracks, lava pouring from each to paint the earth with thousands of fiery slashes—it no longer seems possible to escape any of it. My destruction of this part of the world is growing by the second, and soon there will be nothing left.

People continue to fall. Also gone.

There's a hard tug at my arm. For a second, relief swamps me— *Oliver*—but the fingers dig in with a violence that leaves me stunned, and my heart lurches as I'm pulled close.

I know that perfume.

FIFTY-FOUR

From within the dark: "For this night, Aza, you and your family will pay like you have never paid before."

Saint Willow's elegant voice has gone guttural with pain. I smell smoke and blood, both scents wafting off her just as her perfume does.

All that power. All that scheming and cruelty. Yet here she is, stuck along with the rest of us.

Her fingers are pincers. They squeeze my arm harder, and my rage at her finally unleashes. A wild buzzing fills my head.

"I told you I couldn't control strange magic," I yell into her face as we try to stay upright, the ground shifting and sliding. I wonder how hurt she is, and an ugly and decadent kind of hope washes over me. "But you wouldn't listen. If you had, then Finch would never have gotten this far."

"Full magic," she rasps. Ignoring me. Her fingers keep digging. "Cast right now, and fix this mess you've made. And maybe then I won't destroy your family, won't burn the teahouse to the ground."

"How can you still not understand? Magic has limits, and it doesn't matter how important you think you are—you have to respect that." The idea of casting right now is sickening.

Her lips curl. "Respect? *I saw you cast.* You cast just to show that you're the most powerful. Even more powerful than me."

Now I *do* hear madness in her voice. It's like the lava coming out from somewhere deep in the earth, leaking through the layer she's so carefully kept on top.

I jerk back, trying to free myself from her grasp. I have to find Oliver. Trees are snapping all around me, the ground shuddering while fire pours out—suddenly, Saint Willow feels very small. Very human. As powerless as I am.

She practically hisses as she yanks me closer. "Do you think this changes anything? You owe me everything. Your family owes me everything. *I still own you.*"

The world roars. Tilts like a seesaw. The smell of deep soil being unearthed for the first time turns the air pungent. Too rich. I nearly gag.

The ground crumples beneath one of Saint Willow's feet. She slips, and so does her grasp on my arm. Just enough.

I draw, the motions all instinct. The burn on my palm stings. I barely notice.

In the deepest parts of my mind, a voice is screaming a reminder about Saint Willow's latest threat. That if she dies, her men will come after my parents. A chain reaction that, once started, can only end in one way.

But Jihen is gone. And Luna and Seb—I can't see them anywhere, and they never leave her side. They must be gone, too.

I grab Saint Willow's hand just as she once touched mine. On the table at headquarters. A threat that whispered instead of screamed.

Flesh spell.

I cast.

A long whistle splits the air. It comes from the side, and I picture in my mind what's happening: the tree swinging down through the dark like a knife making its stroke.

Red kisses the tops of Saint Willow's cheekbones as she squeezes my arm again. The wild pulse of fury in her blood, the bright glitter of her eyes—I can never forget her beauty. "Did you hear me, Aza? *Did you*—?"

I watch her expression change as she glances over and up. From fiery rage to freezing terror as the line of the tree cuts across the smog-covered sky. It's a glimpse of her as more human than monster, and yet I feel nothing for her.

I wrench myself free of Saint Willow's hold. The force of it sends me tumbling backward.

The tree crashes into her even as she's turning to try to escape.

Her scream cuts off as she hits the ground with a thud. The tree rolls to lie across one arm, trapping her.

Stuck here in yet another way. She's still alive but also defanged and declawed. She's gasping for breath, struggling to free herself while she glares at me. Her motions are jerky, unbalanced—the least elegant I've ever seen her. Whatever's broken inside her won't simply be shaken off. Will continue to break her even more if she doesn't get out of here soon.

Everything in me says to run. Saint Willow can't hurt me anymore. It's already over. I just need to walk away.

Finish it, Aza. Now's your chance. She's down, but doesn't she always find a way to win in the end? What do you think she'll do to you then?

Casting pain hits as I'm still trying to think. I stumble back a step as agony flares downward from my skull. Only just narrowly do I miss tumbling into the crack behind me. A crack that wasn't there even seconds ago.

The agony dulls to a roar. I'm gasping for breath as Saint Willow still is. Just as she remains pinned, I'm also unable to move.

Cast on her. This is it. Let her go and you'll never be free.

I draw again, nodding to myself, everything inside me shaking just as the earth continues to shake.

"Aza, we did it."

Nima, approaching from the trees. She's either lost her contacts or the orange of her Ivor eyes is being magnified by the lava all around; they're glowing so brightly in the dark. I'm unable to look away as she comes to stand beside me, the fire reflected in her gaze like her own kind of power.

"Look at her," she says as she stares down at Saint Willow. "At my feet and about to beg for *her* life. But it won't matter. It's too late for me to care."

Saint Willow has gone still, a statue while everything erupts around her. Her expression is as indignant as it is furious. It's just not possible that Nima can be a real threat.

"I saved you," Saint Willow says to Nima.

"You destroyed me." The depths of the gatherer's hate comes spilling out. Saint Willow has wronged me, but it's been years of that torture for Nima. "Now it's my turn. No mistakes this time. Not like that night out on the street."

As the ground keeps trembling, I manage to stay balanced. But at her words, fresh unease starts to dawn. It makes me feel oddly lost, like something flimsy getting caught on the wind and simply swept up along with it.

"What are you talking about?" I ask. "The only mistake that night was all those people dying."

Nima shakes her head. "I meant to kill her."

I've never heard the gatherer so calm. So at peace with what's happening.

"The night she made me help you get magic back," she continues, "I gathered the spell as she ordered, but she was meant to die that night with the crowd."

The unease sharpens. A grim understanding—more hurtful than any casting pain—fills me, and I shudder just as the earth does. "All those people—you meant for that to happen? So that she would die when I cast that spell?"

"It was the only way it would work. I'm sorry, Aza. But I was desperate to escape. To get away from her. And if she wasn't going to let me leave, then I had to find another way. I knew you wanted to get away from her, too. And the two of us working together—our chances were better. Stronger. It was my best hope—*our* best hope."

I don't know if it's right to feel betrayed, but I can't help it— Nima had me kill for her to try to escape.

Except how can I condemn her when I was also supposed to get something in the end? To cast my full magic once again. Saint Willow out of the picture. It's not Nima's fault that Finch was the one to cast her latest gathered spell.

But—what was the cost for that?

"How did Finch pay for getting my magic, then?" My thoughts spin as more cracks split the ground. The clearing's now so hot my eyes are burning along with it. "What cost did you gather into *that* spell?" A new possibility slams into me. "Is Finch dead? Is that the cost?"

He was turned into jade stone after I cast on him, but there's no way to know if he survived.

But just as quickly, I know I'm wrong. If Finch died for casting that spell, it would mean Nima was planning for *me* to die.

"The cost was my gathering." Nima's voice is flat. The earth keeps on shaking, but she doesn't seem to notice, all her focus on Saint Willow. The gang leader is dead still, stunned into a frozen silence by Nima's strange gain of power over her. "The spell took away my ability when it was cast. The only magic I had left, and the one thing she wanted from me. Do you see, Aza? You getting your magic back was meant to save both of us. Giving up being a gatherer was *my* cost—the only payback I could offer for everything she ever made me do with it."

No longer a gatherer. No magic at all. The orange glow in her eyes is really nothing but the lava that's everywhere around us.

Nima's free now.

The world roars. A rumble from deep inside. And the orange in her eyes surges—yet more lava.

I go to draw. To cast and finish off Saint Willow.

"Aza, leave. I'll get rid of her for the both of us."

"What?" I stare at Nima, bewildered. I sidestep growing pools of lava. My heart is thundering inside my chest, screaming at me to get away. To find Oliver and leave the pink woods forever. But Saint Willow is still here, still—

"*I'll do it.*" Nima continues to stare at the gang leader. "So go."

Suddenly, Saint Willow laughs. It's as broken-sounding as this part of the earth is. As her body might be. Her plans. But still there's smugness in her laugh despite it all. This hint of madness—it's how she still believes she'll always win in the end. Even when she's losing. She can't ever be wrong.

"*How* will you do it?" she asks Nima, her voice harsh. "You can't even cast."

Nima's calm smile chills even me. She gestures to the lava that's pooling ever closer to where Saint Willow is still lying. Still pinned.

Fear crawls over my skin. The pink woods are nothing now but liquid fire and crevices darker than night. There's no guarantee of escape if she waits.

I start to reach for Nima's arm. "You can't stay here."

Another smile as she finally faces me, this one even more serene. She waves away my hand. "This is the last part of my making things right. I'm sorry you didn't get your magic back. But watching this—knowing she's gone for good—is mine."

I remember her confession. The both of us sitting at the piano in the Tea Chest and her playing while talking to me about fixing wrongs.

Saint Willow pushed Nima to the limit until there was nowhere left for her to go. Until the only way out was to push back.

What if *I* let Saint Willow keep pushing me until I'm out of room?

If Nima could justify all those deaths for the chance to escape, what might I come to accept? Who would I dare to become?

More trembling. A crack opens up in the forest floor at my foot—orange begins to climb from it even as I look—and I pull back. Deciding. I think about how even the Great West Coast Quake eventually ended. How Nima has gone this long working for Saint Willow, figuring out different ways to survive.

I nod at Nima, unsure of what to say. Nothing feels right when everything seems wrong.

But she's already turned back toward Saint Willow.

And Oliver's still out there.

Saint Willow's dark eyes flash at me.

So many last things I could say to her.

You deserve this.

This is your fault.

Everything has a cost.

Instead, I decide on the one thing she might understand.

I tear off the willow-print silk ribbon from my arm and toss it at her.

I'm free, too.

The world roars as I turn to go. To search. I stagger through the dark, pain pounding with each step. My voice goes hoarse as I call—*Oliver, Piper, Embry.* I move along, my hands held out like they can help me see into the night. People are still everywhere, running and searching, too. I try to catch sight of every face moving past.

The rushed graze of fingers on my arm as they pass, as shaky as the ground.

"Aza!"

Relief is dizzying. As sweet as the pink trees once were. "Oliver, we have to—"

"I know, I was just—" Warm hands in the night, searching for mine. The briefest glimpse of hazel eyes and white teeth. "Okay, let's—"

The world roars again. *Thunders.* And a great tearing sound fills the air as the ancient roots of too-close trees shred apart.

The earth behind Oliver yawns open, and a second later, he is gone.

My hands are empty.

An icy coldness washes over me so I can't breathe. I keep reaching out into the dark, denying, denying, denying.

The emptiness against my palm is unbearable.

Oliver.

FIFTY-FIVE

The bell over the door of the teahouse chimes, and I glance up from behind the counter, ready to smile at the customer as they walk inside the shop. Smiling on cue—I don't mind doing it as much as I used to. Sometimes the smile even feels real.

But it's only a courier with a delivery.

I go to sign the form and accept the large box. Fragrance wafts out through the cardboard, telling me it's a fresh batch of dried flower branches—chrysanthemums, wisteria, rhododendrons, and jasmine. Our regular order of the materials needed for a Wu fire. Tonight I'll be helping Mom dry leaves and flower buds over it to make more stock.

The teahouse has yet to be as busy as it was during the month when Saint Willow directed orders toward it. But it's never sunk as low as those times she sabotaged us, either. So there's that.

Wu Teas might never return to the peak of its glory, back when royalty wanted us. But we're still here. Still existing. That can't be said for everyone.

The only customers in the shop have just been served in the dining area, so I take the box of flower branches and head toward the kitchen.

"Delivery," I say to my parents as I step into the room.

"Oh?" Dad looks up distractedly from the paperwork in front of him on the table. He's still figuring out the teahouse's new filing system, constantly lamenting the change.

"Oh, good, it's here—just as scheduled." Mom's measuring blends to be bagged, and the air is rich and pungent with the scents of chamomile and rose—our Content blend. Still not my favorite, but I like it more than I used to. "Mind just leaving the box on the counter, Aza?"

I set it down. "Okay if I leave a bit early? It's only an hour until closing, and I want to pick up some stuff."

It's October next week. The early part of fall. And the end of a summer that I'll never forget for lots of reasons.

"Sure, go ahead." Dad gets up, stretches, and heads for the shop. "I need a break anyway."

"Meeting anyone?" Mom reaches for tea bags. "Oliver, perhaps? It's been a bit, hasn't it?"

Hearing his name again—it's like I'm back in the ring and absorbing a blow.

It's not Mom's fault. She doesn't know what happened. No one does. Oliver and me—what we were, nearly were, wanted to be—it's just my secret now. It sits with me like a wound, some days rawer than others. Another cost of magic.

Finch, Saint Willow, Luna and Seb, Earl Kingston, Vetta, Tau—they're all gone, too. Killed by magic cast by me that I couldn't control. Dozens more, whose faces I can't picture, also swallowed up by the earth.

I haven't heard from Embry since that night. I don't know if his bones shattered or if he somehow survived casting once more and is somewhere here still. Too broken to know who he is, or maybe too broken to want to try. Both options hurt to consider.

Either way, I wish I could speak to him again. To say he really did do exactly as he swore to and that I'm sorry the cost came down to him.

The quake only lasted for a few minutes—a recorded fact that still sometimes feels like a mistake. At the time, it felt endless. A shaking that wouldn't stop until the earth was nothing but crumbled dust.

Now the quake seems small—too short for all that damage to have happened. I wake up in the middle of the night sure I can somehow go back and fix things, reverse it all. Other nights, I wake up with fires and floods still in my mind. Quakes and lightning storms bitter in my mouth. The taste of tragedy in my throat. And I'm glad going back is no longer possible.

Once it would have been, maybe.

But not anymore.

Everyone's bodies are still down there—deep in the cracks of the world, where no one can reach them. The city proclaimed the heart of the pink woods a burial site. The whole area was temporarily blocked off after the quake, and soon the closure will be for good.

Already, all the cracks are slowly closing back up on their own. In a matter of months, the ground will have returned to the way it was. Nothing will remain but seams in the dirt, like scars after a devastating injury.

Decades from now, the Quake of the Pink Woods will be remembered as just one more natural disaster that Lotusland survived. Details as muted as how the woods got to be pink in the first place. Softened with time.

But until then, the quake lives on. Its echoes are still felt everywhere.

Scouts roam the streets, a twenty-four-hour patrol that leaves us all on edge. Full magic wasn't allowed before, but it also wasn't unheard of for instances to be bribed away. Unreported in exchange for a favor.

No longer. Casters have never been in such danger, never so hunted. Rewards are up for our capture, for witnesses caught staying silent. There are whispers of spies in training. For the sake of the future and the earth.

Display Ivors line the blocks. Their howling is a part of the night.

My own magic—the one Finch took—is once again beyond my reach. As with any caster who dies, the magic inside them is released back into the air, ether invisible to the eye. Maybe one day, I'll know of another gatherer.

Maybe it'll even be Nima, come to find me again. Like Embry, I can't be sure what happened to her that night. I have no doubt she stayed long enough to see Saint Willow dead. But whether she stayed too long, I just don't know.

The cost of freedom—of magic—we're all still paying it in one way or another.

"No, it's not Oliver." I grab my jacket from where I left it draped over a chair in the kitchen. City air in autumn remains damp, but it's also brisk as it blows off the Pacifik. The Tea Sector's scents have warmed to make up for the new chill, and now you can detect cinnamon on the wind sometimes. Cloves and mint and oranges.

If I'm not careful, I can think I'm in Spice instead. And it's too easy to linger, searching for ghosts, wishing.

Mom begins filling an oversized ceramic jar with tea bags. "I'm sorry I haven't met him yet—hopefully you'll bring him by soon."

I only nod, my heart still twisting. I finish putting on my jacket. "I'm sorry, too. I'll be back for dinner, okay?"

"Please do." A shadow crosses her face. It speaks of her fear for me because of the Scouts searching out my kind.

Even gang members are being more careful around the cops than normal, sensing how high the tension is in the city. The gangs have seen this before, the ebbs and flows of power. They bide their time, waiting for the city to go back to the way it was.

I don't know if it ever will. There might not be another quake, but disaster in Lotusland comes in all forms. Ill-fitting magic, the thirst for power, the hunger to cast—those are also still here in waiting. Ready to be picked up and set loose.

No one knows that better than I do. So much changed after the quake—for the city, for me—but the lure of full magic remains. The danger of it. The burn on my palm has long healed, but in the right light, it's not hard to make out its spell star shape.

I say goodbye and turn to go.

Mom stops me before I've left the kitchen. "Aza, aren't you forgetting something?"

I stop, my hand on the door frame, unsure. "I don't think so."

"You don't have your starter bag. I didn't think you ever left the house without it."

A pang. Like the shudder of magic, forever calling to me.

"It's okay," I say, wanting to believe, "I don't need it anymore."

ACKNOWLEDGMENTS

My hugest thanks to these incredible people for helping make *Spell Starter* happen:

Victoria Marini, agent extraordinaire and a really awesome person.

Matt Ringler, rock star editor and also a super awesome person.

The entire amazing team at Scholastic, especially Shelly Romero, Josh Berlowitz, Maeve Norton, Sydney Tillman, and David Levithan, for all your work and support for *Spell Starter*.

Jesse, Matthew, Gillian, Wendy, Mom, Dad (miss you!), and more family—thank you always.

ABOUT THE AUTHOR

Elsie Chapman grew up in Prince George, Canada, and has a degree in English literature from the University of British Columbia. She is the author of the YA novels *Dualed*, *Divided*, *Along the Indigo*, *Caster*, and *Spell Starter*, as well as the middle-grade novel *All the Ways Home*, and the co-editor of the anthologies *A Thousand Beginnings and Endings* and *Hungry Hearts*. She currently lives in Tokyo, Japan, with her family. You can visit her online at elsiechapman.com.